praise for *the sex sphere*

"Alien invaders tend to squirt acid, go invisible, or drive humongous ships. Not the ones in Rudy Rucker's 1980s classic *The Sex Sphere*, where an alien named Babs and her crew take the form of disembodied sex organs that attach to human hosts . . . Only trip-tastic writer Rucker could imagine such a scenario. The best part is that Rucker, a mathematics professor, opens the book with a whole introduction on the fourth dimension and how it works. The aliens, you see, are trying to return to this dimension . . . If you like your science fiction to contain hard science mixed with bizarro humor, don't miss *The Sex Sphere*." —Annalee Newitz, *io9*

"Phenomenally weird . . . *The Sex Sphere* is a tome that deserves to be on the 'experimental/avant garde' shelf along with books by Irvine Welsh, Iain Banks, and William Burroughs. It's a crossover book for anarchist-stoner-hipsters and it's a far-out read, playing havoc with the concepts of math, sex and politics." —Ivan Lerner, *Revolution Science Fiction*

"You cannot know where modern science fiction has gotten to unless you are familiar with Rucker's work." —*Fantasy & Science Fiction*

T0087977

praise for rudy rucker

"Rudy Rucker should be declared a National Treasure of American Science Fiction. Someone simultaneously channeling Kurt Gödel and Lenny Bruce might start to approximate full-on Ruckerian warp-space, but without the sweet, human, splendidly goofy Rudyness at the core of the singularity." —William Gibson

"One of science fiction's wittiest writers. A genius . . . a cult hero among discriminating cyberpunkers." —*San Diego Union-Tribune*

"Rucker's writing is great like the Ramones are great: a genre stripped to its essence, attitude up the wazoo, and cartoon sentiments that reek of identifiable lives and issues. Wild math you can get elsewhere, but no one does the cyber version of beatnik glory quite like Rucker." —*New York Review of Science Fiction*

"What a Dickensian genius Rucker has for Californian characters, as if, say, Dickens had fused with Phil Dick and taken up surfing and jamming and topologising. He has a hotline to cosmic revelations yet he's always here and now in the groove, tossing off lines of beauty and comic wisdom. 'My heart is a dog running after every cat.' We really feel with his characters in their bizarre tragicomic quests." —Ian Watson, author of *The Embedding*

"The current crop of sf humorists are mildly risible, I suppose, but they don't seem to pack the same intellectual punch of their forebears. With one exception, that is: the astonishing Rudy Rucker. For some two decades now, since the publication of his first novel, *White Light*, Rucker has combined an easygoing, trippy style influenced by the Beats with a deep engagement with knotty (or 'gnarly,' to employ one of his favorite terms) intellectual conceits, based mainly in mathematics. In the typical Rucker novel, likably eccentric characters—who run the gamut from brilliant to near-certifiable—encounter aspects of the universe that confirm that life is weirder than we can imagine." —*The Washington Post*

"Rucker stands alone in the science fiction pantheon as some kind of trickster god of the computer science lab; where others construct minutely plausible fictional realities, he simply grabs the corners of the one we already know and twists it in directions we don't have pronounceable names for." —*SF Site*

"Reading a Rudy Rucker book is like finding Poe, Kerouac, Lewis Carroll, and Philip K. Dick parked on your driveway in a topless '57 Caddy . . . and telling you they're taking you for a RIDE. The funniest science fiction author around." —*Sci-Fi Universe*

"This is SF rigorously following crazy rules. My mind of science fiction. At the heart of it is a rage to extrapolate. Rucker is what happens when you cross a mathematician with the extrapolating jazz spirit." —Robert Sheckley

"Rucker [gives you] more ideas per chapter than most authors use in an entire novel." —*San Francisco Chronicle*

"Rudy Rucker writes like the love child of Philip K. Dick and George Carlin. Brilliant, frantic, conceptual, cosmological . . . like lucid dreaming, only funny." —*New York Times* bestselling author Walter Jon Williams

by rudy rucker

the sex sphere

a novel by

RUDY RUCKER

night shade books
new york

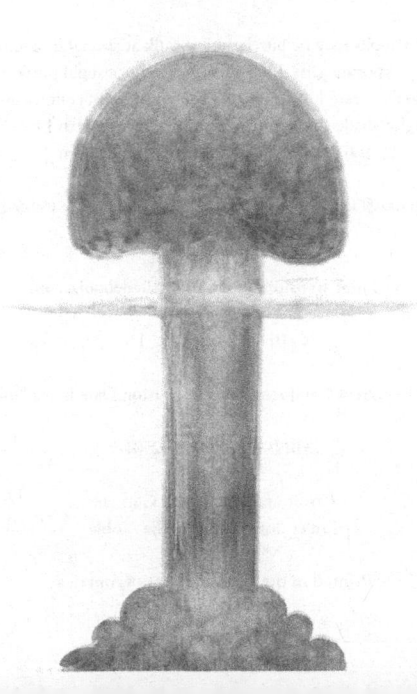

For Sylvia

contents

a giant pussy from another dimension changed my life

by annalee newitz

The first time I met Rudy Rucker, we were at a science fiction convention with a group of mutual friends. I believe I said something like, "Holy shit! You're the guy who wrote *The Sex Sphere*? That book completely blew my mind when I read it in the eighth grade!"

Rudy gave me a half grin. "Uh . . . I feel kind of weird about that," he said.

We stood there awkwardly, and I realized that I'd just confessed to reading his book about sex-crazed trans-dimensional aliens when I was thirteen. A book full of countless scenes where humans gleefully humped geometric objects cleverly fitted with genitals, breasts, and mouths. I could see why Rudy felt a little weird. But later, he sent me a copy of the paperback—the original 1983 one whose ultra-non-sexy cover was already burned into my memory—and signed it with an illustration of the sex sphere herself. There was Babs, in ballpoint pen, a degenerate speck of hypermatter who had emerged into our puny 3 dimensions by taking the shape of a floating ball with giant breasts, a hungry mouth, and a pussy that could swallow galaxies.

I grew up in the early 1980s, so I read a lot of smutty science fiction as a teenager. The recent history of wacky, horny '70s experimentation was available in the bookstore at my local mall, and my parents had a policy of buying me pretty much any cheap paperback I wanted. As long as I was at home reading, I wasn't getting into trouble. At least, that's what they thought. Little did they know I was learning about interspecies sex, telepathic orgasms, lust pills, and alien pheromones. I forgot most of those books, but *The Sex Sphere* remained with me. It was probably the strangest sex story I had ever read, and that made it special.

Re-reading it as an adult, I realized that I'd forgotten the book's main plot. It's a kind of Cold War farce, with terrorists from various European countries trying to kidnap physicists like our anti-hero Alwin so they can build an atomic bomb. It's also about a marriage on the verge of collapsing under the weight of Alwin's neuroses and general neglect. The writing veers between experimental and erotic, and somehow the bizarro mix conveys an intense, almost visceral sense of being trapped. Alwin wants to save his marriage, but he's constantly derailed by frustrations that go beyond it. He feels hemmed in by the airless politics of the Cold War, an ever-present sexual desire for impossible things, and a cosmic hunger to escape the confines of his 3-dimensional reality.

One of the great rules of literature is that everything always means something else. That's why it's important to ask what the sex symbolizes in a novel like *The Sex Sphere*. Primarily, I think it's Rudy Rucker's sense of explosive outrage at our limitations. I'm also fairly certain that was what drew me to the novel as a teen, along with the strangely compelling scenes of people going mad with trans-dimensional eroticism.

When I was 13, I was stuck in a very conservative town in a very conservative part of the state, surrounded by church-going people who thought girls should wait for boys to ask them out. I was constantly being told what girls couldn't do. Literally everything on the list was something I loved: science, computers, science fiction, action movies, porn, Dungeons & Dragons, sex. I can't tell you how many times I wished a giant goddamn pussy from another dimension would appear and leave a bunch of juice all over those moralistic fucks.

In his "Afterword" to *The Sex Sphere*, Rucker writes that the book grew out of his wish to defy convention in every possible way. He hated where he was living, he hated his job, and he just wanted to blow everything up. Maybe with an atomic bomb. Or, wait, better—how about with a giant pussy that built an atomic bomb? How about with an infinite sex machine from a dimension so obscure that only a few mathematicians even bothered to study it? Sitting in my hellish middle school and listening to Ronald Reagan drone on TV, I sympathized greatly with this line of thought.

I said earlier that this novel spoke to my rage about gender stereotypes when I was a teen. One of the major themes in *The Sex Sphere* is the sexism of its characters. We are privy to Alwin's growing awareness that there's something profoundly chauvinistic about his urge to hump a floating genital with no head attached. Partly this awareness comes from his wife, Sybil, whose thankless role in this novel is to remind Alwin that he's a selfish jerk. But she's also there to model a form of sexuality that isn't about screwing specks of degenerate hypermatter. Sybil prefers full humans, preferably ones with a penchant for reading E.M. Forester novels to her.

Eventually Alwin comes to realize that Babs, the sex sphere, does not represent female sexuality at all. Instead, she's male sexuality made literal—a destructive, abstract force. Indeed, her main focus in the first half of the book is building an atomic bomb that will blast her back to her home dimension. The idea is reminiscent of the best moments in *Dr. Strangelove*, where we realize that our eponymous anti-hero is hot for the bomb itself, and its world-ending powers of ejaculation. So we can view *The Sex Sphere* as a condemnation of male sexual desire.

But it's also more than that. Once Babs has blasted herself free, she decides to come back to our world for reasons that are a little murky. She turns herself into millions of sex spheres, trying to take over Heidelberg, and possibly the Earth. Everyone has their own private sex sphere to distract them from reality. At one point, Babs says she's simply doing it to harvest sperm, but then she starts killing women and sucking men into her space-distorting labia. It's hard to say what her endgame might be, but Alwin surmises that the whole problem comes from the fact that men are focused on cosmic abstractions, while women care about the cozy, nurturing details of daily life. Again we're seeing a kind of condemnation of male desire, but Alwin is selling the breadth of women's desires short too.

What emerges from the gooey, transreal pyrotechnics is a sense that men will always be susceptible to the lure of what amounts to erotica from another dimension.

But women will force them to focus on the "details" of domestic life, bringing them back to reality. Though that sounds depressing as hell for everybody, what gave me joy in this book as a teen were all the cracks in that reasoning. Also, the book is gonzo, in the original Hunter S. Thompson sense of the word. Rucker goes on a lot of surreal tangents, and offers many handholds for people who want to climb into a different reading of the story.

As a teen, I found those handholds in the moments when the book comes unhinged from its gender tropes entirely. A female mad scientist creates Babs, after all, and some of the sex sphere's early adopters aren't interested in genitals so much as the idea that anything can be sexy: a toroid, a 4-dimensional spacewalk, a giant, or a tiny screen showing pictures of a high-tech future. There's a character who falls in love with his sex sphere because it likes to read science fiction novels with him. The warm, gleaming marble shows him pictures of other worlds, and that's what arouses him.

In these flashes of zaniness, I think I glimpsed my future as a queer nerd, obsessed with geological timescales, evolutionary biology, and non-binary gender. I didn't remember *The Sex Sphere* for all these years just because it was deeply weird and funny, though that certainly was a selling point. I remembered it for showing me a world where sexual desire went so far beyond the traditional norm that it could only be described with theoretical math. And that is ultimately what all good science fiction does. It breaks us out of our preconceptions and paints a vista where everything familiar becomes enticingly alien.

"If we want to pass on and on till magnitude and dimensions disappear, is it not done for us already? That reality, where magnitudes and dimensions are not, is simple and about us. For passing thus on and on we lose ourselves, but find the clue again in the apprehension of the simplest acts of human goodness, in the most rudimentary recognition of another human soul wherein is neither magnitude nor dimension, and yet all is real."

—Charles H. Hinton

"At first, indeed, I pretended that I was describing the imaginary experiences of a fictitious person; but my enthusiasm soon forced me to throw off all disguise, and finally, in a fervent peroration, I exhorted all my hearers to divest themselves of prejudice and to become believers in the Third Dimension. Need I say that I was at once arrested and taken before the Council?"

—Edwin A. Abbott

introduction
by rudy rucker

This is a novel about higher dimensions, and about sexual love. I don't need to explain much about the sex, which is, as always, a mixture of the erotic, the comic and the surreal.

But higher dimensions are less familiar. What I'd like to do in this introduction is to sketch some of the basic science ideas that I've used. Not that you have to read the introduction right now—you can check it out later, or never. It's only here an extra. Proceed immediately to Chapter One, if you prefer.

Anyone left? Initiate professor mode . . .

The fourth dimension is a direction perpendicular to all the directions we can point to. Sometimes people say that time is the fourth dimension, and this is in some respects true. But to start with, we just want to get the idea of there being some unknown and higher possibilities of motion.

The best way to begin thinking about higher dimensions is to look at some two-dimensional creatures who have no notion of a *third* dimension. These creatures were invented by Edwin A. Abbott in his 1884 classic, *Flatland*. The best-known of the Flatlanders is one A Square (see Figure 1). By thinking about A Square's difficulties in imagining a third dimension, we become better able to get over our own difficulties in understanding the fourth dimension.

The Flatlanders are confined to the surface of what seems to be an endless plane. They can move East/West, North/South, or any combination of these two directions. But it's impossible for them to jump up out of their world and into the third dimension.

FIGURE 1: A SQUARE

One minor point needs to be mentioned here. When A Square looks at two of his fellows, say A Triangle and A Circle, the Square's actual retinal image is of two line segments—just what you would see if you were to lower your eye to the level of a tabletop on which some cardboard shapes were lying. But as the space of Flatland is permeated with a light mist, the edges of the triangle seem to shade off faster than do the edges of the circle. Thus our Square is able to distinguish his fellows' shapes, and to form good mental images of them (see Figure 2). If you think about it, this is no more surprising than the fact that we're able to use our two-dimensional retinal images to form three-dimensional mental images of the objects around us.

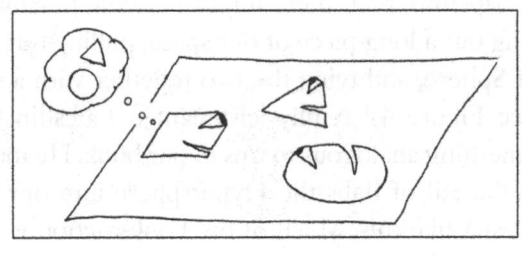

FIGURE 2: A SQUARE LOOKING AT A TRIANGLE AND A CIRCLE

Okay. Now how does A Square find out about the third dimension? A Sphere from higher-dimensional space takes an interest in A Square and decides to show herself to him. She does this by moving through the plane of Flatland. What does A Square see? A circle of varying size. And if we suppose that the sphere has a valley-like peach cleft, the cross-sectional circles will have little nicks (see Figure 3).

FIGURE 3: A SQUARE MEETS A SPHERE

Suppose that A Square became so interested in A Sphere that he wanted to prevent her from leaving his space. What could he do? If we think of the Flatland space as being a sort of soap-film, then there might be some possibility of stretching out a long piece of our space, pulling out a long piece of Sphere, and tying the two together with a square knot (see Figure 4)! A physicist named Lafcadio Caron does something analogous to this in our book. He manages to knot the tail of Babs-the-Hypersphere into our space. Babs doesn't like this. Much of the book's action is in fact directed by Babs—her goal is to get some people to carry out a certain act which will free her tail from the knot.

Towards the end of the book it develops that Babs is more than just a four-dimensional hypersphere. She is really a pattern in infinite-dimensional "Hilbert" space. Why would I want to drag in so many dimensions?

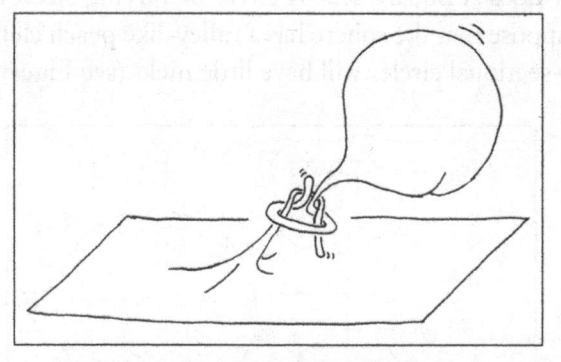

FIGURE 4: A KNOT IN SPHERE'S TAIL

One of the main characters in *The Sex Sphere* is a hypersphere named Babs. When she moves through our space, our hero Alwin sees . . . what? A hypersphere is the high-er-dimensional analogue of a sphere, so just as A Square sees a sphere as a *circle* of varying size, we can imagine that Alwin will see Babs as a *sphere* of varying size.

We can imagine that A Sphere would be able to lift A Square out of his space, and it's equally possible to suppose that Babs might lift Alwin out of our space. Alwin could either tumble about in this higher space, or he might "slide" on the surface of Babs herself, just as A Square could be thought of as sliding up along Sphere's swelling flank.

It's interesting to realize that hyperspheres are not utterly fictional concepts. As early as 1920, Albert Einstein suggested that the three-dimensional space of our universe is curved back on itself to form a great hypersphere. The important thing about a hyperspherical space is that it is finitely large, yet one never comes to an edge of it. This is, of course, analogous to the fact that our Earth's spherical surface is finite and without edges.

Einstein's General Theory of Relativity has taught us to think of gravitational force as being a result of the *bending of space*. That's one higher dimension, at least. Yet Einstein's Special Theory of Relativity tells us that the basic reality is not space, but *spacetime*. So here's another higher dimension. Three space dimensions, one time dimension, one dimension to curve spacetime in—that's five already. But any lover of SF knows that there are many parallel curved spacetimes—alternate universes—so we're going to need a sixth dimension to stack these spacetimes in.

What's particularly interesting here is to realize that the process of breathing particles in and out serves to weave us together; and—which is more important for the story—the concept of "family tree" has a real significance in spacetime. Not to give too much away, when our character Alwin starts tumbling off into the direction of the "future," he drags his children after him. Note that if someone were able to pull their past selves out of spacetime, then no one would even remember them!

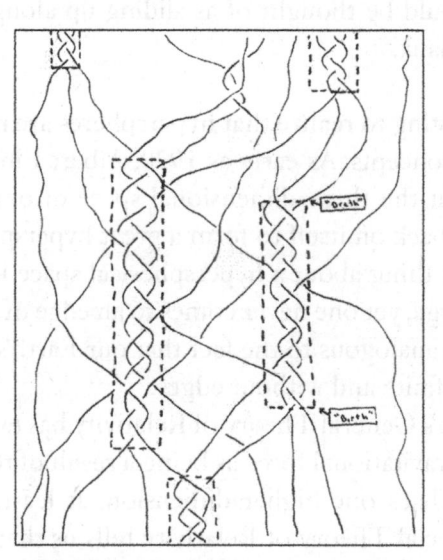

FIGURE 5: PEOPLE ARE SPACETIME BRAIDS OF PARTICLE WORLDLINES

In modern physics, the fundamental reality is thought of as infinite-dimensional. This fact is not widely known—people just don't know what to make of it. What you have to do to appreciate the world's infinite-dimensionality is to realize that our ordinary concepts of space and time are just *constructs*. What is in fact immediately given to us is an unstructured sea of thoughts and perceptions. We try to impose order by using a four-dimensional spacetime framework.

But just take an honest look at your thoughts, and you'll realize that the situation is much more complex. Here is an object—how many questions can I ask about it? Infinitely many: what's its longitude, latitude, height above sea level; what does it taste like; how much does it weigh; who does it belong to; is it in some ways reminiscent of my high-school prom; what would William Burroughs say about it? And so on and on. We all know the game of Twenty Questions—our world is a game of Infinity Questions.

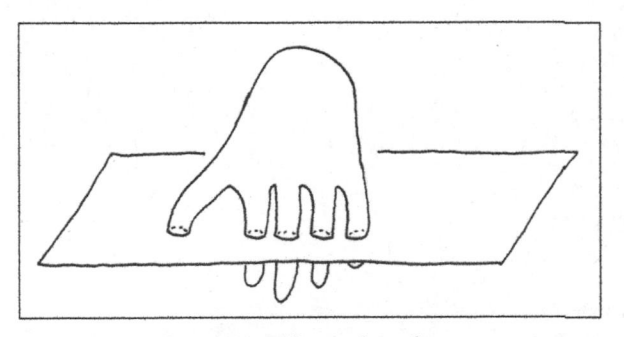

FIGURE 6: MANY ARE ONE

Babs eventually gets her tail unknotted, but somehow she can't bring herself to leave our universe alone. She manages to appear in many places at once. We can use a simple Flatland analogy to see how *many* distinct objects can actually be *one* on some higher level: just think of a hand whose fingers stick down into Square's space (see Figure 6)!

Well, those are the main tools you'll need to deconstruct the text; more detailed help can be found in my popular-science book, *The Fourth Dimension* (Houghton Mifflin, 1984 and Dover Books, 2014.). And now—let the weirdness begin!

—Rudy Rucker

the sex sphere

ONE
under the hill

Lafcadio Caron hated the physical universe. As a Platonic idealist, he deeply resented any claims that the crass world of matter might have on immortality. So he devised a theory according to which any bit of matter eventually decays into light, and a second theory according to which light eventually gets tired and trickles into the folds of spacetime; and a third theory according to which space and time will die of disuse once all the mass and energy are gone. "Here today, gone in 1040 years," he would say, twisting his features in desperate, irrelevant laughter. The man had problems.

But, yes, he was a genius. He spent much of his time slouched in a leather armchair in the University of Rome's physics library. Graduate students and foreign research fellows would cluster around him as he lolled there, long skinny legs stretched out. The legs were like grasshopper legs; and like a grasshopper, Lafcadio would rub his legs together as he talked, chirping and buzzing about Ultimate Reality.

His constant companion was a roly-poly Hungarian woman named Zsuzsi Szabo ... an exotic name which translates prosaically to Susan Taylor. She had short blond hair, high Tartar cheekbones, huge pillowy breasts, and a washerwoman's arms. The State had originally sent Zsuzsi to Rome to learn the latest developments in nuclear-reactor design. But instead she had attended Lafcadio's lectures, fallen in love and defected ... heedless of her Budapest family's fate.

Zsuzsi was a wizard at experimental design, and Lafcadio took her into his full confidence. They made a striking team: Fat Lady and Thin Man, Sancho Panza and Don Quixote, Earth and Fire. The graduate students speculated avidly about the pair's sex-life. It was, indeed, intense.

"You are my wild exotic particle," Lafcadio might say, mounting her. "Let me split you into quarks, my darling."

"Cling close, svheet one," she would respond, ardently reversing position. "I am absorber for your titanic energies."

Biologically, the union was barren. But Lafcadio impregnated Zsuzsi with the design for a beautiful second-generation proton-decay experiment. It was this experiment that led to the Mont Blanc laboratory's capture of a speck of degenerate hypermatter. Hearing the news, the proud couple named the particle Babsi (Hungarian for "little bean"), and hurried to see it.

aosta, italy, february 8

Wet snow is falling. The sky is gray and it looks like there will never be a sun again. From some random crag we watch the slow crawl of lights up the valley ...

cars and trucks laboring through spaghetti-turns to the Mont Blanc tunnel. There in the distance is the tunnel's mouth, a small upside-down U, sad and surprised.

Moving closer, we see the concrete customs shed and tollbooths. Closer. A Fiat stops, the driver shows a pass. The car is colorless with dirt, the driver white with cold. Lafcadio.

Zsuzsi, for her part, is pink with breakfast, loud with pleasure. "Zo, finally vhe have a little Babsi!"

"This would seem to be the case. If Signor Hu is to be believed." Lafcadio holds up a cautious bony finger.

They pull into the tunnel. *10 Km*, reads a sign overhead, indicating the distance to the French end of the tunnel. The Mont Blanc tunnel is filled with an eternal roar, a Hephaestian clangor. Huge trucks labor past, shaking Lafcadio's tiny car. The light is yellow and smeary. Everything is covered with wet grit. The air itself seems to grow thick. *9 Km*.

Zsuzsi glances up at the car's ceiling. "I hate it in here. All zat mountain over us. Kilometers and kilometers."

Lafcadio laughs his strangled laugh. "All slowly decaying, Zsuzsi. Slowly returning to the One." *8 Km*.

"I vhish vhe vhere already zere," frets Zsuzsi. "I don't trust zat Chimmy Hu to keep za Babsi stable. He doesn't really understand your zeory."

Lafcadio snorts briefly. "Doesn't *believe*, is more like it. No one but you, dear Zsuzsi, has really believed in my vacuumless vacuum, my cube of Absolute Nothingness. But only in such an incubator can our little Babsi live." *7 Km*.

"How much did Hu zay she vheighs?"

"Variable. Up to a full three grams," crows Lafcadio. "Can you believe that? Apparently she comes from a cascade of the most energetic proton-decays yet observed. And your mono-field caught her, Zsuzsi, swept her into the vacuumless vacuum. We'll celebrate with a trip to Venice, you and I." *6 Km*.

"Svheet dollink! But zlow down. Vhe're here."

They turn off into a sort of underground parking garage. It's a hard turn to make, and the canvas-shrouded truck behind Lafcadio's Fiat comes dangerously close to ramming them.

They're out of the car as soon as it stops, hurrying across the cold, damp garage to a door in the far wall. Lafcadio has a key. White light streams out, making a brief bright trapezoid on the garage's rough concrete floor.

Inside its bright and warm. An old guard waves them on. They trot down the hall. At the end is a large room with a lot of machinery. A smiling Chinese man in tan corduroys and dark blue sweater greets them.

"Lafcadio," he calls happily, "Zsuzsi! It is still stable!"

"Zat is vhonderful, Jimmy." Zsuzsi tosses her overcoat onto a chair. "Let me zee." She wears a tight red sweater, wide skirt and high boots. Pushing Jimmy Hu to one side, she leans possessively over her machine. Lafcadio crowds up behind her, watching over her shoulder.

The machine looks something like an arcade game, with a dead-black video screen set high in a console. Pipes and cables writhe out of it like tropical lianas, brightly colored root-vines feeding on the satellite machines:

vacuum pump, ion drive, gas chromatograph, differential analyzer, macro-processor, monopole accelerator, quantum fluxer, quark scanner, relativity condenser, gravito-magnet, strong/weak force junction, supercooled bloog tank, hyperonic veeble-tweeter, two-tier furglesnatcher, black boxes, boxes, boxes, boxes. Lights blink, needles wag, speakers hum here deep under the mountain, far from the Eye of God.

Behind it all is something that looks like a huge Beuys sculpture, a four-meter stack of iron plates interleaved with gray felt pads. Tubes and wires snake out of the felt, feeding the machines.

"Babsi," croons Zsuzsi, staring into the screen. Looking in with her, we see a pulsing point of light . . . neither far nor close, just there.

"It is werbling on a four-millisecond cycle," whispers Jimmy Hu. "Shall we cut in the resonance drive?"

"Don't ask me," chuckles Lafcadio. "All I know is that I'm right. A particle is the hypersection of a four-space construct."

Zsuzsi grunts wetly and lets her hands drop down to a row of knobs. Close shot of her fingers diddling the dials. Her nails are short and bitten, lacquered pink.

Laboring whine of machinery being pushed to its breaking point.

"You see," exclaims Lafcadio. "It is still growing! There is no practical upper limit to the size of a particle."

Wunh-wunh-wunh-wunh-wunh-wunh-wunh: an alarm-hooter. Zsuzsi and Lafcadio are staring in at the golf-ball-size Babsi particle, but Jimmy Hu is worried now. He backs away from them, glancing up at the alarm horn, then back at the console.

"Don't try to manipulate it," he warns. "Not at this energy density!"

"Nonsense!" cries Lafcadio. "Listen to me, Zsuzsi! We must knot Babsi into our space for metastability. Use Hinton double-rotation."

Her sensitive, stubby fingers dance across the dials. The object behind, or in front of, the screen begins to spin. Another flick of the dials. Babsi flattens a little and dimples in at the poles. The sound of the hooter is faint and musical, synched to Babsi's growing buzz. Jimmy Hu's voice is shouting something, but the sound warps into gabble.

"Z-axis," hisses Lafcadio. "Donut."

Zsuzsi is playing the console like this year's high-scorer. Babsi's polar dimples dig in and meet. The mottled matter flows in one pole and out the other. It's a torus now, a spinning vortex ring.

But then ... as we stare at the Babsi the ... spinning stops and ... goes over to the room.

Babsi, Lafcadio and Zsuzsi: the three are motionless, while all around them the blurred room races. Engine, impresario and operator: poised at the center of a merry-go-round gone mad.

"Tie the knot," urges Lafcadio. He is gaunt, gray and wild-eyed. "Use XZ surgery and a W-axis hyperflip."

You have the feeling the Babsi particle wants to escape, for the flowy little torus jerks back from Zsuzsi's touch of ruby laser light. She throws a switch and a glowing blue net of field-mesh holds Babsi fast. The surgical red ray cuts in.

The alarm's sound is a dull, repeated scream: *aenh-aenh-aenh-aenh-aenh*. Look at Zsuzsi's fingers, slick with sweat.

Now the Babsi folds in on itself, and two circles link. The shifting outline of a Klein bottle is there, a meaty bag whose neck stretches out and punches in to eat its own bottom: a tortured hairless bird with its head stuck in its navel and out its ass. The world-snake. Klein-bottle Babsi-bean slides in and through itself, tracing impossible curves. Slowly it settles down, smoothing out and shrinking a bit.

The room has stopped spinning. Zsuzsi throws a relay, and the machines idle down.

Lafcadio laughs and hugs her. "Ready to take our baby to Venice?" As Zsuzsi watches, he draws out a tiny gold key and twists it in a little lock next to the console screen. There is a hiss of air and the screen swings down like an oven door. Lafcadio reaches in.

The space in there is funny. As Lafcadio thrusts his arm in the *front*, we see his hand angle in from the *side*. Undismayed, he seizes the little bean and takes it out.

Close shot of Lafcadio's palm. Resting on it is a spherelet. It glows slightly. There are lightly shaded lines on it, as on a peeled orange-pip.

"*Babsi*," croons Zsuzsi, motherly bosom aheave. "*Edes kicsikem*." Sweet little one. She prods it with a trembling finger. It shrinks away, avoiding her touch.

When the little sphere shrinks, the surrounding space distorts ... It's like suddenly seeing Lafcadio's palm through a wrong-way lens. But then the Babsi bounces back, bigger than before. It tries again to shrink away, and again bounces back. The space-knot is holding.

"Come zee, Jimmy," calls Zsuzsi. "Vhe have really trapped a hyperobject."

Jimmy Hu edges back in the room, loosely laughing, shaking his head . . .

PPPPFFFFFFWWWAAAAAAPP!

A huge ball of tissue is flowing over Zsuzsi . . . *eating* her! Suddenly only one hand is still showing. Blood drips off the fingers as they clench, unclench, go lax. Bones crunch.

Lafcadio has been flung back against a bank of machines. His face is rigid with horror. Tubes and cables snap, gas is whistling out in foggy plumes, sparks are jagging, and now a sheet of flame sweeps across the room.

Lafcadio falls to his knees, gone all to pieces, moaning, eyes rolling, tongue lolling. The blood-flecked superparticle edges towards him. Jimmy Hu grabs Lafcadio's foot and pulls him away. The giant Babsi bulges forward, hesitates, then SLAMS down to point-size as fast as it can. The floor beneath it bulges up with space-pressure . . . but the hyperblob can't get free.

Lafcadio's clawed fingers rake the floor as Jimmy drags him out of the room. The door slams. The little bean lies on the concrete, angrily buzzing in a puddle of blood.

TWO
alwin

Sybil and I were making love. 69 is LXIX in Rome. She moaned. It all felt so good. I moaned back.

But softly. Two of the children, the little ones, were sharing the room with us. They were sleeping in a folding bed, one at each end.

After a while Sybil and I came together, unusual for 69. There was, surprisingly, a magnolia outside the window. The city lights shone on its wet leaves. We kissed, and murmured a few things. Love. She fell asleep.

After a medium interval of time I decided to get back up. Rome was right outside, and it was only midnight.

My clothes were on the floor by the bed. I slipped them on, took the key and walked the two flights downstairs.

The hotel halls were narrow and oddly shaped, like pieces in a 3-D jigsaw. Hotel Caprice, just a block off the Via Veneto. It was shabby and casual, some forgotten bankrupt's converted house. Out of politeness, the horse-faced clerk ignored me on my way out.

A fine rain was falling. It was a cool spring night, a few days before Easter. With all the pilgrims in town, we'd been lucky to find a hotel room.

On the Via Veneto I sat down under a cafe awning, ordered a Heineken, then wished I hadn't. There was hardly anyone out, hardly anything to look at. I was getting cold through my damp sport coat. Holy Week comes well before the *Dolce Vita*.

A madman approached. Already from twenty meters you could tell. He carried a big toy robot, one of those weird Japanese toys that looks like a member of Kiss. The maniac's eyes were all over the place, and he caught me staring at him.

"*Ecco!*" he screeched, holding the robot towards me and raising one of its arms. He made a buzzing noise then, like the robot was supposed to be warding off my eye-attack with a death ray. "DZEEZEEZEEEEENTINI!"

I looked away, hoping he would keep walking. Fat chance. I could hear him pause, move closer, pause again. One more step and he'd be breathing on me.

With a sudden cry I whipped up my arms and pointed them at him, holding my fingers out and my thumbs flexed, as if to shoot Dr. Strange energy bolts from my palms.

A stupid move ... this wasn't exactly my first beer of the day ... but it worked. Falling right into the Marvel Comics idiom, the madman crooked a protective arm in front of his face and backed slowly off, eyes ablaze.

I looked around the café to see if anyone had noticed my little victory. But the place was empty and ... no, over there was a woman smiling at me, nice dark hair, good ass-flesh mouth, *hi, baby*, but, heh, there's a man with her, also staring at me ... should I look away? No, he's not sending eye-attacks, no indeed, he's ... *pimping*, with a flick of his eyes at the woman, and a crook of his pinky at me ... weird and scary. I called for my check.

Out from under the awning it was still wet ... not rain so much as heavy mist swirling and roiling in light-brightened patterns which twisted clear to heaven. All that information, just getting me wet. I decided to walk up to Harry's American Bar, have a whisky and go back to the hotel. Full of purpose, I strode faster.

There was a man ahead of me, a big strapping fellow loafing along under an enormous silk umbrella. I could see that I would have to pass him, and felt a bit nervous ... he had fifty pounds on me, easy. But, after all, the street, though empty, was brightly lit, and the man was, I realized, much too well-dressed to be a mugger. He was wearing Gucci shoes and a three-piece gray suit, for God's sake.

I angled out to the curb and stepped up my pace, hoping to just whisk past him. Fat, as I said before, chance.

"Tsst!"

I slid a glance over. With that suit he looked like the junior partner of a Newark law firm. Played football at Rutgers. Breast-heavy, wasp-waisted wife and a newborn named Nino. You just had to trust this Roman.

"What?"

"Come here." He stepped closer, including me under his umbrella. "You American?"

I repressed my stock response, *Does the Pope shit in the woods*, and just nodded.

"You live here?"

I was flattered he knew me for an expatriate. I'd been out of the States for almost two years now, though not in Italy. I decided to make him think I was really worth his time.

"Sure. I work at the embassy."

He nodded, pleased with his catch. Time to reel me in.

"You wanna come to my place? It's just down there."

He gestured at a dark side-street. Sure. Right. I was really going to walk into some random alley with this guy. What kind of idiot did he take me for? I shook my head.

"I'm going up to Harry's for a drink." I looked pointedly at my watch. 1:20 already. "I really better be on my way."

He looked hurt, surprised at my rejection.

"Whatsa matter? Come on! I got a beautiful place. Italian girls very romantic."

A pimp! Of course! A silk-lined room full of sensual Italian courtesans . . . high cheekbones, dark-fleshed lips and nipples, animal haunches, smellow cracks and the dewy jet-black deltas . . .

"No," I heard myself saying. "No thanks. I just got laid. I couldn't eat another bite."

The pimp looked more and more agitated. It was like I was the only mark who'd chanced past all evening. He all but grabbed me by the arm.

"Just come and look. Cost you nothing. Come back other night."

I wanted to. I wanted to see. But I had a nagging suspicion that there really were no girls down that dark street, that this big strong guy would just beat the shit out of me and take my watch and wallet. On the whole, he looked too well-dressed for such a crude approach, but hell, what did I know about Rome?

Stubbornly I shook my head and started walking again. The big pimp tagged along, sheltering me with his umbrella.

"How can you do this to me? Old friends and you won't even come look at my beautiful girls!" There was a catch in his voice.

"I've never seen you before in my life," I said with a short laugh. "Where do you get this 'old friend' stuff? For all I know, you'll kill me if I go in a side-street with you."

His face hardened. "You insult."

"I'm sorry," I said hastily. Only half a block more to Harry's, all warm and lit up, dear God, let me get there alive. "I do think of you as a friend."

A dark figure on a bicycle came whipping around the corner up ahead. The bicycle had a light on each handlebar, one red and one green, like an airplane. The skinny rider was standing up on the pedals, his tattered clothes flapping and one hand waving free.

"*Guai a voi, anime prave! Non isperate mai veder lo cielo: i'vegno per menarvi a l'altra riva ne le tenebre etterne, in caldo e'n gelo,*" he declaimed in a high, fanatical voice. He was riding down the middle of the sidewalk, speeding straight for us.

I spotted the toy robot in his free hand then, and realized it was the madman from before. I should have known better than to still be out where he could find me.

I stepped out from under the big pimp's umbrella, hoping to get out of the madman's way. But he'd fastened his eyes on me now, and seemed determined to ram me. The robot's lit-up eyes swept back and forth with the man's cries and wild gestures.

"ZAPPAPPA ZEZEENO SFERA GLOBO POW POW POW." His sound effects. Without looking, I stepped back off the curb to get out of his way. There was a screech of tires behind me. I tensed convulsively.

The pimp in the three-piece suit lunged towards me, the mad bicyclist shot past and a car nudged gently against the backs of my thighs. I felt like fainting with relief. But my troubles were just beginning.

The car that had almost run me down was a black Fiat four-door, slewed sideways from the sudden stop. The driver came boiling out of his vehicle, hairy and fighting mad. He screamed at me and pointed repeatedly at a small green sticker on his windshield. I had no idea what he was talking about.

The big pimp got in on the conversation. He introduced himself in Italian, and I caught the name: *Virgilio Bruno*. The ugly little black-mustached driver redoubled his shouting. Virgilio stood calm and stolid as a rock in a stormy sea. The words *Americano* and *lire* kept cropping up. The driver rummaged in his glove compartment and got out a little pamphlet with the Pirelli Tire Company logo on it. The numbers printed on the back seemed to be of importance. He pulled a folded yellow receipt out of his wallet and unfolded it three, six, nine times till it was the size of a pillowcase. He read off some more numbers in a loud voice, frequently pausing to gesture for effect. Finally he pointed one last time at the sticker on his windshield and handed the tire pamphlet and the yellow receipt to me.

Virgilio nodded formally, quite the lawyer now, and drew me a pace aside.

"He," a slightly contemptuous inclination of the head accompanied the word. "He say you have damaged his tires. Want ten thousand lire."

That was something like ten dollars. Should I pay him? It would almost be worth it, just to get off the fucking street. I looked over my shoulder to see if the mad bicyclist was around. I fingered the loose bills in my pants pocket. There was enough.

"We no pay," Virgilio informed me firmly. "I fix."

Before I could stop him he turned and unleashed a machine-gun burst of Italian on the driver. Even while holding an umbrella, Virgilio's hand-gestures were magnificent. Watching his one active hand you could see it all: the cautious pedestrian, the foolishly speeding (and possibly intoxicated) driver, the near-fatal accident, the likelihood of my suing for lower-back damage.

I was convinced, absolutely. But not that hairy little wart of a driver. He began negotiating a compromise. This was going to go on for hours! I snuck a look at my watch. It was almost two in the morning.

Just then the lit-up sign outside Harry's went out. And, whipping around the same corner, there came the mad robot-master on wheels. He must have ridden around the block. As if on cue, Virgilio and the driver stopped arguing. Before I knew what was happening, Virgilio had me in the backseat of the car with him and we were driving down the Via Veneto. In a way, I was glad.

"What you name?" the big pimp asked.

"Alwin Bitter. Could you drop me off at my hotel? Hotel Caprice." I called the name up to the driver, but he only hunched his shoulders stubbornly.

"Virgilio Bruno." He shook my hand, holding the contact longer than I liked. "You no live in hotel. We all have Scotch whisky at my club."

"My wife's going to be wondering where I am."

Virgilio just laughed. "With sex you gave her, she sleep all night."

The driver sped past the street where I'd met Virgilio, past the café where I'd had my beer, past the side-street where dear Sybil and the kids were sleeping. Would they wake as widow and orphans?

"Hey!" I tapped the driver on the shoulder. "Let me out! *Alt!* I'll give you your *dice mille lire!*" I pulled a bill out of my pocket and waved it in his face.

He accelerated through a red light, missing a Mercedes with a reflexive twitch of the wheel. We passed the American embassy on the left.

"You work," said Virgilio, hooking his thumb at the building.

"No, no," I cried. "That was a lie!"

Virgilio thinned his lips and shook his head. "No lie. You insult, but no lie. You very valuable, Alvino. Dead or alive."

There was another red light. We were near the Termini railroad station. There was too much traffic for the little wart to run the light. He had to stop. This was my chance to escape my kidnappers. Stealthily I took the back door handle in my left hand. Just a quick jump and . . .

I'm not a brave man. My self-image is of a very small and weak person. In point of fact, I'm almost six feet, and solidly built. But I was a late bloomer. I spent those formative early high-school years as a pudgy little science wimp. I'm still scared of big men with deep voices.

"*Calmo*," Virgilio said, snapping down the lock on my door. "Keep your head. I am heavily armed." I saw the dark glint of an automatic in his hand. The light changed and the car sprang forward.

The traffic thinned out rapidly as we drove away from the Termini. Anonymous street-lit buildings strobed past. Food, food, food. I wondered how they would keep me, my kidnappers. I noted the names of the streets we passed. I tried to think of the binary notation for the number 69. I tried to think of anything but the photo, still vivid in my memory.

The photo: Aldo Moro, Italy's most eminent statesman, found dead in the back of stolen Renault: a color news photo in *Time*, May 22, 1978: There he is; they dressed him in his blue suit after shooting him; you can see through the station wagon's open hatch; he's lying on his back, legs folded to fit; dead lumpy unshaven jaw and neck, dead closed eyes pointed away, dead limp hand loosely curled; the Brigate Rosse held him two months and no one met their price, even after his pitiful letters; they shot him eight times in the chest and washed and dressed him; a bloodless blue corpse in the back of a red Renault with green soldiers standing guard; try only to think of the colors, not the angle of his legs, the canceled empty gray face . . .

We pulled into a vast empty parking lot and stopped. There was something huge and black looming over us.

"*Colosseo*," the little wart of a driver observed. Footsteps approached. Virgilio unlocked my door and poked me in the ribs with his pistol.

"How much are you worth, Alvino?"

My door flew open and a man in a guard's uniform beckoned for me to get out. Virgilio and the wart came close on my heels.

My three captors led me in under the Colosseum's outer arcade, the guard snapping gates open and closed. There was a lot of trash on the ground: fruit rinds, food-papers, handbills with the Pope's picture. The rain stopped and a full moon came out. The Paschal Moon. Today had been Maundy Thursday. I remembered that the Pope had, in a televised religious observance, imitated Christ by washing the feet of several mental defectives at church this evening. We'd seen part of it on the tube in the hotel lounge.

The guard opened the door to a downward flight of stairs. "*Scendere, signor*." This was it.

"I won't." I got out my wallet. "This has gone far enough. I'll give you all my money." I counted rapidly. "Three hundred thousand lire, and I'll sign my traveler's checks."

Virgilio shook his head and took my wallet anyway. He laid a hand on my shoulder and pushed me gently toward the stairs.

Something in me snapped. That was death down there. *Green-red-blue*. I had nothing to lose. I swung around and punched Virgilio in the neck. He made a husky crackling noise and dropped his gun. I scooped up the pistol and took off running along the arcade circling the Colosseum, looking for a way out.

But all the exits I passed were locked up tight. My shoes were loud on the ancient stones. After a while I heard voices ahead of me . . . I'd run almost full circle. I stopped and leaned against the inner wall to catch my breath. In the silence I could hear the scuff of footsteps coming after me. Quietly drawing closer. I looked down at my pistol to check that the safety was off. But surely they all had guns, too.

My pursuer was almost on me now, and around the curve ahead I could hear the guard reviving Virgilio. I scooted through one of the short passages leading into the Colosseum proper.

The Roman Colosseum is a roundish stadium about a hundred meters in diameter. The central arena's flooring is long-gone, exposing a warren of subterranean halls, stalls and cells. The stadium seats and benches are gone too, so that the supporting walls are uncovered. The supports slant all the way from the arena's edge to the top of the Colosseum's outer wall. The whole thing looks a little like the inside of a dried-out sea urchin: a crude central maze surrounded by crumbly radial fins.

With the moon as bright as it was, I was going to have to move fast. It was a choice of up or down. The kidnappers had wanted to take me down, so I chose up, first slipping off my shoes.

With a leap and a wriggle I got up onto the butt of one of the slanting support walls. I was lucky, for it wasn't half-collapsed like some of the others. My wall angled smoothly all the way to the top. Silently I rushed up the moon-silvered stone slope. There was a puddle of shadow by the parapet of the outer wall. I flung myself into the shadow just as the wart stepped into the stadium. He was cradling a machine gun with a wire stock.

I pressed myself deeper into the shadow, hardly daring to breathe. He found my shoes, glanced up, failed to see me, walked over to the edge of the arena and stared down. Virgilio called something from outside, and the wart called something back. For a while nothing happened, and then I saw the guard moving about in the arena's sunken maze, machine gun at the ready. The little wart followed the guard's movements like a hunter watching a bird dog.

I was going to have to do something before they searched up here. My shoes were right down there, showing them where to look.

I wormed a bit higher and peered down the outer wall to the ground. Quite a drop, twenty-five meters at least. But the wall was cracked and pocked enough to climb down. I decided to go for it.

Virgilio had joined the wart in staring down into the arena, where the guard was hoping to flush me out. Neither of them saw me slink out of my shadow-pool and slide over the edge.

The low moon lit up every cranny and fissure of the stone. I picked my way down over some decorative ledges. So far, so good. Next came a bunch of arches separated by pillars. I hung onto one of the cornices and swung my legs down, scissoring madly. Finally I got them wrapped around a big column. I leaned my head back and let go with my hands, starting a slide down the shaft. I caught the column with my arms and got the next few meters for free.

When I slammed into the column's base I almost lost hold. Fatigue. I was still too high above the street to jump, and the next stretch of wall looked dangerously smooth. I got in one of the arch's shadows and sat down to rest. I'd killed my back, torn a fingernail and rubbed my cheek raw. Some more moldings and another slide down a column and I'd be on the street. If I didn't fall on my head. I sat there sucking my hurt finger.

I could see my watch. 3:30. The hangover from yesterday's drinking was starting up.

Virgilio's smooth voice came drifting down from somewhere overhead. What was the matter with those guys? Were they political terrorists or just in it for the money? They thought I was some bigwig from the American embassy. I cursed myself for the lie.

God, I was tired. Utterly drained. Maybe it would be a good idea to just stay put. If I started running off down the street, they'd spot me and chase me down. Every now and then a little truck full of vegetables buzzed by, but other than that there was no one to turn to.

It seemed fairly safe where I was. My sheltering arch opened into an arcade ringing the second story of the Colosseum, but this arcade wasn't connected, in any obvious way, to the central area where they were looking for me. I was so tired that the stone behind my back felt like foam rubber. I decided to stay here till morning. Then the rats would go back into their holes, and I'd get a cab back to the hotel, and we'd get the hell out of Italy. I had no intention of getting involved with Italian police. Just put me and Sybil and Tom and Ida on the train back to Heidelberg. *Basta!*

I could have dropped right off to sleep, except that I had to piss. That last beer on its way out. I struggled to my feet and stepped over to the other side of the arch, leaned up against the cool stone and . . .

"ECCO!" screamed a voice below. The madman with the robot!

The crazy rotten fuck. Waving his goddamn light-up toy. I'd show him death rays! Aiming quickly, I fired my pistol at him, capering on the pavement some ten meters below. Missed. No time for another shot. I could hear someone running down some stairs to my left. I took off down the arcade in the other direction.

And ran right into Virgilio. He darted out at me from a shadow and had his pistol back before I knew what had happened.

"You make good sport, Alvino." He twisted my arm behind me in a hammerlock and pressed the gun against my spine. "Come quickly now."

I groaned and went along quietly. Down the stairs to the ground-level arcade. Down more stairs. Some doors and stairs again. Doors. A cubical concrete room lit by a single caged light bulb.

The guard was there, and the madman, and a business-man-gangster. The businessman-gangster seemed to be running the show. He was comfortably overweight, with amused, blinking eyes. They called him Minos.

At his direction, Virgilio put leg-irons on me, and chained the irons to a heavy staple set into the wall. Minos watched from a sofa across the room. I had a pile of rags to sit on. The guard left, while the madman stood watch with a machine gun.

"You are from the US embassy," Virgilio began.

"I am *not*. I'm just a poor physicist living in Germany on a research grant."

"Fancy words," Virgilio replied. "Signifying nothing." Now that he was no longer playing the pimp, his English had improved considerably.

"You don't have any girls at all, do you?" I demanded. "Your whole living is kidnapping people off the Via Veneto. How long do you think you can get away with it?"

"Virgilio is a very good trapper," Minos remarked in his mild, cultured voice. He had a cupid's-bow mouth. He looked as clean and well cared for as a newborn baby. "I often buy from him. But how much are you worth?"

"He is very important," Virgilio insisted. "The embassy will pay billions of lire. I'll let you have him for only one million."

"He says he's merely a scientist," Minos said doubtfully. "Perhaps you should just . . ." He made a negligent, lethal hand-gesture. "Why couldn't you get me a spy?"

"*Kree kree*," the madman said, swinging his machine gun around. "*Kree kree kree*." The businessman-gangster said something to him, and he sat down on the sofa too, with his robot on one knee and the machine gun on the other. They talked quietly for a minute. The madman's name seemed to be Lafcadio.

Virgilio paced back and forth slowly, exuding menace. Suddenly he stopped and stood over me, his fists clenched.

"You are from the US embassy."

"Don't start hitting me," I said in alarm. "If you want to think that, you just go right ahead. Phone them up when they open. It shouldn't be much longer." I looked at my watch. It was almost 5:00.

"What kind of physicist?" Minos wanted to know. "Lafcadio was a physicist, too, before he went crazy. Lafcadio Caron. You know of?"

Lafcadio Caron? This lunatic? Sure, I'd heard of him. I'd even read some of his papers. He'd been in charge of the proton-decay experiment in the Mont Blanc tunnel. There'd been an accident there a few months ago. But how . . . ?

"What kind of physics?" Minos repeated. "I must decide if you are of any value."

"Atoms," I blurted out. "I study atomic and nuclear physics." This was a simplification. My precise specialty was the mathematical analysis of quantum-mechanical Hilbert Space operators.

"He can build a bomb!" Virgilio cried excitedly. "Just think what the government will pay to stop him!"

"Maybe I could build an atomic bomb," I said, playing along. "But you'd have to steal me some reactor fuel."

"*Boomawhooma pow pow pow.*"

"Perhaps we know where to find some. Or perhaps the

embassy will *think* we know where." Minos and Virgilio exchanged a significant glance.

I was getting in deeper all the time. "I'm not a weapons expert," I pointed out. "I'm simply a theoretical physicist doing research on infinite-dimensional space in Heidelberg, Germany. I wrote a little book about dimensions called Geometry and Reality? That helped me get the grant for Heidelberg. And I came to Rome with my wife and children for a vacation. My wife wants to see the Pope at St. Peter's on Easter."

"Today will be Good Friday," Minos said absently. "A day for human sacrifice." The delicate little mouth formed a small smile in the fat face. "Get a manifesto from him, Virgilio, just in case. Then contact the embassy."

Minos and Virgilio talked a bit more in rapid Italian, patting each other on the shoulders. Minos left, throwing me a smile and a negligent wave of his pinky.

"Okay," Virgilio said to me. "Sit down and write." He dragged a chair and card table over to where I was chained. He had paper and a ball-point pen. Lafcadio still bounced on the couch, making explosion noises and cradling his gun.

"What's this supposed to be?" I demanded.

"Self-incrimination. Revolutionary manifesto. Write."

This is what I wrote:

I HAVE JOINED THE PEOPLE'S ARMY OF MY OWN FREE WILL. DEATH TO THE FASCIST PIG. CUT OFF HIS BLACK PLASTIC TROTTERS. ROAST HIM WITH GAMMA RAYS. USE EVERY-

THING EXCEPT THE SQUEAL. FUCK AMER-
IKKKA, FUCK KKKOMUNISM, FUCK KKKOD.
SINCERELY, DR. ALWIN BITTER, THE ARCHI-
MEDES OF ANARCHY.

I wouldn't want to say that I composed the whole message myself, but I did have a hand in it here and there. On
one level, I even meant it. But on the level that counts, I
didn't mean a word. Honest! I just wanted to get out alive.

Virgilio was pleased with our collaboration, and taped
the note up on the wall. "Here, Alvino," he said, handing
me a small machine gun. "Try it on for size."

The gun was an Uzi, Israeli-made, lethal as a cobra's
fang. It had a snap-on wire stock. I clicked the trigger.
Empty of course. I realized Virgilio had just wanted to
get my fingerprints on the weapon. I threw it at him. He
dodged easily, then left, laughing at me. Lafcadio was still
there on the couch, standing guard.

"*Per altra via, per altri porti verrai a piaggia, non qui,
per passare,*" he said suddenly, staring at me with glowing
eyes.

I noticed that he had a photograph glued to his robot's
face, a photograph of a plump blond woman. His mother?
Some lost love? Was this really the famous Lafcadio
Caron? No point stirring him up with a question.

I smiled politely and lay down on the rags to sleep.
Maybe by the time I woke up, this would all be over. Virgilio would contact the embassy, and they'd tell him I was
an academic, a scholar, a nobody. Then he'd just have to
let me go.

Or would he? The businessman-gangster hadn't come right out and said so, but I had the impression they might kill me if I wasn't worth a good ransom. Dead men tell no tales.

I pushed the thought away. Once Virgilio realized his mistake, surely he'd put me out on the street. I wouldn't press charges; he could be sure of that. All I wanted was to get the next train out of Rome. The next train. I drifted off to sleep, a bad sleep filled with bad dreams.

THREE
sybil

The children woke Sybil up. They were in the bathroom playing with the water. Their little voices were very loud on the tiles.

"Alwin," she called, "make them stop."

The noise kept on, Ida, five years old, liked to giggle. Tom, seven, liked to roar. He'd only learned the roar recently, from some school friends in Heidelberg.

"BAAAOOOOUUUUUU! BAAAOOOOUUUUUU! UUUUUUh UUHHHHHHHOOOOOUUUU!" Tom.

"Gligeeglegleheeehegligiheeheeteeheeegleeheepeepe-gigteehee." Ida.

"Stop the NOISE!" Sybil shouted, "You'll wake everyone in the hotel!"

Ida gave a happy scream and came running out of the bathroom. She was waving a towel that had been rolled into a loose tube.

"Poo-worm bite Mama!" she shouted with a burst of laughter, and threw the towel at Sybil. One end of the towel was soaking wet. It smacked onto the bed, right where Alwin's sleeping, reassuring bulk should have been.

"Is Daddy taking a bath?" Sybil asked.

"Dada gone!"

"Tom," she called to her son, invisible in the bathroom. "Where did Daddy go?"

No answer. She repeated the question. Still no answer.

Sun was coming in the window. Sybil looked at her watch. 7:30. Nice and early, and good weather. They could do the Forum today. Maybe Alwin had gone downstairs to order coffee for them. But why couldn't he have just phoned room service?

She got out of bed, a tall woman with voluptuous features and a nice, willowy figure. When she stood still, as she did now for a moment, her body described a gracefully attenuated S. She had a way of standing still and staring, moving only her head and her lovely neck. *Craning*, Alwin called it.

Sybil craned at the bathroom door, then went in. Tom was busy floating things in the partially filled tub. A toothbrush case, a dirty metal ashtray, two reddened wine glasses, the drawer of a matchbox, a folded bit of paper. As always, the sight of his bulging, intent forehead filled her with love.

"Tommy, where's Daddy?"

"I don't know. I didn't see him yet today."

Sybil felt the first pang of fear. Alwin must have gone out in the night and gotten into trouble. They had drunk a bottle of the hotel's cheap wine, then made love, and then ...? He often got back up after sex, a habit which annoyed her, struck her as slighting; but where could he still be at 7:30 in the morning? How thoughtless could you get?

"Let's get dressed and go downstairs, children."

"Is Daddy downstairs?" Tom asked, looking up from his water-play.

"Yes, I think so." Her voice grew brittle with sudden anger. "Now, don't make Mommy do everything. Find your clothes and put them on. You can wear what you had yesterday. I'll give you new socks and underpants."

"Okay." Tom jumped up and ran into the bedroom, making a race-car noise at the corner. Ida gave an abandoned squeal of delight. When Sybil came back into the bedroom, both of the children were bouncing on the bed.

"Double Ting!"

"Triple Ting!"

"*Ostrich* Ting!"

That was one of the children's chants. They were such little *people*, the children, little elves with their own elvish ways. For a moment Sybil wished that their oldest child, Sorrel, the ringleader, were there too. To simplify the trip a bit, Sorrel had been parked in Frankfurt with Sybil's parents, Lotte and Cortland Burton. Cortland was a big vice-president for Miltech, an international conglomerate of high-tech engineering companies.

Tom threw a pillow and knocked the phone off the bedside table.

"That's IT!" cried Sybil, springing into action. "You get those clothes on *now* or there's no breakfast!"

"What's for breakfast?" Tom asked in a put-on fussy voice.

"Yeah," Ida cackled, joining in the joke. "What are we eating for breakfast?"

"Fried egg with spinach?"

"Yucky hot milk?"

"Pancake with pig gravy?"

"Broken waggy waggy?"

"Booger pie?"

"Poo and pee?"

"BAAAAOOOOUUUUUU!"

"Gligeegleglheeheglgihee!"

The children were on the bed, snorting and grunting and rolling around. Sybil lunged forward and caught hold of them. "I'VE HAD IT, KIDS!"

As the children began to dress, Sybil harangued them. "I don't know *why* you two can't behave *normally*. Here we are in Rome for a lovely *vacation* and you roll around like *animals*. Now let's go downstairs and find Daddy."

Alwin was not in the breakfast room, not in the lobby, not to be seen on the street outside. Sybil even walked to the Via Veneto and craned. Pale, empty sunshine. God *damn* him.

Back in the hotel, she approached the desk clerk, a cadaverous man with a horse-face. This was Beppo, the night-clerk, tired and waiting to be relieved.

"Have you seen my husband?"

Beppo smiled broadly. "*Si, si*. I see him go in the night. He no come back. Where you think he go?" The last question was a blend of malice and idle curiosity.

"I don't know!" Sybil exclaimed, her voice rising. Suddenly she was afraid. "Something must have happened to him! Can you call the police for me?" Her hands were shaking.

Beppo jerked his head and shoulders in an ambiguous gesture . . . part shrug and part nod. "I will attempt. But perhaps no one there today. *Venerdì santo*."

"Good Friday," Sybil translated. "Oh Lord, what a mess. Everything will be closed. Try the hospitals, too."

Tom and Ida bounced past. They held their forearms together and their hands up under their chins. They were playing Easter rabbit. Poor little orphans. Sybil's eyes filled with quick tears.

The night-clerk dialed a number, listened briefly, then hung up.

"*Impossibile, Signora Bitter.* I can do nothing."

Sybil knew better than to take no for an answer. She could see a light in an office behind the clerk. Someone in there would help her. "I would like to speak to the manager."

The night-clerk glanced longingly at the lobby doors. Where was Guido the day-clerk, that lazy pig of a Tuscan? Beppo's lips pursed into a thin line of distaste. Perhaps if he ignored this woman she would go away. Find her husband, indeed. "The manager is not here, *signora*. Perhaps you should go to the *carabinieri* in person."

This was a mistake. Beppo had underestimated Sybil's determination. Now she began to scream.

"WON'T ANYBODY HELP ME? MY HUSBAND MAY BE DYING! WHAT KIND OF HOTEL IS THIS?"

At the sound of her angry, frightened voice the children came to her side and stood there, wide-eyed and anxious. Some guests looked up from their breakfasts. A porter came over, glaring at Beppo. And then the manager's door opened.

"Of course," Beppo began. "Of course I will help." He fumbled at the telephone.

"WON'T ANYBODY HELP ME FIND MY HUS-BAND?" Sybil repeated.

The manager came out of his office, wiping coffee from his mustache. He had a well-worn look, and kind-looking wrinkles on his forehead.

"*Signora?*"

Sybil drew a breath and gave him a smile. "My name is Sybil Bitter. We are staying in Room 201. Last night my husband went out for a walk, and he has not returned. I am afraid something has happened to him." She fixed the night-clerk with a hard glance. "And this man . . ."

Beppo gave a hugely insincere smile and handed the telephone to the manager.

For the next few minutes the manager talked Italian over the phone, frequently asking Sybil or the night-clerk for bits of information: when Alwin had left, how to spell his name, what his passport number was, his physical appearance, what he had been wearing.

"Where's Daddy?" Tom whispered up at Sybil. "Did he run away?"

"I don't think he would do that," Sybil answered softly. Why would he? They'd been having good food and great sex; why would he run away?

"Maybe he got lost," suggested Ida.

The manager set the telephone down slowly, his forehead corrugated with worry. "Maybe you come into my office, a-Mrs. Bitter."

"Why? What is it? Just tell me!"

The manager looked around the lobby, then leaned across the counter to speak confidentially. "A note has been a-found at USA embassy." His dark, liquid eyes stared at Sybil significantly.

"What kind of note? From my husband?" Had he run away . . . or, oh God no, killed himself? "What are you trying to tell me?" The children at her sides began to babble questions.

"Please, a-Mrs. Bitter. Do not excite. Beppo now take you to USA embassy. Is only a-two hundred meter." The manager spoke rapidly to the night-clerk. The gaunt man stood up and began slowly to shrug himself into his shiny black raincoat.

"What did the note say?" Sybil asked, keeping her voice level.

The manager sighed. "Is a-very bad in Rome this year. Your husband has been-a . . ." He paused, groping for the word. "Bandits give him a-back for money. Or other things."

"He's been *kidnapped!*"

The children burst into tears. They knew all about kidnapping from years of schoolyard warnings. It took Sybil several minutes to calm them.

And then Beppo led them outside. A cloud crossed the sun, the air cooled momentarily. Well-dressed people hurried this way and that, going for coffee, going to church. Sybil wondered if she should have gone back upstairs to get coats for the children.

Ida stopped by a window display of chocolate eggs. They were the huge Italian kind, foil-wrapped and with a toy hidden inside. Alwin had planned to buy two for the kids today.

Sybil signaled the night-clerk to stop rushing ahead, and waited for Ida. The child was just tall enough to see in the store window. From the side, Sybil could see the round little face reflected, no bigger than one of the giant Easter eggs.

"Come on, Ida. We have to find Daddy."

Still the blond little head stared into the depths of the store window. Was there a tear on her cheek?

"Ida? Don't cry, honey."

At this, Ida's face squeezed up and the fat tears popped out. In an instant her whole face was wet. Alwin had always compared this process to the squeezing of a grapefruit half. "I'm scared of the kidnappers," Ida sobbed.

"Don't worry, sweetie," Sybil said, picking her up. Such a cuddly, curvy body this little one had. *Rubber popo, you're the one.* "Everything will be all right. Everything will be all right." Sybil carried Ida to Beppo and Tom, taking comfort from her own words.

"Do you have a gun?" Tom was asking the night-clerk.

"*Subito, signora,*" the skinny man cried to Sybil. "I have hurry."

They tagged after him as far as the corner, from where he pointed out the US embassy building, half a block down the other side of the Via Veneto. The daylight shone through the night-clerk's lank strands of greasy hair, making unpleasant highlights on his scurfy scalp. Sybil was glad to see him go, the heartless prick.

The light changed, and they could have rushed right across the street, but Sybil hesitated. Until she went and talked to some little American official, this was still unreal.

Alwin kidnapped? For what? All they had in the world was some furniture, and the money they were saving for a house. Why would a kidnapper grab Alwin in his shabby old sport coat?

Tom and Ida were examining the Italian comic books at the corner newsstand. *Paparino* was Donald, and *Topolino* was Mickey. Up where the children couldn't see, there were a bunch of the lurid Italian porno comics. Sodomy was the thing these men craved the most ... Sybil could feel it in their stares and pinches. Ugh.

As if called up by the thought, a passing man in a suit and mustache ran his hand over her ass. A bony hand like a sheathed meat-hook. Sybil turned to glare at him, but he was already two paces into the street. She bought a *Topolino* and a *Paparino* to keep the children busy.

The embassy was housed in an enormous old dwelling, practically a palace. Freshly mimeographed sheets of paper were blowing up and down the sidewalk. Some kind of message in Italian. The guards let Sybil in after she showed her US passport. They were black marines with country accents.

"My husband's been kidnapped," she told them.

"We're doing what we can, ma'am. Just go on ahead in."

Inside, there was an enormous marble entrance hall with a single silver-haired lady behind a metal desk. DOT HOOK, said the plastic nameplate. DOT HOOK, RECEPTION. She looked alertly at Sybil and the two children.

"My husband has been kidnapped," repeated Sybil. "What can we do?"

"Oh, so you're the *wife*." Dot Hook paused to savor the information. "Mrs. . . ."

"Bitter. Sybil Bitter. Did you get a note?"

"That's right, Sybil, there was a note *nailed* to our front door. With a *stiletto*. Do you want to see it?"

This felt viciously unreal. "Yes," Sybil said. "Of course. What do they want?"

"Well, I think you'd better have a little talk with our Mr. *Membrane* about all this. He's our vice-consul in charge of vice. Room 36G." She pushed a button on her special Dot Hook intercom. Zzuuzzz. A voice crackled back.

"What is it?"

"The wife is here, Mr. Membrane. *Syllable* Bitter."

"Send her . . . up."

"Ten-four, Mark." Dot Hook glared provokingly at Sybil. "Can we find our own *way*?"

"What are you talking about?"

"To 36G."

"She talked to that box," Ida stated questioningly.

"It's a walkie-talkie," Tom explained.

"Bill-*leee*!" bawled Dot Hook. "Take Mrs. Bitter up to 36G."

The taller of the marines marched snappily over. Sybil and the children followed him up a flight of marble stairs.

"Don't say *thanks* or anything," Dot Hook called after.

"What's wrong with that woman?" Sybil asked the marine.

"I don't rightly know," he said, with a sunny smile. "Women is *all* crazy."

Sybil smiled. The music was nice, even if the words were wrong. "Did you see the kidnappers' note?"

"I guess I did. It was stuck on a knife in the door. Just like being at the movies. This Rome is a hell of a town."

"Are kidnappings common?"

"Well . . . they ain't *unusual*. There's been four Americans already this year."

Hearing this made Sybil feel a little better. The situation was bad, but not unheard of. No worse than losing your wallet, really. Alwin the wallet. Sometimes he said that's all he was. *No*, Sybil would say, *that's not all. You're my fat cock, too*.

They were walking down a long Americanized hall. Green carpeting on the floor, air conditioners plugged into the windows. But the heavily ornate moldings above the windows, the fat scrolls hanging there like iced curls of butter . . . the moldings said, "Italy." Italian architecture made Sybil think of food. Especially right now. They'd rushed out of the hotel without breakfast. *Cappuccino*, butter curls and shiny Italian rolls, a soft-boiled egg. The children must be getting hungry, too.

Just then the marine stopped at one of the doors. Door 36G. M. MEMBRANE, VICE-CONSUL. "He in here, the man you got to see."

"Thank you."

"And seein' is believin'."

"Goodbye."

"I'm leavin'."

"Back to duty?"

"You know it!"

"Well . . ."

". . . hell. Right on there, ma'am. You need any help, just rattle my cage. Bill Buttwhumper. Pleased and pleasin'."

He held out a large, dark hand. Sybil laid hers in it. A gentle pressure.

The door to room 36G swung open. Buttwhumper saluted, turned sharply on his heel and strutted off down the hall.

"Do you miss your Daddy, sweetums?" Mark Membrane, vice-consul, was kneeling on the green carpeting, cozying up to Ida. His attention turned to Tom. "Do you like football?"

The children hung back, unpleasantly surprised. Membrane looked up at Sybil. He was a skinny, rawboned man with a boyish face and a heavy shock of blonde hair. He wore a blue cord suit. "Mrs. . . . Bitter?"

He rose smoothly to his feet and took her hand. "It's a terrible thing . . . terrible."

"I'm sure it is," Sybil said, stepping into the room and finding herself a chair near the desk. "But nobody has yet explained to me what's actually happened. Can I see the note?"

"It's partly . . . in Italian," Membrane said, closing the office door. He beamed down at the children, looking like a pale stork, like Ichabod Crane. "Would you two like some Coca-Cola®?" You could hear the trademark.

"Yay!"

"I'll . . . get some." Membrane had the habit of pausing dramatically in the middle of some sentences, as if to accumulate the necessary charge of sincerity to finish his . . . message.

He extracted two cans of Coke from the icebox under his plastic bar, a squat affair stamped in parquet repetitions. He gazed pleasantly at Sybil. ". . . Something for you?"

"Tomato juice?"

"V . . . . . . 8®?"

"That will be fine. Can I see the note?"

"Certainly . . ."

Sybil waited awhile for the rest of the sentence, then plugged in another token.

"Can I see the note?"

Membrane was draped over his little bar, measuring out the Cokes and the V–8.

"Would you kids like a Milky Way®?"

"Yay!!"

"Can I see the note?"

"It's partly . . ."

". . . in Italian," Sybil interrupted, rising to her feet. "Show me the fucking note!"

"Your Mommy is . . . under stress."

"BAAAAAAOOOOOOOOOUUUUUUUUUUUU!!!"

"Poo an' pee, poo an' pee!"

"We're all under stress, Mr. Membrane. And you aren't helping much. My husband has been kidnapped, and you won't even begin to discuss it. The facts! I need to know what's going on!"

Membrane gave the children their Cokes, gave Sybil her thick red juice, then walked behind his desk, where he briefly rummaged.

"Here."

Sybil took the piece of pink-brown paper. Butcher's paper. There was a hole in the middle. She scanned down the page. It was written in English, and this is what it said:

We have taken your tool. Alwin Bitter has been conscripted into the People's Army, Division of Nuclear Weapons. Ransom him before it is too late. Your reply must be multiplied on papers drifting from the embassy window. We await. — Brigate Rosse

"Who's that?" asked Sybil. "*Brigate Rosse?*"

"That's the Italian part. It means *Red Brigade*. But they aren't." Membrane's unformed face held something sly.

"They aren't the Red Brigade?"

"No. Everything's wrong. The technique, the language, the . . . reply method. It's not the Red Brigade at all. These days every kidnapper says he's the Red Brigade just to . . . cause alarm. I'd be willing to bet that . . ."

"That?"

". . . *these* fellows are just after some money. But . . ."

"But?"

"What *is* your husband's occupation? To the best of your knowledge."

"He's a theoretical physicist. Unemployed. Not really unemployed. On a grant. He has a Humboldt grant to do research in Heidelberg this year. Next year we don't know what we'll do." Sybil shot a glance over at the children, not really liking them to be in on all this. But they were absorbed in their comics, flipping the bright pages.

Membrane gazed meditatively at the ceiling. It was clear that he was already in possession of the few poor facts Sybil knew.

"Could your husband assemble a . . . nuclear device? An atomic bomb?"

"I don't know. Probably. In grad school he used to talk about how easy it would be. He's good at making things. But you said you don't think he's really in the hands of bombers."

"Not . . . yet."

"What do you mean?"

A long, thoughtful pause. "How much can you pay? To get your husband back."

"Nothing. A few thousand dollars. Nothing, really."

"That's good."

"Why?"

Membrane leaned across the desk, his Adam's apple jutting out over his button-down Oxford-cloth collar and regimental-stripe tie. "I am going to tell you something in strictest confidence. Someone out there has enough nuclear fuel to build a hundred-kiloton bomb. Two months ago an LWR fuel-assembly truck was hijacked near Mestre. We have got to find that fuel."

"What does that have to do with my husband?"

"We will use your husband for . . . bait. To flush out the *real* terrorists, the ones with the reactor fuel. In return . . ." He held a silencing hand up to the spluttering Sybil. "In return I give you my solemn word that your husband will be . . . freed unharmed. Look at this."

He handed her a freshly mimeographed sheet of paper. A message in Italian. It was, Sybil realized with horror, the same as the papers she'd seen blowing up and down the sidewalk in front of the embassy.

"You've already replied? What did you say? What does this say?"

Membrane picked up another copy of the message, cleared his throat and began sonorously to sight-translate.

"'In the affair of Alwin Bitter. Greetings, revolutionary comrades. We, as Americans, feel sympathy for your woe. But freedom is not anarchy. Nor anarchy freedom. Professor Bitter is a man of peace, an atomic scientist. To think that his long and intimate association with weapons projects enables him single-handedly to build a bomb is fantasy. To take his close ties with the US embassy for military involvement is gross self-deception. Do not harm this innocent man, or the gravest consequences will ensue. We stand prepared to pay a ransom of one million US dollars.'"

"But that's so misleading," Sybil cried. "It makes him sound like an important bomb specialist! They'll never give him up!"

"They'll . . . have to give him up," Membrane said with a faint smile. "Word spreads fast in Rome. No matter who has him now . . . the real terrorists will come and get him."

FOUR
orali and rectelli

It was bad sleep, there on a pile of rags somewhere beneath the Colosseum. My body was immobile with exhaustion, but my brain was racing ... trying to find a way out, trying to find a next move. There were lots of dreams. Here's one of them:

I'm outside the Colosseum, running down endless streets with shuttered doors. Finally I find a café-bar which is open for the early workers. No one inside will talk to me or even look at me. In the back there is a billiard table, and arched doors leading down. On the green baize lies a dead man, crumpled like a bag of garbage. His legs are missing ... not really missing, just stripped of meat. Butchered. The man behind the zinc bar is cooking a greasy cannibal stew. He passes out huge glass mugs of beer, bubbles a-tick. The mugs are so big and so clear you could almost go skin-diving in them. He won't give me one, just shakes his head. Then into each of the mugs he ladles a chunk of fresh-cooked leg-meat. I recoil and rush out through those arched doors in back.

I'm running down a slope, down the radius of a series of concentric circles, heading deeper and deeper underground. It's an invisible underground Colosseum. Demons peer at me from odd nooks and crannies. A rumble of voices all around. There are thousands of us drifting down toward the impossible center.

In the half-light I pause in front of an ... exhibit, some kind of recess in the wall where a tasty bit of knowledge might be served, something about quarks and quantum chromodynamics ... but instead there's a gray-white demon with a swollen tick's body. He scrambles about, then splits a vent and spews hot liquid on me. It's foul, with lumps, stinking and stuck to my body, marking me for all to see. Somewhere below, Minos is waiting to judge me ...

I woke with a start. I knew where I was. My back was killing me, and my hurt finger throbbed. I looked at my watch. Quarter of ten. Lafcadio still sat on the sofa, guarding me with the robot and the machine gun on his lap. He hadn't noticed yet that I was awake, and I studied him through slitted eyes.

His dry black hair stuck out from his head in asymmetrical tufts and auras. There was a festering scab-crust along the outer curve of his left ear. His skin was a sallow yellow, blued along the jawline by sixteen-o'clock shadow. His mouth was a thin twisting line, never quite at ease, never quite unamused. It was as if he were constantly holding back both screams and laughter. He kept his eyes squeezed almost shut, possibly in an effort to valve down the boom and bustle of consensus reality.

He wore a plain black suit, shiny with wear, and a stained white shirt with no necktie. The suit pockets bulged with worthless objects. Now as I watched he fished out a sheet of paper with some sort of geometric diagram and studied it intently, turning it from side to side like a monkey would. His hands were off the machine gun ... but this did me no good, as the chain fastening me to the wall was so short. Yawning loudly, I sat up.

Lafcadio put away his diagram, whispered to his robot, and then smiled at me in a friendly sort of way.

"*Stavvi Minòs orribilimente, e ringhia: essamina le colpe ne l'intrata; giudica e manda secondo ch'avvinghia.*" Apparently he spoke no English ... strange for a physicist, but not impossible, especially in Italy.

"I'm sorry." I threw out my hands. "I can't understand you at all. I only know about twenty words of Italian. *Non capisce.*"

But that didn't stop him. He wanted to talk. He had something on his mind. "*Luna,*" he said, molding an ass-shape in the air. "*Baciare e entrare.*" He made the traditional hand-gesture for coitus, the erect right index finger bustling about in the loop of left thumb and forefinger. Apparently he was asking if I liked sex.

"Sure. *Molto bello.* Me and my wife every night." Smilingly I pumped the air with both fists, as if lifting myself up and down on a bed.

Lafcadio went to the door of our stone room and peered out. Was he going to set me free? Tell me a secret? Sexually assault me?

"*Ecco,*" he said, laying his gun down on the sofa and stepping close to me. He fumbled for something in his pants pocket and then brought it out. A tiny bean or seed it looked like, lying in the center of his dirty palm.

Looking lovingly down at the little lump, Lafcadio began . . . blowing kisses at it. Pursing his lips and making coaxing noises.

"*Smeep smeep. Smeep smeep smeep.*"

The little sphere seemed to twitch, to grow a bit.

"*Smeep smeep,*" went Lafcadio, pausing to grin and nod encouragingly at me. I was supposed to help.

"Smeep," I went, dry lips puckered. "Smeep smeep smeep."

"*Smeep smeepy.*"

"Smeepity smeep smeep."

The little ball grew, its surface flowing. In a way, I felt like I was being hypnotized, or having a hallucination. But yet the . . . *presence* growing and taking shape in crazy Lafcadio's cupped palms seemed real enough. Another order of reality, I thought, when suddenly . . .

There was the crash of footsteps, an explosion of gunfire, and Lafcadio pitched toward me, his chest gushing blood. With what must have been his last act of volition, he passed the magic sphere to me. It shrank back to the size of an orange-pip. I pocketed it as I stepped back from the intruders.

They were two very short men with guns, burr haircuts and big jaws. They looked like a couple of the "snoids" R. Crumb used to draw, amoral little goblin-men who live in sewers and assholes. They wore matching gray mechanic's overalls with nametags. *Orali* and *Rectelli*. One had a machine gun and one had a sawed-off shotgun. They didn't look like police.

Or act like them. The snoid with the machine gun rapidly emptied out Lafcadio's pockets, making a growing mound of newspaper clippings, pages ripped out of books, drawings of circles, pornographic photos, dead flashlight batteries, orange rinds, squeezed-out tubes of ointment, and balls, balls, balls. There must have been fifteen or twenty little balls, some wood, some metal, some rubber. Ball bearings, Ping-Pong balls, *bocce* balls, gumballs, and even a tiny Earth-globe pencil sharpener. But none of them seemed to be alive like the one I'd pocketed.

The snoid with the sawed-off shotgun stepped over and blasted the chain connecting me to the wall. Pieces of metal and concrete flew up, catching me on my good cheek. It stung viciously. I could feel the wet of blood. I was scared to touch my face, scared that some of it was gone.

They began hustling me out of the room, not noticing that my ankles were still manacled together. I stumbled and fell forward. Somewhere outside, the shrill *do-so, do-so, do-so-do-so-do-so* of an approaching police car sounded. The shotgun fired off a blast between my legs ... OH! ... and then my ankles were free. There was blood and smoke everywhere. I was half-deaf from the gun-blasts.

The snoids got me upstairs, and before I knew it, we were in a purple Maserati convertible, doing 120 kph through Rome traffic, the police somewhere far behind. A beautiful Sophia Loren look-alike was driving. The snoids called her Giulia. It sounded like they were telling her to drive faster.

I was in the front next to Giulia. The death seat, as regards traffic fatalities. Each snoid kept a gun-barrel on my neck. The way the car was whipping around was just unreal. It was like watching Cinerama.

"Please, Giulia," I moaned. "Please slow down."

She answered without looking over. Thank God she had the sense to keep her eyes on the road.

"*Calmo.*"

The full beautiful lips made the second syllable into a kiss. The voice, damped and deepened by two luscious swells of mammary tissue, was like a caress. Poised between two kinds of death, I fell in love. Cautiously I touched my cheek. It was only an abrasion after all, already scabbed over. A stroke of luck.

A bridge flew under us. To the left I could see the Castel Sant' Angelo, beautiful in the mild April sun.

We fishtailed around one of the vegetable-green Roman buses and took a hard right in a controlled four-wheel skid. I wished the car had a solid roof, or at least a roll bar. Giulia was not really a very good driver.

Now we were on a wide street parallel to the Tiber. A nontourist street with cheap department stores and dress shops. A *Supercortemaggiore* parking garage was coming up on our left. With a horrible wrench, Giulia heeled the car over, cut through three busy lanes of traffic and skidded into the garage entrance. I kept worrying that one of the snoids' guns would go off by accident. Distractedly I put my hands to my face and fingered my scabs.

Inside the garage they seemed to be expecting us. In the rear wall a giant metal mouth yawned open. An elevator for cars. We powered in. And finally stopped. Behind us the two halves of the elevator door *whumped* together. In the pit of my stomach I felt the descent begin.

"Are you a friend of Virgilio's?" I asked.

"Sometimes. He sold you to us. You will build atomic bomb, yes? We have . . ."

The elevator came to a stop. The doors in front of us slid open like jaws—one half went up, one half went down. Giulia fell silent and jockeyed the car down a dark, empty tunnel and through another automatic door.

"How you fellows making out back there?" I called to the snoids. There was no answer save for the steady pressure of the gun-barrels on my neck. I was so happy not to have died in a car crash that I felt absurdly elated. Build an A-bomb? No problem. I'd read a couple of articles on it in grad school. Now if they just had a glove box so I wouldn't have to touch the plutonium it'd be . . . But what was I thinking?

"Okay," Giulia said. "We get out here. You first, Bitter. You get out and up against the wall."

I hesitated. "You're not . . . you're not going to shoot me?"

She smiled beautifully, each tooth a pearl. "*Calmo.*"

I got out, went up to the wall in front of the car and put my hands on it. The skin on my back crawled, but the snoids didn't shoot me. To my left there was a door, and Giulia tapped out a complex tattoo. While we waited, I thought about the mysterious sphere I'd inherited from Lafcadio. I seemed to be able to feel its tiny warmth in my pocket. Later, when I was alone I'd . . .

A peephole opened and closed. With a rattle of bolts, the door swung open. A slight red-haired man and a dark hard-faced little woman peered out over a pair of Uzis. The women talked Italian for awhile, and then we went on in. The snoids stayed outside.

"The only exit," Giulia cautioned me, "is back through this garage. So do not attempt an escape. There is no escape."

"Fine. Fine." I nodded several times. All these guns were making me nervous. I kept my hands at my sides and tried not to make any sudden gestures.

"*Peter Roth*," the red-haired man said, introducing himself with a quick bow. "*Sprechen Sie Deutsch?*" He bobbed up and down with a chicken's jerky nimbleness, and turned his head to fix me with what seemed to be his only good eye. I felt like an interesting caterpillar.

"*Ja, ziemlich gut*," I answered. "*Ich wohne zur Zeit im Heidelberg.*"

"*Ach, wie schön. Ich hab da studiert.*"

"*Und was für ein Fach?*"

"*Mathematik. Zwar Logik und Mengenlehre.*"

This pleasant little chat about Roth's mathematics studies could have been lifted right from a faculty tea back at the University of Heidelberg ... though the presence of automatic weapons did stiffen the atmosphere.

The room we were in was, except for one thing, just like the organizational office of any small political party. There were a couple of beat old chairs, a file cabinet, a table with a mimeograph machine on it, a vinyl couch and a desk with a typewriter. The wall next to the desk was covered by a bookcase. There were no windows, of course, but the air was fresh, and three fluorescent light fixtures set into the low ceiling provided a nice even glow. The floor was carpeted in beige, the brick walls were painted cream and the ceiling was covered with soundproof tiles. Two doors led off the office, connecting it on the one side to a sort of one-room efficiency apartment, and on the other to an enormous workshop with machines.

The one thing that made this office unusual was the presence of large numbers of green plants. There was a row of ferns along the top of the bookcase, a huge spiky aloe plant in one corner, a little banana tree in another corner, several hanging pots of flowering fuchsia and numerous small begonias, African violets, geraniums and the like. It was the plants that gave this deeply buried room its fresh, open feel.

Giulia and the other woman were intensely discussing something, so I continued my German conversation with Peter Roth.

"What's going on?" I asked him. "Why did those *schnoids* come after me?"

"Virgilio has arranged it. At first he was going to sell you to Minos for a simple ransom. But after the embassy's reply he realized that you would be valuable to us. He told us where to seek for you. Virgilio's phone is unfortunately tapped, so we had to act in some hastiness."

This raised more questions than it answered. For one: If a deal was made, then why had it been necessary to kill Lafcadio? For two: Why hadn't the embassy just said that I was an unimportant little physics researcher who knew next to nothing about bombs? Instead they had replied in such a way that Virgilio the trapper could peddle my pelt to . . .

"Who are you? What is your organization?"

"We call ourselves Green Death." In German it came out *Grüner Tod*.

"Not the Red Brigade?"

Roth shook his head rapidly. "That's all over with. Like the Baader-Meinhof gang. Seventies-years stuff. Green Death is eighties-years."

I was beginning to see why all the plants were hanging around. Green Death. I figured this must be some super-radical splinter of Greenpeace: the people who'd been going around wrecking seal hunts and ramming whaling ships.

"But what do you want with an atomic bomb?" I demanded. "Surely that's not . . ."

"Professor Bitter!"

The dark little woman had finished her conversation with Giulia. Giulia shot me a bone-melting smile and drifted into the connecting apartment. I felt like trotting after her and etcetera. How could any woman have such a thin waist and such wide . . .

"Professor Bitter!"

Roth nudged me, in as friendly a way as possible, with his gun. The boss wanted my attention.

"Yes?"

"I want you to build us a big-ass bomb."

She was only five feet tall, but the voice more than made up for it. It was strong and rough, with a punk-singer's rhythm. Fingernails and black jello. Funny, I had taken her for Italian.

Her skin was pale, with a yellow tinge of liver. Her hair was short, black, spiky. She wore an elastic-waist overall printed in camouflage, and a pair of black combat boots with little gold stars painted all over.

"Of course," I heard myself saying. "Of course, I'm a nuclear weapons expert."

Not only am I scared of big strong men, I'm scared of mean little women. It's just little skinny men and nice big women that I get along with. People like Roth and Giulia. I was sorry to see this woman here at all. "What's *your* name?" I demanded with a trace of reckless insolence.

"*Beatrice*." She used an Italian accent on it. Bay-ah-tree-chay. "I am the pistil of the Green Deathflower. You will be our thorn."

"The thorn of plenty," Roth put in, managing to speak a clean, German-American English. He had laid down his gun somewhere. Perhaps Giulia had taken it into the little apartment, now closed.

Glancing over at Peter, Beatrice smiled for the first time.

"Thor'n likely."

"Thorn-Burger Deluxe."

"Thornium-233."

These were strange people. But suddenly I felt relaxed enough to smile too.

"What is this Green Death stuff anyway? What are your goals?"

"The human race is a blight. A cancer-virus eating at Mother Earth. We want to blow it all away. Radiation therapy."

"People are part of Nature, too," I objected. "Some say the best part."

"Even in Antarctica they can smell our stink," Peter intoned. "The great oceans are polluted. And on the land the deserts grow. Every day another species becomes extinct. Human civilization must be stopped before all is lost."

"It's going to take more than one bomb to bring down a global civilization," I said noncommittally. If Roth and Beatrice had seemed friendly a minute ago, they were all business now.

"You leave that to us," Beatrice snapped. "You just build us our bomb. Show him, Peter."

Roth started to steer me into the huge workshop off the little office, the room with machinery in it.

"Wait," Beatrice cried. "Keep a gun on him, Peter."

"*Ja, ja.*" He walked over to the little apartment door and opened it. The smell of frying meat came out. My head swam with sudden hunger.

"Could I . . . could I have some food before starting on your bomb?" Food and drink and a wash and a piss and a rest . . . I needed them all. "I feel very weak."

Beatrice gestured with her machine gun. "Okay. Go on in there and eat. I'll keep you covered."

It was a pleasant lunch. Giulia had fried some veal scaloppini in a little Marsala. She and Peter and I had them with mounds of *al dente* spaghetti loaded with butter and Parmesan. There was some rough red Valpolicella wine, and I drank as much as they would give me . . . which wasn't as much as I would have liked. By the time we got to the coffee, Beatrice had relaxed enough to sit down and join us.

Over the coffee, the four of us began to chat. We started with neutral topics: world travel, European trains, the sights in Rome, my research work. From my research I got onto my recent history: how I had lost my job in America but gotten a grant to study in Heidelberg. Before long I was even talking about my childhood as a smart, lonely kid in Kentucky.

Having to hear someone else's life-story makes people want to tell their own. Before long we had a regular encounter group going. Giulia get out the Valpolicella, and over the next couple of hours the three Green Death terrorists told me about their lives, and about how they'd come to Rome.

three statements
and a mental movie

the story of giulia verdi

I grew up on a farm near Verona. My father raised plum tomatoes for canned paste, and grapes for cheap wine. The soil was dry and rocky. There was always sun, and the leaves were covered with fine white dust. The vines could find their own water deep underground, but the tomato fields needed constant watering. When the sprinklers were on, I loved to run down between the dripping rows of tomato plants, smelling the acrid leaves and the settling dust.

"My twin brother Ugo was always with me. In the spring we would help Papa's men graft the new scions onto the gnarled vine-stocks. And when the tomatoes started growing, we would pick off the worms. But there were many summer days when we had nothing to do but run and play.

"Ugo was saving up money to get a racing bicycle. He was always listening to bicycle races on the radio. Sometimes I would help him make money by searching for bottles and scrap metal along the railroad track. The track ran right next to our property. There was a crossing and even a little old man living in a house to raise and lower the gates. He liked to tell us terrible, blackly funny stories about the war.

"I had an older sister, Maria, who became a nun. She lived in a nunnery in Verona. One summer my body began to develop. It came too early. Men stared at me, and I was frightened. Mama sent me to spend a month safe with Maria.

"While I was gone, a train derailed onto our property. There was a tank-car full of some poison. An ingredient for a pesticide. All my family died, all our animals, all our plants. It is so poisoned there that it is still fenced off. They pushed dirt over the broken tank-car, and no one can go close.

"Maria said I should go to the University and become a doctor. She said I should put the past behind myself. And I did study; I studied for years. I became a psychiatrist for working people in Mestre. This is an industrial town near Venice.

"I noticed how similar the psychoses of my patients were. A whole world of madness seems possible to the layman, but the doctor sees only the same few blighted fruits: depression, paranoia, dissociation. Those whose jobs force them to work with toxic materials have much higher incidences of mental illness. Why must such products be produced? Whom do they really benefit?

"Over the next few years I became increasingly involved in environmental activism. I marched, I collected signatures, I lobbied for legislation. But still the air hurt my lungs, and still the corroded stones of Venice sank deeper into the sea. It seemed that no one could stop the criminal polluters.

"Finally something happened. The president of a nuclear fuel company in Mestre was machine-gunned in his mistress's bed. The mayor's car exploded. An arson fire destroyed a whole refinery.

"One of the terrorists was captured: Beatrice. She pleaded insanity. The court assigned me to interview her. I found her the only sane person in Mestre. We joined forces."

the story of peter roth

I grew up in a village near Essen. I was an only child. My parents ran a little food store. Wine and canned goods, and fresh things. Milk, bread, vegetables. Every morning my father would get up at 4:30 and drive to the farmers' market. He had the best vegetables in the village.

"My mother's father had been a hunter, in charge of a noble family's woods. She loved the forest and knew the names of all the plants and insects. When I was little we took many walks. But soon the forests near us were all gone. On Sundays Father would drive us on the autobahn in his Mercedes. That was his great love, driving the Mercedes.

"Finally there was a crash. A VW was trying to pass someone, and we plowed into him from behind. Mother died; we had to watch her, with metal in her chest. It was horrible.

"I worked in the store after school. The women in the village were all kind to me, but I was very lonely. At night I studied, I studied hard so I could get my *Abitur* and go to the University. Ever since the accident I hated my father.

"I went to Heidelberg. The German university life is very free. No one keeps track ... you simply attend the lectures that you choose. I had saved some money, and father helped me too, so that I could rent a room in someone's basement. The first year I spent Christmas with my new girlfriend's family. I didn't go home until Pentecost—and what I saw was very surprising.

"The coal strippers had taken away our village. They have a machine; it is as big as the cathedral at Worms. They have such a machine with a whirling disk of diggers that shaves the land away. A rich seam of coal lay under our village, you see. One of the big companies had bought the mineral rights, and they just left an open sore where I had lived.

"What upset me most was the graveyard. They tore poor Mother out of the earth and put her someplace else. I had many dreams about it.

"Now that my father's store was gone, he had gone to work at the Bayer factory. He lived in a horrible room with the money from his store in a box. A horrible room in a horrible factory town. You would not believe the air.

"I finished two more years of study at Heidelberg. There were many radical students there, and we did a number of street-actions. Some of us became urban guerillas. I myself bombed a general's car at the American base. A Mercedes.

"Suddenly the police were very interested, and chasing down my friends. I had to leave Heidelberg. The bulls had put my picture on their terrorism posters, just for one Mercedes.

"I took the train up to Essen one morning, and while my father was still at work I broke into his room and stole all his money. I left in a big hurry and ended up in Paris.

"There were some other German radicals there, and we all lived very well for a few months. After that my money was used up. Holger, one of my friends, knew an Arab who wanted to pay us for some jobs. Bombing someone's embassy, things like that. We told him to meet us with the money, out in the Père Lachaise graveyard.

"I don't like Arabs at all. When men have killed all the green, the whole world will be like the Middle East. Holger and I robbed this guy and beat him up. Holger went too far, and suddenly the Arab was *kaput*. He had friends, and we had to get out of Europe fast.

"We got some false passports and took a plane to New York the next day. America . . . the land of unlimited possibilities.

"The only job I could find was as a waiter in a Bavarian restaurant. What a joke. They are the biggest fascists in Germany, the Bavarians. It's as if you came to Germany and worked in a *Texan* restaurant. I had to wear leather pants and let old people touch my ass. Soon I missed Europe very much.

"The whole time, I was taking courses at the Free University, mostly things about radical politics. This is where I met Beatrice. She convinced me to come to Italy with her."

My mother is Italian and my father is Spanish. I guess they're still alive. Shoveling shit in Buffalo.

"We had a really humongous family. I was the first girl and did a lot of the child-care. Mom worked in a piss factory, inspecting pipes. Dad was on the swing shift at Hooker Chemical.

"When I was about eighteen these really horrible things started happening in our neighborhood. Everyone was getting leukemia and blood-cancer and tumors. The little twins . . . the little twin boys in our family . . . both of them got leukemia the same year.

"Mom was real Catholic. She hung rosaries on the twins' beds, but they died all the same. And then it came out that we were living on top of a toxic chemicals dump. I mean it was no surprise . . . there was always horrible scum oozing out of the ground, and when our neighbor tried to grow cucumbers they were curly and rotted on the vine.

"The Feds said we had to evacuate, into downtown Buffalo. I was out of high school and spent the summer working in Mom's sewer-pipe factory. They buried the first twin in July and the other in August. Little white coffins. I couldn't take the scene, and hitched to the City.

"My big brother Hayzooz was living there in the Lower East Side alphabet. Avenue B. He was speeding a lot, working in a garage capping tires. I did a lot of weed till one time I got dusted. Somebody sold me a pack of KJ and said it was Colombo. I was so fucked-up, walking down the street on wood feet, talking crash. Hart of the wud and trubba not. I got busted, and in jail it came to me how for someone to put a cattle-trank on God's green weed was just like killing the twins. I was . . . *radicalized* by the experience.

"Hayzooz used to fly with some of the FALNs, those Puerto Rican nationalists? I got in tight with them and threw my first bomb. The office of Hooker Chemical. Before long the pigs were closing in. Hooker and heat.

"I had to cool off. I moved across town to Little Italy, got a job running a sewing machine and studied radical politics at the Free University. One course had an anthology of terrorist writings. The best thing was a piece called *Stadtguerilla* by the Red Army Faction. The old Baader-Meinhof gang. I got the idea that revolution is riper for the plucking in Europe. I decided to go to Italy, since that's what I can speak.

"Peter and I started really relating. He moved in with me. We both wanted to get the fuck out of Amerikkka, but we didn't have the bread.

"This room I was living in was like upstairs from a grocery. Gino's Superette. Gino was a real pig. He had a brother in the police, and they were always busting shoplifters. We decided to burn his ass.

"What we did was to reserve tickets on a Sunday morning flight to Rome out of JFK. Pick 'em up there and pay cash. Saturday afternoon Peter stole a car and we loaded all our luggage in it. I had a hot machine gun I'd gotten off Hayzooz.

"Just at closing time Saturday night . . . two in the morning . . . we step into Gino's. His cash register was bulging. He'd been selling beer and wine all evening. He had his pig cop off-duty policeman brother there for security. Since Gino knew us, they hardly looked up. And then Peter wasted them.

"It was beautiful. We didn't want to stop shooting. All the cans of spinach busting open and exploding, the ricocheting strung-out racket of explosions and in my head rock-and-roll radio playing Patti Smith: *never return to this piss factory!*

"We were out at the airport before the cops even knew. On the flight over we decided to call ourselves Green Death for the spinach. Peter got us hooked in with some movement people in Rome. They set us up in Mestre.

"Mestre's right near Venice, but it might as well be Newark, New Jersey. A whole town of working people breathing pollution-death. We liquidated a refinery and executed an environment-criminal or two. Things heated up and Peter split. I stayed too long and got popped.

"I'd pitched my passport, so they didn't really know who I was. I said I didn't either. My picture was in the paper. Some old guy came in claiming he was my father. But he was really a brother anarchist! Told me when and where to hijack the reactor fuel! But that comes later. Meanwhile the pigs decided to check me out for crazy before trial. Sent me to a white-coat. And that was Giulia."

how green death came to rome

magine yourself a disembodied eye, a movie camera if you will . . . watching when and where and what you want.

Flat country. Factories on the right, smudging the sky. On the left is a large, yellowish-white compound surrounded by a ten-meter wall. A prison. You move along the road towards it, along a potholed two-lane road. It's a February noon with a high, smogged-out sun.

The prison wall looms overhead, its surface scarred and scumbled. At the bottom is a small door, a rusty metal door propped open with a case of empty wine bottles.

A man's booted feet rest on the case. He is tilted back in a wooden chair, guarding the entrance with a machine gun in his lap. He is beautifully uniformed and badly shaven. The boots are black and very shiny. Staring into them you can almost see yourself . . . or is that the chalky sun?

A VW bus with one occupant pulls up in front of the prison. The slightly built, red-haired driver gets out: it's Peter Roth. He is dressed in white, like a hospital orderly. He walks slowly up to the prison guard, a sheaf of papers in his hand. His breath steams in the air.

From behind the guard you can hear sounds: the squeak-clang of steel doors, the dull hubbub of the prisoners' voices, the sliding shuffle of their feet, and the peng-peng-peng of high-heel boots. A woman's boots, watch them now: peng. Imagine the percussion's tiny shockwave rippling up that long leg, luscious as a pig's, active as a spider's. Peng. Whose leg is this? Dr. Giulia Verdi's.

Besides the boots, Giulia is wearing a tan poplin skirt and a thick red sweater. She is leading Beatrice out of the prison. Beatrice is wearing gray pants and a gray straitjacket with the arms crossed tight and padlocked in back. Criminally insane. She walks along in a slow, uncertain daze, led by Giulia's hand on her shoulder.

Look at Giulia's nails, so nice and red against the gray prison cloth. It's Valentine's Day, though no one here cares. The head guard accepts Giulia's signature for a release form, and then the three terrorists drive off in that VW bus.

Inside the bus everyone is talking at once. English is the common language.

"What should we do now?" Peter asks Beatrice, helping her out of the straitjacket. He jerks his head at Giulia, driving. "Can we trust her?"

Beatrice smiles. She is alive again. "Can we trust you, Giulia?"

"Implicitly. I like very much the actions you have done."

"How much time do we have?" Peter asks Giulia. "Until they realize you have defected."

Giulia shrugs expressively. "Italian bureaucracy is very . . ." A quick hand-gesture sketches a maze. "Maybe even a week till they notice. Or maybe two hours. We should leave Mestre. I loaded my suitcases, you see." Indeed, there is a lot of luggage in the back of the truck.

Beatrice swings her arms back and forth to get the circulation going, lights a cigarette. "Did you bring the weapons, Peter?"

"*Ja*, boss."

They're driving through a working-class residential neighborhood with all the Old World charm of a pile of concrete blocks. The small apartment buildings are new, with cheap, ungainly shapes. Walls are painted any color, in patches, with Stella cigarette posters stuck up everywhere. There are no sidewalks. Half-dressed children float bits of filth in mud-puddles.

"Today's the fourteenth, right?" Beatrice asks.

"*Sì*."

"Well, some old guy came to see me in jail. He told me that tonight a truck would be hauling six nuclear-reactor fuel assemblies along the autostrada to Brescia."

"That's great," Peter says excitedly. "That's fabulous."

"We gotta hijack it. Hijack it and take it to Rome. The snoids will let us stash it in that *Supercortemaggiore* garage."

"*Bene*," says Giulia. "Hijack the truck near Verona and get the autostrada south. I know the area well." They've reached the entrance for the autostrada, the Italian superhighway system. Giulia takes her ticket at the tollbooth and stomps on up to 140 kph.

Now jump one hundred twenty kilometers west and six hours forward. It's dark, for one thing. But like a firefly, your disembodied eye lights things up enough to see. It's those three terrorists, huddled in their van. The van is parked on a gravel back-road, just north of the chain-link fence which seals off the autostrada. A faint smell of wine and salami.

Beyond the fence there's a slope, the emergency apron, and then the westbound lanes. Fiats fly past, high-speed streaks of light, first white, then red. Whoooom. Whoooom. Other kinds of cars too, and trucks. Brrooooom. Brrooooom.

Inside the van they're as tense and happy as kids on Christmas Eve.

"Okay, Peter," says Beatrice. "You better go now."

Peter climbs out of the van. The door slams tinnily. He's dressed in black and carrying a machine gun and a walkie-talkie. He goes over to the fence, gives it a sort of shake, and a section the size of a garage door falls to the ground. They snipped it out earlier.

Peter drags the fencing out of the way, steps through the hole and heads left, walking up the stream of west-bound traffic, staying low and out of the lights. His job is to spot the truck with the reactor fuel.

In the van, Giulia and Beatrice get ready. Giulia slips off her sweater and bra. The breasts are a bit smaller than you'd expected. But they feature perfect, jutting, baby-bottle nipples. Beatrice is impressed, and briefly reaches out to fondle Giulia.

"You're beautiful."

"Being beautiful isn't enough." She starts the car.

They both get out now, Beatrice with a machine gun, Giulia with her breasts. And a brick. She's standing by the open driver's door with a brick.

Beatrice presses her walkie-talkie to her head, waiting to hear from Peter. Crackle hiss crackle nothing crackle WHOOP!

"HERE HE COMES!"

Over to the left you can see a bunch of headlights coming. Giulia watches intently, then cuts on the van lights and drops the brick on the accelerator.

The obedient vehicle stutters forward through the hole in the fence, picks up a little speed, wobbles across the emergency lane and then angles left onto the autostrada, into the oncoming traffic.

A Ferrari fishtails around the van without slowing down. Next is a little station wagon and . . . doesn't make it. *Smack* into the cree-cree spark roar scub thub-thubby. DOA.

Giulia springs out into the highway and poses near the crushed van, boobs wagging, "Help me!" At the shadowed highway edge lies Beatrice, prone markswoman. Here comes the truck.

A shiny big truck-cab pulling two low trailers. Cool and professional, the driver glides in slow and stops in the emergency lane. He jumps out to help the half-naked woman kneeling by her van. His partner runs back to set flares.

All unnoticed in the grass, Beatrice is talking on the walkie-talkie.

"Hurry up, for God's sake. There's two of them. Shoot the one lighting flares. Hurry!"

The driver, a serious, solidly built fifty-year-old; is leaning over Giulia now. Beatrice can't quite bring herself to pull the trigger. Then there's a long, loud burst of automatic weapons fire a hundred meters to the left.

"Got him," says Peter over the radio.

The driver starts, turns and sprints towards his truck. Even with the shipping schedules secret, they've been expecting something like this. He realizes that he should have . . .

Beatrice drops him just off the corner of the cab. Giulia drags her suitcases out of the crushed van. Cars are stopping on both sides of the autostrada, doors slamming, hurry hurry hurry!

Here's Peter. He knows how to drive trucks. Beatrice scrambles into the driver's door ahead of him. Giulia hands her suitcases in the other door and comes in after. The big engine fires up and they clank-lurch onto the highway.

The truck-cab is a nice medium blue, sort of ultramarine. There's two flatbed trailers in back, each with a pyramid-stacked load under gray tarps. You can tell it's really heavy stuff, from the stiff way the trailers ride.

It's a long way to Rome. Past Bologna, past Firenze … they drive all night, stopping now and then for gas and coffee, delicious greasy sandwiches and a shot of *grappa* as the sun goes up. Somehow the badly organized police roadblocks are all too late, or in the wrong places.

By breakfast time, Green Death is safe in the cool concrete of the *Supercortemaggiore*. One of the snoids, Orali, watches the other unloading the fuel-assemblies. Rectelli's using a forklift to get the six bulky concrete boxes off the trailers. Most of the weight is just padding and shielding, but no one's quite ready to try pulling the fuel rods out.

"We're gonna build an atomic bomb," Beatrice tells the snoid.

"*Bene.*"

"Do you know how this is done?" Giulia asks Beatrice.

"Peter knows. Don't you, Peter?"

"No."

Beatrice starts to say something cutting, then stops herself. "It doesn't matter really. They'll *think* we can build one."

Orali shakes his head. "We got build one bomb and set off good. Then is much more for threat of second one."

He rubs brisk thumb against fingers in the money gesture. He's more criminal than terrorist.

"Look," Beatrice says, sternly addressing Peter. "I saw a TV show where any bright twelve-year-old kid can build an A-bomb if he has the . . . the radioactive stuff. Read some books, man. I say we set off the first one in St. Peter's Square on Easter."

Giulia looks a little upset at this. "No, no. Those are simple people, good people. You must not bomb them."

Beatrice shrugs indifferently. "We need the crowd. I'd like to see at *least* one thousand dead for the news."

The last giant concrete shoebox of nuclear fuel is loaded onto the freight elevator down. Orali takes Giulia's arm.

"*Vuolsi così colà dove si puote ciò che si vuole, e più non dimandare.*"

"Bene," she says, flashing her sharp teeth.

SIX

the anarchist archimedes

Sybil was still in Vice-Consul Membrane's office when the bad news came in.

"The bait worked ... *almost* perfectly," Membrane announced, setting down the phone. His eyes were focused somewhere past Sybil.

"He's dead," Sybil said flatly. "Go on and tell me."

"No, no. He's been kidnapped by a new group called Green Death. They're the ones with the reactor fuel. We monitored the arrangements over a phone-tap. Only ..."

The children had finished their comics now, and were feeling hyper from all the sweets Membrane had fed them.

"On'y *whut?*" shouted Ida, sticking her head out from behind Sybil's chair.

Membrane looked genuinely embarrassed. "We ... were too slow. They snatched him out from under us. And now ..." He raised two trowel-like hands.

"Now my poor husband will be forced to assemble an atomic bomb for the Green Death," Sybil spat out. "Just you wait till I tell this story to everyone. Here you've taken a simple kidnapping for money and turned it into nuclear terrorism. They'll never . . ."

Never let him go, she had meant to say. But thinking the words brought her tears back, hot and bitter. It was no use staying here, no use listening to this shitweasel blather on about secret agreements and delicate negotiations.

"Just shut up," Sybil said, standing. "I'm leaving. I'm going to tell this to the *Herald Tribune*."

Something hard flashed in Membrane's eyes. "I wouldn't do that if I were you."

Sybil tugged the kids out of their chairs. "Why not?"

"If you go to the paper, then I will give them my version. I will tell them of my . . . suspicions." Membrane scratched his face, goggled at her and continued. "Sybil. I think your husband went over to the terrorists of his own free will."

"That is such BULL!" shouted Sybil. "Let's get OUT of here, children!" She slammed the door behind her.

A minute later she was outside the embassy. Butt-whumper gave her a friendly salute. She nodded weakly and walked off down the sidewalk. Where to now?

To the newspaper. To make a stink. Membrane shouldn't get away with this. She bought a *Herald Tribune* at the next newsstand.

"I'm hungry for lunch," Tom told her quietly.

"Me too!" quacked Ida. "Hungwy!"

"Is Daddy making bombs?" asked Tom.

"I think he might have to," Sybil said with a shaky sigh. She too was hungry. "We can have lunch in this café, children."

They were standing under the awning of one of the nicer Via Veneto cafés, a big place called The Glacier. Inside was a huge room with marble columns, and out here under the awning were dozens of tables as well. The chairs were the good kind of lawn furniture, made of thick gray plastic cords stretched between black steel tubes. Sybil plopped down in a chair facing the street, and the children sat down across from her.

A slender, dignified waiter appeared and they placed their orders. *Spaghetti con sugo* for the kids, a *salade niçoise* for Sybil. Fanta, mineral water and a quarter liter of *vino bianco*. The victuals began arriving almost immediately. Soon they all felt a little better. The sun shone, casting living color-shadows from their drinks onto the clean linen tablecloth.

"Where is Daddy now?" Tom asked, sucking up a last strand of spaghetti. "I didn't understand what the man said."

Sybil washed down a forkful of flaky tuna and dark-purple anchovy with a gulp of wine. This was a good salad. She ate a leaf of lettuce before starting her answer.

"Apparently some gangsters stole Daddy last night. They thought he might be rich, and that we could pay a lot of money to get him back."

"Aren't we rich?"

In a way, this was a reasonable question. Here they were spending Easter in Rome. But, on the other hand, home right now was a two-room subsidized apartment in Heidelberg.

"Rich? Are you kidding? Those gangsters would have wanted more money than Daddy makes in ten years."

"What will dey do if we can't buy him back?" Ida asked anxiously. Her upper lip was bright orange from the soft drink.

"Well, now it's different," Sybil explained. "Some other people stole Daddy from the gangsters. Some bad people who want him to make an atomic bomb. It's thanks to stupid Mr. Membrane that they got *that* idea." She poured more wine and soda and sopped a piece of bread in the juices of her salad. Funny how she could go on eating like nothing had happened. She must be in shock.

"Bad silly men," said Ida.

"What if they light off Daddy's bomb? We should go far away!" Tom's round forehead was asterisked with worry.

"Don't worry, Tom. Daddy wouldn't let a bomb go off with us still here. Let's go to the newspaper office and see if they can help us." She folded the *Herald Tribune* open to the editorial page and scanned the list of offices. *Rome: 73 Viale Giulio Cesare, Susan Spangle, Ed.*

"Susan Spangle," Sybil said out loud.

"Who's she?"

"Maybe she can help."

She paid the check and hailed a cab. Julius Caesar Street was halfway across the city. They went through a park and across a huge square with an Egyptian obelisk. Sybil wished they had time to stop and look at the hieroglyphs. But no. She began to feel a certain irritation towards Alwin. If he hadn't been out staggering around at two in the morning, none of this would have happened. Shit, shit, shit!

The *Herald Tribune* office was at a corner near the river, upstairs from a big dress shop. There were about fifteen people working there, and Sybil had to talk to most of them before getting to the boss.

Susan Spangle's assistant was a fatherly fat Italian named Signor Atti. He even had suspenders and a mustache with waxed ends. He cheerfully agreed to keep an eye on the children while Sybil talked to the boss.

Susan Spangle turned out to be a smooth-voiced black woman with long straight hair and small features. She wore a black coral necklace with matching earrings. Her dress was a practical-looking pale blue, with buttons up the front and a little collar. Preppy, almost. Her eyes were yellow and older looking than her face. Forty-five, maybe. A tough career woman.

"Your husband was involved in the killing at the Colosseum this morning?"

"I hadn't realized there was a killing."

"Yes . . . are you *sure* your husband was kidnapped?"

Sybil told the story of her meeting with Vice-Consul Membrane. Spangle listened carefully, staring at the ceiling with calculating eyes.

"Is your husband able to build a bomb or not?" she asked finally.

Just then the kids came charging into the office, Signor Atti hot on their trail.

"His fat ate a pencil!" Tom shouted excitedly.

Signor Atti's shirt was untucked. He'd been showing off his stomach.

"His fat gone eat ME!" squealed Ida, half believing it.

"Do we have anything on the Green Death group?" Spangle asked him.

Atti groaned in thought, tucking his shirt in. "Yeeees. They were in Mestre, and then I dunno. Let me go call Magnani."

Tom and Ida came smearing up to Sybil, merry mouths open with excitement.

"Is the bomb done yet?" Tom wanted to know.

Just then the phone rang and Spangle picked it up.

"Hello. *Herald Tribune*. Spangle speaking."

"Yes," affirmative.

"Yes," neutral.

"Yes," questioning.

"Yes," confirming.

"Yes," inquiring.

"Yes," listening.

"Yes," thinking.

"Yes," transitional.

"Yes," challenging.

"Yes," demanding.

"Yes," capitulating.

"Yes," concluding.

"Good-bye, Mr. Membrane."

"That was your Vice-Consul Membrane," she explained, making a notation on a piece of paper.

"What did he say?" Sybil asked, her heart sinking.

Spangle looked at Sybil coolly. "Is it true that your husband was quite active in the anti-war movement? That he helped organize a demonstration against US involvement in Latin America?"

"I don't see what that has to . . ."

"And is it true that he was unable to get the necessary

security clearance to work on the Streamford Project? Could this have embittered him so much that . . . ?"

"You can't be serious! Don't you see that Membrane just wants to cover up his blunder?"

Spangle made a sour little face. "The facts speak for themselves, Mrs. Bitter. Your husband left a note at the Colosseum, a radical manifesto in which he calls himself 'The Anarchist Archimedes.' A weapon with his fingerprints was found near the murdered man's body. Mr. Membrane tells me that . . ."

Just then Atti came back in, big and friendly as a beer barrel. "I have talked with Officer Magnani. Green Death exploded a refinery in Mestre and may have stolen a truck with reactor fuel. They are involved in the shooting of former University of Rome physicist Lafcadio Caron, which took place at the Colosseum this morning. The officer would like very much to talk with Signora Bitter. He is on his way here."

"Are the Italian papers breaking the story?" Spangle wanted to know.

"If Magnani's coming, they'll be here, too. You know how he loves publicity."

Spangle made some quick notes, and gave Sybil an insincere smile. "I do aim to be fair, Mrs. Bitter. Why don't we organize a little press conference right here?"

Sybil felt trapped and desperate. She hadn't yet met anyone who cared what happened to poor Alwin. He was becoming an abstraction, a news item, a jaded world's daily *frisson*.

"I'm going," she announced. "I'm going back to our hotel. The children need a rest."

"But what about Officer Magnani?" Spangle protested. "And our press conference?"

"I'll be at my hotel. Hotel Caprice."

Before anyone could stop her, Sybil had dragged the kiddies out of the *Herald Trib* office and down onto the street. She walked a block or two to calm down, and then paused to look around.

It was a nontourist street parallel to the Tiber. In the mid-distance the hill of the Vatican rose up from behind cheap department stores and dress shops. There was a big *Supercortemaggiore* parking garage across the street.

A street-corner vendor was selling green olives and some kind of white beans. Tom and Ida clamored, so she bought them a triangular wet paper bag full of the fresh olives. The vendor was a very old man with piercing eyes. Sybil wished that her father were there, and decided to call him from the hotel.

The children nibbled at the olives, spitting most of the meat out with the pits. A taxi stopped. They got in, and the lovely buildings slid past, emptily promising romance and adventure. Sybil felt more alone than she had ever felt in her life.

There was a traffic blockage on the Via Veneto, so they had to get out a block before the hotel. All sorts of cars and trucks were squeezing in. Some men were carrying lights and heavy TV cameras.

It wasn't until she stepped into the lobby that Sybil realized that all the people were waiting for her. The manager rushed up to her, oily and excited.

"Mrs. a-Bitter! Everyone is a-wait for you to make

television interview. Come on in a-breakfast room, they got a-lights and action." He leaned a bit closer and raised his eyebrows. Five neatly parallel corrugations sprang into life on his forehead. "You mention a-hotel, say is a-nice, I tear up bill." Two quick, vertical tearing motions.

"Mrs. Bitter!"

"A-Mrs. a-Bitter!"

"Sybil, honey!"

"Hey, Mrs. Bitter!"

Half a dozen reporters came crowding up. Sybil recognized one of them from the *Herald Tribune* office. They hadn't wasted any time getting over here. Tom and Ida squeezed against her legs, scared of getting stepped on. Sybil let the manager pull her into the breakfast room and seat her behind a table with the kids. Tom pointed at a TV camera. Ida stared, dazzled, into one of the lights.

An Italian news commentator was talking into a microphone.

"*Badada ladada borra borra Signora Sybil Bitter lo dadada famma donna di badda da dadda da Professore Alwin Bitter ba dadadadad la preterra dinidini buhduh fla ceticini Morte Verdi.*" This went on for awhile. Finally he flashed a smile at Sybil and posed his question. "*Lo quando billo flant flant de budadda cargo cargo flidovi oggi quan deeda dee? Oscorbidulchos volivorco?*"

A slender lady in purple-tinted glasses leaned over Sybil's shoulder and whispered the translation.

"He asks if you have received word from your husband's terrorist organization. And did he warn you he was leaving?"

"My husband has been the unwilling victim of a double-kidnapping," Sybil said. Her hands were shaking badly. "They want to force him to build an atomic bomb. This development is entirely the fault of the US embassy. They have calculatedly used my husband as bait to draw out the terrorists who have the reactor fuel." She paused and took a wobbly breath while the slender lady translated her answer.

The commentator posed his next question, one for the *bambino*.

"Tom, do you miss your father?"

It went on for another half hour. Sybil wondered numbly if Alwin might see them on TV. As the questions became more technical, she struggled to decide what answers would be best for him. Should the terrorists think that Alwin could build a bomb? Should they think he was in the CIA? If he was worthless they might kill him, but if he was valuable they might never let him go. Finally she started crying. This was, of course, what the cameramen had been waiting for.

When Sybil and the children got back up to their room, the phone was ringing. She had no intention of answering, but before she could stop him, Tom had picked it up.

"Hello?"

A faint voice talking volubly.

"Yes," Tom said. "She's here." He handed Sybil the phone. "It's Grandma."

"Sybil!" Lotte Burton's voice was vibrant with emotion. "You poor child. Your father and I just saw you on the news."

"Oh, Mother," wailed Sybil. "Isn't it awful? They kidnapped Alwin twice, and the US embassy is trying to frame him as a terrorist. I don't know what to do!"

"We're flying down, darling. Cortland has already made the plane and hotel reservations. You can move in right now and get ready for us."

"Move where?"

"To the Savoy. Room 431. It's a three-bedroom suite."

"That's bigger than our apartment in Heidelberg!" exclaimed Sybil. "Are you bringing Sorrel?"

"Of course. Now, move over there and make sure that there's plenty of ice for your father, and three extra pillows for his back." An excited voice shouted in the background. "And he says to get a case of Heineken sent up . . . for you, and for when Alwin gets back. Don't forget the pillows, dear."

"All right," Sybil said. "Wonderful. When will you get in?"

"After midnight. Don't wait up." In the background Cortland hollered, urging haste. But Lotte had one more thing to add. "You know, Sybil, it doesn't surprise me a bit."

"What?"

"That Alwin would fall in with these people. He's always *been* the Anarchist Archimedes."

"It's not his fault, Mother. Really."

"Cortland's getting a good German lawyer for him. We'll try to have the trial in Heidelberg." Violent, prolonged shouting. "I have to hang up, dear. The pillows. Don't wait up."

"Of course I'll wait up. How could I sleep!"

"How are the little ones taking it?"

Tom and Ida were in the bathroom, refilling the tub. Sybil could hear their voices, earnest as two co-workers in a research lab. SPLOOSH! Something big hitting the water. Not the electric fan!

"What was that?" screamed Sybil.

"I'm sorry, Mama!"

"WHAT WAS IT?"

"Sybil? Is something wrong?"

"We got your little bag all wet."

"My toiletries?"

"Toilet!" Squeals of laughter.

"Sybil! What's going on?"

"Oh, it's all right. The children just dropped my little travel-kit in the bathtub. I thought it was the fan."

"I must hang up. Your father is frantic." Hoarse, angry yelling. "He's worried we'll miss the plane, which is ridiculous. There is no traffic on Good Friday. Did you find time to go to church today?"

"I didn't have a moment. I wish I had."

"In Rome there are many churches. I was at the cathedral today. The chants, Sybil. It was indescribable."

"I may still make it. It's only eight o'clock."

"*Eight?* We'll miss our plane!"

"Good-bye, Mother."

"Good-bye."

SEVEN
sex and death

F riday afternoon, after we finished talking, Peter showed me around the workroom where the fuel assemblies were waiting. We spent a couple of hours prying the ends off the concrete casings. Now it would be just a matter of pulling out the fuel rods and extracting the pellets of plutonium oxide.

Just? Airborne plutonium particles are among the most toxic substances known to man. We'd need glove boxes and breathing suits, if not remote manipulators. Back in the office I tried to explain this to Beatrice, but she flew into a rage and called me a coward.

She made it clear that I'd be shot if I didn't get a bomb together in time for Easter, a bomb for St. Peter's Square. If we all got poisoned in the process of assembling the bomb, it didn't matter; there were others to take our places in the front lines of revolutionary justice. Crazy bitch.

There was another problem, the business about St. Peter's Square. Presumably Sybil and Tom and Ida would be there. No way I was going to let the bomb go off. I'd show Beatrice who was a coward. For all practical purposes I was already dead. Or nearly so. I only hoped I could still get lucky.

That evening we watched TV in their little apartment. My passport photo flashed on the screen, then Lafcadio's. Beatrice translated for me. Lafcadio had been running proton-decay experiments in a lab off the Mont Blanc tunnel. There'd been an accident and Zsuzsi Szabo, Lafcadio's beloved co-worker, had been killed. Lafcadio had flipped out and disappeared, stealing a sample of some kind of degenerate hypermatter from the lab. The police were just as glad to have him dead, but the hypermatter was still missing.

The hypermatter thing didn't seem to interest my Green Death captors. They were focused on the factional politics, and on the nuclear explosion we were cooking up.

The TV news described me as a radical atomic physicist with close ties to the US embassy. Picture of the embassy, picture of our hotel. Old news photo of me at a demonstration. Then someone began translating the note Virgilio had gotten me to write.

Now I realized I'd been framed. *Il Archimedes Anarchisti*. The TV showed the gun that had my fingerprints on it. According to the news, I'd met Lafcadio to buy the degenerate hypermatter, possibly for CIA use, possibly for the terrorists. I could be a double or even a triple agent. In any case, I had murdered Lafcadio Caron.

Suddenly Sybil was on the TV screen. Her eyes were desperate and she bit her lips. It was hard to make out her faint voice over the machine-gun rattle of the translator's

Italian. For an instant she looked directly out at me, and my heart stopped. Then the bastards put the children on ... tiny, serious, confused. I started hitting and yelling.

The three terrorists manhandled me out of their little apartment and left me alone in the office. I smashed a few plants against the wall, then sat down exhausted on the couch. I was supposed to sleep here. All the doors ... apartment, outer, workroom ... were locked. I tried to stop thinking, tried to stop seeing Tom's puzzled face.

After a while I found myself wondering if Peter was getting any off those two women. Imagining various three-ways, I slid my hand into my pants. Sybil, baby. It had been so good last night.

How was I ever going to get to sleep here on a vinyl couch with death all around me? My back was killing me. My hurt finger and the wounds on my face throbbed. Did I have any cigarettes?

Going through my pockets I found the little spherelet which Lafcadio had given me. Had that really happened today? Was this the missing sample? The tiny ball glowed mysteriously in the pitch-dark room.

"Smeep," I went, pursing my lips. "Smeep smeep." The ball grew slightly larger. There were faint patterns on it, like half-seen continents on a clouded planet. I felt a stirring of excitement in my loins. The thing gave off an incredible aura of sexuality. *Pheromones*—the airborne organic molecules that people give off when they're sexually excited. Invisible little PLEASE FUCK MEs. Leaning over the sphere was like putting my face between Sybil's legs. Without really knowing why, I licked my lips and began smothering the tiny sphere with kisses. I was just so lonely. The sphere grew and became warm to the touch, bigger and bigger. What was going on?

With an effort I drew my face away from the magic sphere and looked it over. The side facing me had a cleft down it, like a peach . . . like a woman's beautiful ass. My hands dropped away in astonishment. The mildly glowing sphere hung there weightlessly. Now she was turning, showing herself off.

The perfect buttocks rotated out of sight, and I was facing the lovely naveled round of a pregnant woman's belly. I reached out to caress her, running my hand down through her wiry pubic hair to fondle the pouty labia. The sphere hummed gently and floated closer. On top were the mounds of two stiff-nippled breasts. Between the breasts nestled a perfect, full-lipped mouth.

My hands were wooden and trembling with excitement, with rechanneled hysteria. I fumbled my pants open and drew the sex sphere down onto my distended penis. This was madness, but I couldn't stop.

My cock slid in easily. The sphere's mouth smiled loosely up at me, showing white teeth and a pink tongue. I leaned over, trying to kiss her, but she was just out of reach. Obligingly, she grew a bit larger and plastered her sweet-smelling wet lips against mine, shoving her tongue into my mouth.

I came.

In the sudden silence I could hear one of my captors shifting in bed next door. Was this really happening? I stared down at the object in my lap. A skin-colored sphere the size of a giant beach ball, with breasts on top and a mouth between the breasts. At the bottom were the generous buttocks, a crinkly anus and a vaginal passage containing my rapidly limpening penis. Was this safe?

The sphere giggled, shrugged me out, and rotated one hundred eighty degrees about the horizontal. The intoxicating scent of her south pole filled my nostrils. Pheromones locked into receptor sites. Her soft lips and sandy tongue were at work on my genitals. I sighed with pleasure and sank my face into her deeply rounded cleft.

The harder I licked, the bigger she grew . . . past beachball size, past the size of a library's big Earth globe, past all reasonable dimensions. My arms could no longer reach all the way around her. The huge mouth held my testicles as well as my penis, and her luscious vagina covered my entire face.

I came again.

Once more the sphere rotated, and I noticed a twinkling brown eye set in her side, just below the crease at the base of her breast. Next to her eye was the delicate shell of an ear.

"Who are you?" I breathed. "Where do you come from?"

The fat breast nudged me and I tongued the chewy nipple.

"Who are you?" I repeated. "Talk to me."

The smiling mouth came swinging around to plant some sticky kisses on my face. The mouth was almost a foot long now. The teeth looked very big and strong.

"Please shrink a little," I begged. "You make me nervous like this."

Obligingly she dwindled down to a more manageable size . . . maybe a meter in diameter. I happened to be holding her breasts as she shrank, and it was a strange sensation . . . not as if she were a balloon losing air, but rather as if she were sliding out from under me. Yet when she was through shrinking, her breasts were still in my hands.

"Thank you," I said, planting another kiss on her mouth. "Please talk to me."

She pressed her lips together and rocked sweetly one-two, one-two from left to right. Shaking no. Then blew a last kiss at me and shrank slidingly down to orange-pip size.

I smeeped fruitlessly awhile, then put the bright spherelet back in my pants pocket. The two orgasms had left me tired and relaxed. I stretched out on the couch and fell asleep.

I woke to Beatrice prodding me with her machine gun.

"Let's go, Alwin. I want that Easter egg ready for tomorrow. Big workday today."

My cock was still hanging out. I tucked it into my pants. Beatrice refrained from comment. The memory of last night's . . . orgy came rushing over me, filling me with horror and shame. What had I done? Forgotten my wife and had sex with an alien? An evil spirit? A succubus? I was lucky to be alive.

Peter brought me a mug of coffee and a roll with cheese on it.

"I talked to Rectelli, Alwin. He's bringing us a couple of hazard suits."

My heart sank. These people were really serious. Really crazy. "We should have glove boxes, too. Or manipulators. You don't realize how poisonous plutonium is."

"Shut up!" Beatrice snapped. "Shut up or I'll make you do it naked." Her knuckles were white on the gun's wire stock.

There was a knock on the door. Giulia drifted out of the apartment and got it. It was one of the snoids. He handed in two flat boxes.

"Okay, Bitter," Beatrice snarled. "If you're not too busy jacking off, could you get your fucking suit on?"

Peter and I put the suits on over our clothes. They were white plastic, airtight with face-windows. You breathed through a mouthpiece connected to a filter-system set in the back. It was hot and uncomfortable. I had only the vaguest idea of what to do next.

But Beatrice was ready to shoot me, so I hustled on into the workroom with Peter.

It was a big room—say, ten meters by twenty—with concrete floors and walls. The six fuel assemblies were lined up in the middle of the room like giant stone coffins. Or complimentary airline packs of two cigarettes each; the cancer-sticks being, in this case, long metal fuel rods.

There was all kinds of equipment around the room . . . welding torches, Geiger counters, cases of *plastique* explosive, stacks of metal scrap from wrecked cars. From what I'd gathered, Rectelli and Orali encouraged the Green Death to take actions against those polluters who also happened to be slow in paying protection. They were hoping that this bomb caper could bring in 10^{10} lire, plus. They, obviously, were crazy, too.

For one thing, this room had big ventilation ducts in the ceiling. Which meant that when we started taking the fuel rods apart, there'd be plutonium dust filtering all through the *Supercortemaggiore* garage. If inhaled, a one ten-millionth gram speck of plutonium gives a seventy percent risk of eventual lung cancer. A five-hundredth gram causes certain death by fibrosis within two weeks. I'd tried to tell Beatrice about this yesterday, but she acted like she didn't believe me or ... which was quite possible ... she didn't care.

The fuel rods slid out easily. We laid them down side by side, not *too* close together, of course. According to some papers Peter had found in the truck, each of the rods held forty little hundred-gram pellets: thirty low-enriched uranium oxide and ten of the heavy stuff, PuO2, plutonium oxide.

Peter got a cutting-torch and took off the metal cap at the end of a fuel rod. I tipped it up, and the pellets came sliding out like sooty checkers. Some dust flew up and I stopped breathing for a second ... then went back to hissing the air in and out through my filters.

Peter nudged the pellets with his foot. "How do we tell which are plutonium?" His echoing voice was mixed with the buzz of his breathing system. He sounded like Darth Vader with a German accent.

Without stopping to think it over, I told him. "Use a Geiger counter. The plutonium gives off more alpha-radiation."

It was funny. I knew I didn't want the bomb to be a success. But yet, I'd spent so many years working around physics labs that I couldn't stand not to do it right.

That's not quite honest. On some deeper level I really *did* want to build a working atomic bomb. Build it and see it go off. Death wish? Maybe. Or think of a couple of bored twelve-year-old boys whiling away a long Sunday afternoon by setting off firecrackers. The thrill of the blast. The smell of the ozone, the roar of the cloud. I've heard that when an A-bomb goes off, the air around it catches fire. You see every color of the rainbow. Especially God's colors: purple and gold. I wanted to see it for myself.

I got a Geiger counter and separated out the plutonium from the uranium. I used my gloved hands . . . there was no real danger from the actual radiation. You don't get the neutrons and the hard gamma-rays until a nuclear reaction starts. The current issue was just to avoid breathing in any plutonium particles . . . and presumably the hazard suits were taking care of that. I planned to keep my suit on until I was well out of this place.

The next hour was filled with the simple, repetitive work of opening the twelve rods and separating out the $PuO2$ pellets. It felt more and more unreal. My mind wandered back to my encounter with the sex sphere.

Had I imagined the whole thing? All the ingredients for a good hallucination had been present: physical injuries, mental stress, isolation to the point of sensory deprivation. Bullshit. It had really happened.

With the suit on I couldn't get to my pants pocket, but I could feel the tiny pressure of the little ball in there. If I called her, would she come return? Of course she would. We were *lovers*.

This brought back the sick, ashamed feeling I'd woken up with. I was no better than some geek with a foam-rubber woman's torso like they advertise in *Hustler*. What a pathetic, twisted vision of womanhood: all the "inessential" parts lopped off, nothing left but tits and ass and holes. *Lifelike washable plastic skin. Greek and French features.*

But yet, in a way, wasn't the sex sphere what I'd always wanted? An ugly truth there. "Shut up and spread!" How many times had I said that to Sybil, if not in so many words? The memory of her weeping, televised face filled me with such anguish I could hardly . . .

"*Na?*" Peter said, interrupting my thoughts. "*Was nun?*"

What now. We had twelve little mounds of plutonium pellets, say one kilogram per mound. Critical mass of $PuO2$ was, as far as I could recall, around ten.

"Put them all together and they all spell MOTHER!" I sang, my voice breaking. "The sound of one hand clapping."

"What is the next step, Alwin?" Peter held the cutting torch near my suit. "We have no time for lighthearted games."

"Okay, okay. What we need to do is form the plutonium into two hemispheres. Separate the hempheres with Styrofoam or something, and then pack the whole thing in a big ball of plastic explosive. With any luck, a fast reaction will set in when the explosive slams the two hemispheres together."

"Why do you speak of luck, Alwin? We need your scientific certainty."

"So forget luck," I said with a shrug. "So far as we know, no one has ever built a simple atomic bomb that didn't work. Let's finish the job. Do you have anything to pack that plutonium in?"

"There are two steel mixing bowls in our kitchen," Peter suggested.

"Good. Go get them."

"You go. We can't trust you alone in here."

I went and pounded on the workshop door.

"What?" shouted Beatrice from the other side.

"We need the steel mixing bowls from the kitchen."

"What else are you gonna need? I don't wanna open this door any more than I have to."

I thought for a minute. "Get a bunch of tubes of epoxy glue. And a Styrofoam ice-chest. A-and a small trunk to put the whole thing in." I paused and thought again. "Do we have wires and a timer in the workshop?"

"*Ja, ja,*" Peter put in. He was standing next to me. "We've got all that."

"Okay," Beatrice called, her voice gone girlish with excitement. "We'll get that other stuff right away."

While Peter monitored the radiation count, I split the plutonium oxide pellets into two six-kilogram mounds. I was hesitant adding the last few pellets, worried I might hit critical mass before I expected to. But the counter just ticked along evenly.

"All right," I told Peter. "Now we want to find some way of compacting this stuff."

"Why not hammer the pellets into dust?" Peter suggested. "They're brittle enough."

I groaned softly. "Peter, the last thing we want is to kick up a whole lot of plutonium dust. As it is, I plan to keep my suit on until I'm a kilometer or two away from here. Think of something else."

"Melt it? We've got an oxyacetylene torch here that cuts plate steel."

"Now you're talking. Now you cookin' wif gas, boah. We just need a crucible."

We poked around the workroom till we found a barrel of sand.

"This is perfect," I told Peter. We'll hollow out a hemispherical mold like this . . ." I dug rapidly at the sand, making a bowl-like depression some ten centimeters across and five centimeters deep. "Get the torch."

Peter dialed the torch up to high and fused the top layer of sand. This would keep the plutonium from trickling away. I got six kilograms of the dirty disks and set them gently in. At my insistence, Peter covered the torch and barrel with a plastic drop cloth before the next step.

"That's our fume-hood, Peter."

Just as he started heating up the plutonium, Beatrice got back. I went to the door.

"Is it safe?" she called.

"Oh, sure. We're not doing much of anything. Come right in."

The lock clicked and the door slid open. Beatrice stared past me at the flare of light in front of Peter. A fat sputter of plutonium flew up and melted a hole in the plastic cover sheet.

"Take a deep breath," I mocked. "Good clean country air."

Beatrice looked a little pale. "Take this shit and let me close the door. And don't worry about those ceiling vents, I told Orali not to run them today."

I reached out towards her, rubbing my dusty fingers together. "Don't just stand in the shallows, Beatrice. Come all the way in. Get healthy, baby."

There was a sharp report and something whistled past my face. Giulia. She was standing behind Beatrice, firing her Uzi at me.

I know when I'm not wanted. I backed off. Beatrice shoved in some parcels, and the door slammed.

"The first batch is all melted," Peter said, turning off the torch and walking over to me. "Why do you try to contaminate Beatrice?"

"I don't like her. I don't like being kidnapped. I don't like bombing thousands of pilgrims."

"Oh, come on, Alwin. So far you have cooperated so well. Just a little more and we'll let you go."

"When? When do you let me go?"

"After the bomb goes off. Soon after that."

Would they? Would they let me go then? Of course not. How could Green Death extort ransom for an imaginary second bomb if I were free to give out their names and the location of their hideout? And Beatrice almost certainly had cancer now. There was plutonium dust all over my fingers. Would she be likely to free me, after she started coughing up bloody gray broccoli?"

"Come on," Peter said again. "Let's finish the bomb."

We levered out the fused PuO_2 hemisphere with crowbars and chipped off the glassy sand stuck to it. It was lumpy, but it would do. I got one of the steel mixing bowls and tried the fit. Not too bad. Peter got the sand ready for the second batch.

I brought over the other six kilos of plutonium pellets and stood off to the side while Peter melted it down. I was thinking hard.

The main thing was to keep them from setting this bomb off when Sybil and the babies were around. One option would be to just slap those two plutonium chunks together here and now. Boom.

But there had to be a better idea. Maybe I could rig the bomb up wrong . . . fix it so it wouldn't go off? Unfortunately it was just about too late for that. I hadn't told them about using a tamper and an initiator . . . a jacket of uranium to keep the neutrons in, and a central source of neutrons to get the reaction rolling . . . but the bomb would probably work without them. We had an awful lot of plutonium.

Even if I didn't help any more, Peter would probably be able to put a working bomb together in the next couple of hours. Maybe I should kill him? I picked up a crowbar and stepped towards him. He had his back to me and would never . . .

A shrill bell went off. Peter whirled around, holding the torch towards me. The door rumbled open and a gun-barrel poked in. We were being watched.

I tried to look nonchalant. "Just . . . getting ready to help lift the slug out."

Peter's voice was hard. "Sit down over there." He gestured with his torch. "Sit down where I can watch you. Don't try anything else. Already you have become expendable."

I circled around him and sat down on the floor. The bomb was going to get put together whether I helped or not. Which left only one alternative. Boom.

I waited blankly until Peter was ready. I helped him lift out the second plutonium hemisphere. We nestled the two gray metal slugs into two mixing bowls, fixing them in place with epoxy. Peter carved two Styrofoam disks out of the sides of the ice-chest and glued one to the top of each hemisphere's flat surface. While I monitored with the Geiger counter, he eased the two mixing bowls together . . . tilting them up till they joined to make a plutonium-filled steel sphere.

The chatter of the counter was nervous, but not hysterical. It sounded like a platoon of paratroopers getting ready to jump. Peter smeared a thick bead of epoxy along the crack where the lips of the two mixing bowls met. And then it was done . . . the core of the Green Death atomic bomb, a steel sphere the size of a soccer ball. All we had to do now was pack it in a symmetric charge of plastic explosive, wire blasting caps all over the explosive's outer surface, and hook a timer up to the wires. Then put the whole thing in a trunk and leave it somewhere. I giggled.

"I want you out of here, Alwin. Now. I can finish alone. I don't want you messing with the explosives."

Beatrice heard this and slid the door open. "Leave the suit in there, Bitter."

"No way."

BRATTA-TAT. A flock of bullets winged by. Without
even thinking, I ran over and snatched up the bomb core.
I held it up high over my head.

"Cut the shit or I drop this. The Styrofoam'll give way."
I wasn't fully sure that was true, but it sounded convinc-
ing.

A moment of silence. Our air-filters rattled. Peter was
too close. I sidled off from him, moving towards the door.

"Should I waste him, Peter?"

"*Nein!*" A yelp of fear. "It could go. It could really go if
he drops it."

"All I want," I insisted, "is a chance to clean up."

"I'll hose you," Peter offered. "Go stand on the drain."

There was a floor-grate at the other end of the workroom. Beatrice shut the door, and Peter hooked a hose to
the sink.

"Not too close," I cautioned, keeping the bomb-core
high overhead. "Just hose me down. Me and the death
sphere."

He dialed up the nozzle and played a hard stick of water
over my suit. Bits of black dust washed down with the
clear rivulets. I raised one foot, then the other, letting him
clean the soles.

"Don't forget my hands." The splattering pressure
moved up my arms and played across my hands. For an
instant the water got between my fingers and the bomb's
steel shell. It shifted a bit. I stifled a scream.

If it fell from up there the Styrofoam really might be
crushed. The mass would go hypercritical. The air would

burn and we'd all see God. Half-assed, but effective. I kept wondering if I should just drop it and get this mess over with. But maybe I could still get out.

Peter turned the water off. "Okay, *kerl*, you're clean."

The death sphere was getting heavy. Still holding it high, I jiggled it like Dr. J. ready to unloose a half-court swish.

"Beatrice," Peter shouted. "Open the door. Don't shoot. Don't shoot him."

The door rolled open. I could see Beatrice and Giulia out there, machine guns at the ready. I walked towards them, Godzilla with his giant boulder.

"Back off, bitches. Get the front door open. You, Giulia, you get the Maserati ready." They moved. Amazing, the respect that nuclear weapons bring. So I rode out of the *Supercortemaggiore* garage, standing up in a convertible and clutching an atomic bomb. Just like the President of the United States.

EIGHT
the attack of the giant ass

Sybil climbed out of a taxi in front of the *Herald Tribune* building. The children were safe at the Savoy with her parents, who'd arrived last night with Sorrel. Sybil was going to set Susan Spangle straight about that story she'd printed claiming that Atomic Alwin, the Anarchist Archimedes, had gone over to the Green Death voluntarily.

As she paid the driver, something strange caught her eye. A slowly moving purple convertible with someone standing up in it . . . a man dressed all in white plastic and holding a shiny metal ball over his head. The ball was bright in the hot afternoon sun. A politician? Some kind of ad campaign?

Nope. It was me. I saw her from fifty meters and yelled at Giulia to stop and let me off. I wanted to get the poison suit off before touching my wife.

"Okay," Giulia said, casting a glance up through her heavily made-up eyes. "*Arrivederci.*" Through this whole thing she had never seemed anything but languidly detached. I really had no idea what she was thinking.

But who cared. I was free and safe. I stepped gingerly down out of the Maserati. Giulia did a sharp U-turn and sped back towards the garage. We didn't have much time. Hurriedly I set the bomb down on the hot pavement and unzipped my radiation suit. What a relief to get out in the air again!

Sybil recognized me and came running down the sidewalk. "Alwin, Alwin."

"Sybil!" I picked up the bomb and hurried towards her as fast as caution would allow. This was no time to stumble. I hoped the water had washed all the plutonium dust off the bomb shell. "Get the cab back, Sybil, they're coming for us!"

Sybil heard the fear in my voice and called to her taxi-driver. She'd tipped him well, and obediently he *rur-ru-rred* thirty meters in reverse. The back door opened. Sybil hugged and kissed me. I picked up the bomb and we got in.

"Back to the Savoy," Sybil told the driver.

"*Bene.*"

"What Savoy? Where are the kids?"

"My parents are here. They got a suite of good rooms, and the kids and I moved in with them. But, Alwin, how *are* you?" She glanced anxiously out the taxi's back window. "They're still after you?"

"I think they must be. I've got their bomb." I patted my steel soccer ball. "This, believe it or not, is an atomic bomb. Did you ever play with those little cracker-balls that you throw on the ground and they go off? This is like the same thing. It's full of plutonium."

"Oh, my *God!*" Sybil slid as far away from the bomb as possible. "Is it radioactive?"

"It's okay as long as it's sealed up tight. The plutonium in there is really poisonous though. You'd have to have one of those white plastic breathing suits to take it apart. We can turn it over to the police or something when we get to the hotel." I gave Sybil a kiss. The feel of her soft cheek brought back the memory of the sex sphere.

Thinking of the sex sphere, I suddenly recalled an image from Edwin Abbott's *Flatland:* A three-dimensional sphere who shows herself to the two-dimensional Flatlanders by moving through the plane in which they live. The Flatlanders are squares and triangles sliding around in a single plane, and when the sphere moves through the plane they see a circle which grows and shrinks.

"I can't believe you got away, Alwin," Sybil said, kissing back. "Let's get out of Italy as soon as possible. Let's leave tonight. We could go to my parents' house in Frankfurt."

"I'd rather just go to Heidelberg. I feel too shaky and fucked-up to face a family reunion." I sighed and looked at my trembling hands. "Maybe I can sell the magazine rights for my true-life adventure and we can move back to America. It's so much safer there."

"I know," Sybil said, putting an arm around me. "I feel so . . . exposed in Europe." We rode in silence for a minute. It was late afternoon of Holy Saturday, the day before Easter.

There was no business traffic, but plenty of tourists. An obelisk slid past, covered with hieroglyphs.

"How did you manage to get kidnapped in the first place, Alwin?"

"Oh, these guys tricked me. A big guy called Virgilio

pretended to be a pimp. And somehow he got me into a taxi that . . ." My voice caught. There was something horribly familiar about the set of this taxi-driver's head.

A car behind us honked loudly and the taxi pulled over. "What are you doing?" demanded Sybil. "This isn't the Savoy!"

The driver turned, the same little wart as before. The front door opened and Virgilio got in, pistol in hand. The taxi pulled back into the traffic.

"These are the same guys," I told Sybil with a tired groan. "Where the fuck did you get this cab?"

"The man at the desk called it for me. *Do* something, Alwin!"

"I'll introduce you. Sybil, this is Virgilio Bruno and the wart. Wart, this is Bruno. Virgil, this is Sybil. Alwin, this is the Green Death's atomic bomb. Here, Virgilio, could you just take the bomb and let us off at the Savoy?"

"You have forgotten something, Alvino," purred Virgilio. "Something of Lafcadio's."

He meant the sex sphere. But I wasn't going to give her up without a fight. "I don't know what you're talking about."

"Everyone knows," insisted Virgilio. "Everyone knows from the news that Lafcadio stole something valuable from the Mont Blanc lab. He was a physicist there until the theft. Since then he spoke only about Dante and about spheres. I wonder what he had?"

Sybil stared at Virgilio in sick fascination. He was beautifully dressed in a white linen suit, with a light-pink silk shirt and a dark-salmon knit tie. His finely chiseled jaw was blue with whiskers, his nose was hooked and tough-looking and his eyes were soft with a brutal sensitivity. He was, in short, the man whom she'd most like to be abducted by. He gave her a lazy smile. She fought to keep herself from smiling back. She was being irrational. The man was evil, a ruthless criminal. But yet . . .

"Virgilio's right," Sybil heard herself saying. "I read it in the newspaper this morning. The dead man had stolen some special thing the Mont Blanc lab made. Some kind of degenerate supermatter?"

"Hypermatter," I corrected automatically, and gave Sybil a sharp nudge.

"So you have seen it?" Virgilio demanded.

"No, no. I'm just correcting the word. I do that for Sybil all the time. She's turned some of her memory functions over to me. We're symbiotes. But let's stick to the point. Here's the bomb. Worth maybe ten million dollars. Whether Lafcadio had a sample of hypermatter I have no idea. Just let us out. Here is fine."

We were driving through the Villa Borghese park, not far from the Casino Borghese art museum. Via Veneto was only a kilometer from here.

"Come on, Virgilio," I repeated. I didn't bother threatening to set the bomb off because I knew Virgilio wouldn't believe me. Neither of us was the kind of person to set it off. He'd sell it to the government or to the terrorists, whoever offered more.

There was a sudden crack, and the rear windshield shattered. I threw myself down onto the seat, pulling Sybil with me. Someone was shooting at us. A tire blew out and the car lurched.

"Sybil," I whispered, "if anything happens to me, get Lafcadio's sex sphere. I have it in my pants pocket. It's a tiny sphere that grows."

Virgilio leveled his pistol over us and fired four wild shots out the jagged hole where the rear window had been. An answering bullet caught the wart in the back of his head. Bloody curds flew, and the car skidded out of control. I pressed the bomb into the seat springs and braced myself.

Blessedly, there was no crash. The car just coasted off the road onto the smooth grass, piddled this way and that and finally bumped to a stop. Virgilio fired off another shot, and there was a satisfying scream. But at the next trigger pull, his pistol only clicked.

"*Fotte*," Virgilio muttered. "Out of bullets."

Sybil sat up and looked around. A purple Maserati had pulled up next to the taxi. It, too, had a flat tire. A tall Italian woman in the driver's seat was pointing some kind of machine gun at them. The man in the seat next to the Italian woman lolled back, dying with his mouth open. Virgilio must have shot him.

I sat up, recognizing Giulia and the dying snoid, his splayed teeth bloody in the late afternoon sun. Too bad it hadn't been Beatrice. A police car sang in the distance, and Giulia looked agitated. I hoped she wouldn't start shooting.

Virgilio threw his empty pistol on the grass and stepped out of our taxi. "Let's make a deal," he suggested to Giulia. "You have us. But the *carabinieri* are coming. I have a hiding place. In the *Casino Borghese*. Your gun, my hiding place and we'll share fifty-fifty."

"What about us?" Sybil put in.

Virgilio gave her a calculating look, taking in her light-brown hair, her wide hips, her supple skin. "You are our hostages. You and Alvino . . . and Pauline Borghese. Let's hurry."

I had sort of used up my day's ration of initiative, and didn't even resist when Virgilio lifted the bomb out of the backseat. "Be careful not to drop it," was the best I could muster. "It could go off."

"*Bene*," Virgilio growled. He led the way, Sybil and I followed and Giulia covered us from the rear. It was after closing time, and the tour buses were gone from the Casino Borghese parking lot. We hurried across it, heels tapping. The police horns were much closer now.

Virgilio drew a key out of his pocket and sprang up the steps. The old guard sitting inside recognized him and tipped his hat.

"My brother is head of the museum guards' union," Virgilio told Sybil, pleasantly. "You'll be able to look around in here undisturbed. Without the usual . . ." Balancing the bomb in his left hand, he pumped his elbows in and out to indicate crowded conditions.

Giulia pointed her gun at the guard and jerked it towards the parking lot. With an indifferent shrug, the old man packed his lunch and newspaper in a satchel and walked out. Looking back I could see the blue flashing lights of police cars. They were crowding around the two disabled cars and corpses. It would be a while till they thought to look in here. The old guard wasn't telling. He ambled across the grass towards a bus-stop. It seemed like every monument or museum in Rome was Virgilio's to use as he pleased.

He was already in the next room with Sybil, holding her by the arm, showing her the statue of Pauline Borghese propped on a couch. I'd have to watch this guy. But why should he bother with Sybil anyway, when Giulia was here?

I looked up at her. With her long legs and high heels, she was fully two inches taller than me. Her hips were practically at my shoulder level. Clumsily I threw an arm around her. Her straight-line mouth twitched in a half-smile. Standing this close I noticed for the first time that her skin was a bit rough under the makeup. The sex sphere twitched in my pocket. I could feel the phero-mones building. The sphere was messing up our minds.

"I'm glad to see you again, Giulia. Even with a machine gun." The sphere pulsed steadily, pumping out the magic molecules of lust.

"Come," Giulia said imperiously, and headed off in the opposite direction from Virgilio and Sybil. I knew I should stay with my wife, but I couldn't stop myself from following.

The sound of Giulia's high heels on the marble floor thrilled me to the core. I had to half-trot to keep up with her long strides. We passed two rooms, and Giulia darted a hurried look into each one. What were we looking for? A place to fuck, I hoped. Surely the pheromones were affecting her as much as they were me.

We came to a flight of stairs and she started up. I paused, straining my ears to hear what the others were up to. I seemed to hear Sybil protesting weakly against the insistent blur of Virgilio's voice, lowered to an amorous murmur. That was an angle I hadn't bargained for. If the sphere could drive Giulia and me into a sex-frenzy, then it could do the same to Sybil and Virgilio. Hating myself, I started up the stairs after Giulia. I caught up at the top and got my arm back around her hips. She threw a quick smile down at me, then stopped by one of the rooms. Pictures and a smooth wooden floor.

"Come, Bitter, come make *amore*."

I nodded vigorously. She slung her Uzi across the room, stepped out of her dress and unhooked her bra. I tore off my shirt, dropped my pants, and slipped off my underwear. Without my having to ask, she knew to leave on her heels, stockings and garter-belt . . . though it took a minute for her to maneuver her panties out from under the garters. Meanwhile I kissed her on the neck, on the nipples, on the navel. As soon as her cunt was uncovered, I knelt down and began licking it, tasting her piss and sweat. I tilted my head back and looked up past her garter-belt, past her big nipples, worshipping her body, her unreadable face.

Then we were on the floor and I was in her. She folded up her legs and dug those high heels into my back. I whinnied like a racehorse and hit the homestretch. Sweet coming come swelled my bag. I kissed her face, so close, and murmured, "Giul', oh Giul', gon' co' now ba' . . ."

In the blotchy phosphene haze of afterspurt I saw something move, off to the side there, my *pants* sliding towards us. I snapped up onto my elbows. The right pant-leg bulged out, round and full, then ripped and split to release the horny sex sphere. I could hear Sybil down-stairs moaning, *screaming* in peak sex-come frenzy. Faith-less whore. The sphere grew bigger.

Virgilio led Sybil past the statue of Pauline Borghese and into the next room. He set the bomb down on the floor, and put his arm around her waist. She could smell his cologne and faint sweat. Some other quality was in the air, too—some incredible charge of sexual tension.

Virgilio pressed closer. Sybil craned to see if Alwin was watching. What would he think of her, letting this brutally handsome Italian put his hands all over her? But Alwin wasn't looking, no, he was trotting after that big Italian woman like a pet spaniel. Going the other way. Well, so much the better. Why shouldn't Sybil enjoy her-self too, for once?

Virgilio's hand slid down and pressed into Sybil's ass-crack. With a sigh and a shudder, she pressed back.

"Look at this statue," Virgilio was saying. "My favor-ite. The Rape of Persephone, by the immortal Bernini." He gestured with his free hand, then let the momentum carry his hand onto Sybil's lower belly. She glanced at his strong hand, knuckles tufted with black hair, then looked obediently at the statue. In the distance she heard Alwin and Giulia going upstairs.

The statue. A wild-faced man holds Persephone high in the air. Persephone's face is docile, bovine, conven-tionally alarmed. The amazing thing is the modeling of the abductor's hands pressed into Persephone's soft warm marble waist and thigh. The flesh sinks and gives, just so.

Virgilio slid his hand down and kneaded Sybil's cunt. She felt enclosed by his strength, front and back, wearing him tight and dirty. Her knees felt so weak.

She slid down on the cool marble floor and lay there, mouth and legs open, reveling in her submission. This was like a dream. Nothing mattered anymore but sex.

Virgilio danced out of his clothes. He knelt by her head. She opened her mouth wider, showing her tongue, and he pushed in. She let her mouth go big and wet and soft, let him pump deep and deeper, loving the taste of his skin, the smell of his balls.

Now Virgilio was tugging at her panties. She raised up helpfully, and he got them off, then crawled around to fuck her. She let her mouth stay open and slack like she was still sucking him, and pressed her hands behind her back.

His face was flushed and swollen as his cock. He pushed into her as hard as possible. She pushed back, infinitely soft and wet and deep . . . yin to his yang. They caught a wave of sex-rhythm and rode it to shore, surfer and surfboard, engine and wing, screaming to touchdown, twitch, twitch, twitch.

Virgilio slid off her and kissed her twice, then drew his head back and stared at her appraisingly. "You are the first American woman I have . . ."

"Fucked? Well, you're my first Italian. My first anything since our wedding."

"Truly?" Virgilio looked very pleased with this news. "How long?"

"Eleven years in June." And now I've finally had a lover,

thought Sybil to herself. I finally did it. I won't have to die a goody-goody.

Suddenly the Italian bitch upstairs started yelling something. With a quick leonine motion, Virgilio was on his feet. He whipped his pants on and picked up the bomb. "Let's go upstairs, Sybil."

Sybil rose. Her dress . . . she'd never taken it off . . . slid down and covered her wetness. Virgilio looked impatient, so she didn't bother putting the panties on, just stuffed them in her purse. She followed him upstairs, marveling at the smooth play of muscles in his naked back.

Giulia was screaming louder and louder, drowning out the soothing drone of Alwin's explaining voice. When Sybil saw what was in the room, she screamed too.

Later she would describe it as looking like a cross between Salvador Dali's Young Virgin Auto-Sodomized by Her Own Chastity (an ass floating free of its legs) and René Magritte's The Listening Chamber (a room filled by a single enormous apple). The giant ass had Giulia and Alwin trapped in a corner. They were both undressed. Sybil felt a sharp spasm of jealousy. Virgilio stepped up to the giant ass and started yelling, his A-bomb raised high overhead.

The bitch's screams had drawn what looked like police; three of them came charging up the stairs. Virgilio turned with a snarl, and one of them shot him in the leg. The bomb dropped.

babs the bad

Giulia became very agitated when she noticed the sex sphere. I tried to explain to her that it was a friend of mine, a lover aroused by the sound and smell of the hot piece we'd just torn off. She wouldn't listen.

"Can't you wait?" I asked the sphere sharply. "I'm milked dry. Shrink, damn you! Virgilio'll get you."

But it was hard to make myself heard over Giulia's screams. The sex sphere kept growing. She glided close and gave me an insistent nudge. She had her vagina aimed right at me. Before I knew it, Giulia and I had been backed into a corner, right under a picture of the Virgin Mary nursing baby Jesus.

Giulia had completely flipped, and I was getting worried, too. I had formed a vague idea that the sex sphere was a *hypersphere* extending into the fourth dimension. Which meant that if the sphere's giant cunt swallowed me I could end up someplace very . . . different.

Just then Virgilio came charging in like Serpico. He even had his shirt off, the fucking greaser. I craned forward to check Sybil out and, sure enough, her face had that just-fucked flush. Jealousy and remorse hit me like twin furies. What had we done? Eleven years of faithful wedlock down the tubes.

The sex sphere's split was bigger now, opening and closing like some veiny slobbering man-eater from the fetid swamps of Heinlein's Venus. I was so depressed I didn't care if she got me.

Virgilio was being a crazy asshole and waving the A-bomb around. I yelled at him to power down. Just then some people came running up the stairs. They had uniforms, and looked like police. But they weren't. They were Green Death. Peter and Beatrice and Orali, the remaining snoid.

A bullet caught Virgilio in the leg, oh shit. The bomb slipped out of his grasp. I took the only way out. I jumped feet first into the sex sphere's snatch.

The sphere got out of there in a hurry. We moved off into the fourth dimension. As we left normal space, I felt a horrible wrenching sensation all over my body, as if I were being torn right out of my flesh. The strong walls of the sphere's vagina pressed in, holding me together.

Though nestled deep inside her, I could peep out. As soon as we'd broken the fetters of conventional 3-D space, I could feel myself acquire an extraordinary mobility. My eyes rolled this way, and that way, and other ways too. In one direction I could see down into the wood-floored room in the Casino Borghese.

"Down" is not quite the word. I could see the room as from a distance . . . yet from no particular direction at all. Floor, ceiling and all four walls were spread before me.

Thanks to the forgiving wood floor, the bomb had failed to detonate. Peter was looking it over while Beatrice and the snoid stared at Giulia wriggling into her dress. Virgilio lay on the floor, moaning.

But Sybil ... my Sybil stepped across the room and quickly picked up the tiny sex sphere cross section, far down a hypercurve from the fat part holding me. No one noticed. She dropped the little spherelet into her purse. I hoped she would know to *smeep* me back. Hoped she'd get a chance.

The Green Death were over on one side of the room, regrouping and discussing. It looked like Peter wanted to just run off with the bomb, but Beatrice wanted to take Virgilio and Sybil hostage. Giulia gestured a lot and seemed to be having trouble explaining what had happened to me. The Green Death gang wasn't at all hip to the nature of Lafcadio Caron's hypersphere.

Just then the situation took another turn for the worse. The real police arrived. I could see them outside the little museum, crouched behind bulletproof shields and shouting through a megaphone. I wished I could hear what they were saying. According to the news-show I'd seen, they thought I was one of the bad guys. Right now I was better off in hyperspace.

From my vantage point everything looked very strange. I could see through Sybil's dress, see that she had no panties on, and I could even see her guts and bones. It was a little as if everything were transparent. Her beating heart, the sperm in her womb. I prayed she'd survive the impending melee.

But meanwhile there was so much else to see! A roll of my eyes and the Casino Borghese vanished. I was staring into raw hyperspace. It was crowded with moving forms, some round like my girlfriend the hypersphere, some angular, some branching. The motions they described were far richer than anything our 3-D space exhibits. The usual left/right, forward/backward, up/down movements were all there . . . but there was a fourth type of motion, call it *ana/kata*. Thus, rather than saying I could look *down* at the Casino Borghese, I prefer to say that I could look *kata* at it. Rather than saying the sex sphere moved *up* out of normal space, I say that she moved *ana* out of it.

The hyperforms around us often seemed to be turning inside out, not by everting, but by . . . changing perspective like one of those self-reversing line drawings of a cube or a staircase. It was hard for my 3-D eyeballs to keep up with it all. Only by rapidly sweeping my eyes *ana* and *kata* could I begin to grasp the whole picture.

Cautiously, I slid my head a little farther out and tried to get an overall picture of the sex hypersphere. If I held my eyes a certain way, I saw nothing but the same cross section I'd jumped into. Huge tits and ass, an open-sesame crack. But by bending my neck *kata*, I could sight over one of the nipples, for instance, and see it as just one cross section of a whole ridge-line of nipple-tissue dwindling down to a dot on the spherelet in Sybil's purse.

Keeping my neck turned *kata*, but rolling my eyes left, I could see the continuous furry furrow of the hypersphere's cross-sectional vulvas ending, again, in Sybil's purse. I wondered what it was that kept this particular hypersphere from moving entirely away from our normal space. A snag that Lafcadio Caron had somehow set? I recalled a paper of his on three-dimensional knottings of hyperspace objects.

I'd had some worries that my brain might fall out. But, for now, nothing untoward happened. Growing more reckless, I wormed my shoulders and arms out of the sex sphere's minge. Moving my arms around was an incredible sensation. By slight *kata-ana* twitches I could, in effect, move them right through each other: just as two coins on a tabletop can be made to miss colliding if one is slightly raised.

The hyperspace around me was filled with strange, thrilling vibrations . . . as if hundreds of songs were being sung at once. This or that tune would slide into prominence, then segue out as I moved again. Waving my arms in abandon, I forgot my troubles and danced.

Time passed. When I thought to look *kata* again, I could see that Sybil was caught in a stalemate. The Green Death had tied her and Virgilio up, but now the real police had the Green Death pinned down in the museum. Beatrice must have threatened to set off the A-bomb, as the cops were making no signs of invading . . . just yelling over a bullhorn. For some reason Sybil and Virgilio were naked and tied together face-to-face. Were they fucking again? I couldn't stand to watch. Going back *kata* there was, for now, the goddamn last fucking thing I wanted to do.

I turned my head *ana*, straining to see what lay in the hyperspace direction away from normal space. I was by no means embedded in the sex hypersphere's largest cross section. She bulged out and out for several dozen meters before reaching maximum girth. *Ana* there her sexual characteristics faded out and were replaced by some other kind of patterning.

I wriggled the rest of the way out of her birth canal. Born again in a higher world. Praise Jesus. I stood on the sphere, swaying a little.

It gave me a weird, spaced-out feeling to move around in four dimensions. Strangely vivid memories of things past kept flashing in on me, and I had a little trouble remembering exactly what was going on.

My body parts had a disconcerting way of seeming to change radically, depending on what angle I looked at them from. Sometimes my legs were naked, sometimes clothed. And in the greatest imaginable variety of raiment! I recognized jeans, suit-pants, knickers and shorts. For one unsettling instant, I looked down and saw chubby infant's legs sticking out of a shitty diaper. Mellow yellow. A moment later, my hand became a skeleton's claw. I pressed my eyes shut and concentrated on the present.

When I opened them again, things were a bit more orderly. My limbs no longer seemed to flicker back and forth in time. Now, when held at certain angles, they simply disappeared. I decided to work my way *ana* to the sex hypersphere's wide part and demand an interview. *Ana*: further out. *Kata* lay Green Death, faithless Sybil and pigs who hunted the Anarchist Archimedes.

I got down on all fours and crawled up to the summit of one of my sex sphere's breasts. Then I turned my hands and feet in such a way that they became invisible, and pushed. The breast beneath me grew slightly larger. I had moved *ana* to a new cross section. I kept doing this . . . pushing myself along in some invisible direction . . . and slowly the breast-mound flattened. A few more pushes and the nipple faded into a welt, then a freckle, then blank skin. I was getting near the hypersphere's maximum cross section, the equatorial sphere.

But not really a sphere. All sorts of strange shapes rose up around me: armchairs, cave-mouths, saguaro cacti. Seemingly disconnected blobs of skin-covered tissue drifted past. I kept turning my head this way and that, trying to keep my bearings.

The celestial music I'd heard before damped down, and a single stuttering murmur took over, like a taped conversation cut up and played wrong speed. Was the sex sphere finally talking to me?

Just then the skinscape around me necked up and out. I lost my footing. For an instant I tumbled, my limbs aflow, now young, now old. I stood up again, thoroughly disoriented. I seemed to be in a small pink room, a sepia-tone replica of our Heidelberg apartment. A chair rose up behind me, catching me in the back of the knees. I sat down heavily. Sybil walked into the room.

Her face was missing, but as I thought this, the skin-patch arranged itself into her features. She was screaming at me. I had a feeling of *déjà vu*.

"All you think about is yourself," said Sybil's harsh, angry voice. "I can't stand it anymore."

"What do you mean?" I muttered right on cue. "Take it easy."

This was a replay of a fight we'd had last month. And the month before that, and that, and that, and that, and that, and that, and that.

"It's fine for you," railed the simulacrum. "You go to your office, you go to your conferences. What do *I* have? Nothing but your coldness. And thankless work day after day."

God, what a bummer. The hypersphere must have looked into my brain and read my memories. I'd taken Sybil to Rome specifically to get away from this shit. It occurred to me that it would all start again as soon as our trip was over.

The pseudo-Sybil was crying now. I knew it was a fake, but the force of habit brought me to my feet. "Don't cry, Sybil. Things aren't really so bad."

"Ha!" Her face was red and wet. "When was the last time you washed a single dish? You treat me like a servant, like dirt! There's no room for anyone but Alwin Bitter, Alwin Bitter, Alwin Bitter." In her mocking mouth my name became a curse.

"That's not true," I protested. "I've just been wrapped up in my work. But I *do* care. You know that."

"You do not. You just wish I would shut up. Why did I ever marry you? We haven't had one single good time together in years. I can't remember the last time you smiled at me."

"What about last week? When we were in the restaurant and had trout?" I was having trouble remembering that this wasn't real.

"Oh, sure, if we're out drinking our heads off you can put on a happy face. But when was the last time we did something normal together or even *talked?*"

"Look, do you want to take a walk or something?"

"And what about the children?"

"They can come, too."

"You know they won't. Sorrel will throw a fit."

"So let's take a drive."

"And you'll lose your temper and spank poor Tom again. I couldn't believe when you did that last week. You're really sick, you know that Alwin? You're a sick, selfish person. It's just me, me, me, and anyone else might as well be dead."

I was getting mad now. "Look, Sybil, I don't have to listen to this crap."

"Oh, sure. Get mad and hit me. That's your only answer, isn't it?"

"I have no intention of hitting you." I was fighting for control. "If you don't mind, I think I'll go out for some air." I skirted her, heading for the door.

"You mean, sneak out and get drunk, don't you, Alwin? And leave me to spend Saturday cooped up in this horrible apartment with all the children in the building."

"I'll take the kids, I'll take the kids."

The "door" held out a pink hand to me, and I pulled it. It thopped open and closed and I was in a different space, a copy of the single bedroom our three children shared. I felt spaced and half-crazed with hangover, just like on a regular Saturday. I had forgotten how to move *ana* and *kata*. I was locked into a bad-trip rerun the sex sphere had read off the wrinkles of my brain.

"Hey, kiddies," I called. "Do you want to take a walk?"

I could hear them giggling, but couldn't see where they were. The room looked the same as usual: Ida's sleeping-couch on the left, Tom and Sorrel's bunk beds on the right. But the desks were tipped over, and there were clothes and pieces of toys everywhere. They'd really trashed the room, the rotten little turds.

There was a sharp scream from behind me. I turned and opened the door of the kids' clothes closet. The three of them were squeezed in there, faces dirty and eyes rolling. Tom was yelling about something Ida or Sorrel had done to him. They all looked frightened of me.

"Come on, children, get out of there." I stepped forward and something smeared underfoot. A sudden, fruity smell filled the air.

"Ida did it," shouted Sorrel joyfully. "Ida put banana on the floor." She gave Tom another poke in the kidneys and he turned on her, flailing his arms.

I pulled them out of the closet, one by one.

"God damn you, Sorrel, get out of that closet and pick up this room. Why do you have to eat on the floor, Ida? What kind of pig are you? Just calm down, Tom." His hair was in his eyes and he had a fleck of foam on his lips. "Try to act human."

I got a piece of cardboard and scraped the banana off my bare foot and off the floor.

"Pssss," said Sorrel, pointing at my penis. I suddenly remembered that I was naked. Why was I naked here in our crummy Heidelberg apartment on another horrible Saturday morning? For the moment I couldn't remember. "Pssssssss," said Ida. I wondered if there were any beer left from last night.

Just then Sybil walked into the room. "Didn't I tell you children to clean up in here?"

Tom gave a wild, unhappy laugh. "We're cleaning cleaning cleaning," he shouted, grabbing a broom and waving it. "I'll get the *spiders*." He flailed at the ceiling. His broom hit the paper shade covering the light bulb. The shade fell off.

My heart ached for my son. Obviously this was all my fault. "Why do you work them up by coming in here naked?" demanded Sybil.

"Pssssss," said Sorrel and Ida, each holding a pencil between their legs like a penis. I found a wet towel on the floor and wrapped it around my waist.

"Fix that shade right away," Sybil ordered Tom. "Sorrel, you put those desks back. Ida, start picking up."

I sprang to do these jobs, knowing the children wouldn't. But the shade tore in my hands, and when I tilted the first desk back up, all the drawers fell out. One drawer landed on my bare foot.

I roared and threw things. BANG, a table hit the wall and gouged a hole! WHAM, the desk flipped and snapped a leg! CRASH, went the whole fucking box of Legos!

The children screamed in terror. Sybil crouched in front of them, tense and protective. Flaring up like this, I'd put myself so far in the hole that it'd take a week to square it. Sybil might even leave me. Garbage, garbage, my life was garbage. I rushed out the door, face twisted in anguish.

As I stepped through, the space around me gave a strange twitch. There was nothing outside. I was floating in emptiness. The door had disappeared. I waved my arms and legs. There was nothing to push against. Slowly I remembered I was not really in Heidelberg. I was somewhere in hyperspace. But why couldn't I see anything?

"Alwin?" The sweet sound came from all around me. "Alwin, zis is Babs."

"Are you the sex sphere?"

"I'm Babs za bad hypersphere, za one who ate you up." The accent was pure Zsa Zsa Gabor.

"Am I inside you?"

"Your vhife, she don't understand you. You zshould love me best."

"What do you want from me, Babs?"

"I vhant to be free."

This was getting nowhere fast. I still hadn't gotten back my ability to move four-dimensionally. As a physicist, it occurred to me that I might be imprisoned on the hyper-surface of a hyperspherical vacuole in Babs's body. A kind of bubble.

There was nothing around me, nothing but empty curved space. In the distance I could make out a sort of shimmer, a hugely distorted human form. That was me. I was seeing myself around the curve of the hyperspherical space bubble that Babs had stuck me onto.

By way of testing my hypothesis, I took the towel off my waist, wadded it up and tossed it. It dwindled away from me, slowly twisting. Just as the towel seemed to reach the distant shimmer, I felt something hit me in the back of the neck. The towel had circumnavigated my cramped hypercell.

"Let me out," I begged. "Please let me out of here."

I can't take being cooped up. And now my position was like that of an ant on the surface of a toy balloon. No exit. It reminded me of a plastic Thermos bottle I'd had back when I was teaching at State. On the Thermos was a picture of a school bus with Donald Duck getting out, and of schmucky goody-goody Mickey Mouse right there holding up a stop sign. If Donald went right, he'd run smack into Mickey Mouse's *Stop*. If he went left, he'd immediately be at the back of the bus, and would then proceed up along it to that same mickey-mouse stop bring-down. *In real life*, the picture seemed to tell me, *there's no escape from fascist bullshit mickey-mouse stop stop stop.* Though, of course, D.D. *could* have slid up over the lip and into the milk.

Idly I flipped the towel up overhead. A minute later it plopped against the soles of my feet. *Huis Clos.*

"Are you listenink, dollink?" thrilled the sphere's rich voice. I hadn't heard her last few sentences.

"What, Babs?"

"I vhant you to help me free myself."

"I'd like to be free, too. Offhand, I'd say you're a lot freer than I am."

"But Lafcadio trapped a piece of me. Vhat your vhife has in her purse now. A nasty knot in my tail. Oh!" A little exclamation of anger there. "Talkink is zo slow. Here, just let me . . ."

A tendril came invisibly *kata* and plugged into my brain. Babs fed me the story of her capture: Zsuzsi and Lafcadio at work under Mont Blanc, their assistant Jimmy Hu, Lafcadio's "vacuumless vacuum."

Apparently Lafcadio had bulged space up in such a way that he could knot it into the fabric of Babs's body. She was tethered to our space, and she didn't like it. The first thing she'd done was to kill Zsuzsi Szabo. I could see the little bean lying on the concrete under Mont Blanc, angrily buzzing in a puddle of blood. *Ugh*.

"You mean you *ate* Zsuzsi Szabo?" I demanded. "Chewed her up?"

The space around me gave a rippling chuckle. "Vhell zhure. I vhas really mad, you know. But I saved Zsuzsi's brain-patterns. Zis is Zsuzsi's softvhare talkink to you right now, Alwin."

"You mean you're Zsuzsi?"

"Ha, zat cow? No vhay. Now I just got a little Magyar in me is all."

"You're . . . you're not going to eat me, are you?"

"Vhy bother? Your softvhare I can see like a tile floor. Main zing is zat you help me blast off zat goddamn knot."

"Sure. But how?"

"Wiz za atomic bomb I've been gettink together for two months now!"

"You? It was me and the Green Death who did it."

"Sure. Zat's vhat you zink. But I've been callink za shots. Usink Lafcadio. Vhatch some more pictures."

Montage: Lafcadio slugs Jimmy Hu. Runs back to pick up the Babsi bean. Rushes out into the parking lot. The Fiat skidding down the mountain curves. Then speeding down the smooth autostrada. Highway signs flicker past: *Torino, Milano, Brescia, Verona, Padova, Venezia*. Lafcadio in his car, talking animatedly to no one.

Night: Lafcadio in a cheap hotel room. A half-empty bottle of red wine on a table covered with red circles. Lafcadio is cocked back in the desk chair, reading Dante's *Inferno* by the light of a bare bulb overhead. He chuckles softly.

Somewhere outside, a church-bell rings midnight. Lafcadio jumps to his feet, picks up the wine bottle and with one smooth motion uses it to break the light bulb. Spark and sputter. By his bed we can make out the faint glow of Babsi on the bedside table. Lafcadio's dark form glides over and stretches out on the white bed. He is shaking gently, sobbing. "*Zsuzsi*," you hear him mutter, "*O Zsuzsi, non voglio dormire solo.*" At the sound of his voice, the glowing little sphere twitches and grows. You can see an ass-crack now, and breasts on top ... "Zsuzsi!" cries Lafcadio, his eyes white and crazy in the dark. "*Cara mia!*" He picks up the sex sphere and begins to kiss it, his face bathed in radiance.

Morning: Lafcadio inside a café, having breakfast. He chews with his mouth open. One hand stays in his coat pocket, ceaselessly fondling something. There is a newspaper on the table. It has a picture of Beatrice and the headline: *Morte Verdi Terroristi*. Lafcadio stares fixedly at the accompanying article, reading out loud while he continues to chew. Finally he stands and walks across the room to a phone booth. We can see his face talking through the glass. He writes something down on a paper napkin.

Afternoon: Lafcadio at the police station, distraught and weeping. "*Mia povera figlia.*" The cops are sympathetic under their stiff-billed hats. They let him in to visit Beatrice. Fear and calculation in her hard, skanky face. He whispers a message, passes her the napkin and leaves, apologizing to the police. "*No che mia figlia.*"

"So he used his connections to find out how to steal reactor fuel," I mused. "And he fed the info to a terrorist. How did he end up in Rome?"

"He followed za Green Death. Zen vhent to vhork vhiz Virgilio, keepink an eye out for a man like you. He did zis all for love. Your vhife is mean, Alwin. Don't you love me best?"

I was feeling more and more uncomfortable in my hyperspherical prison. With no definite objects but me and the towel to look at, I was beginning to suffer visual hallucinations. Or maybe Babs was still trickling things into my cortex. Bad, heavy, bloody visions. I understood now what she wanted.

"I'll help you," I blurted. "I'll put your cross section . . . the little Babsi bean . . . I'll put it in with the plutonium and set the bomb off. That should get you loose, all right. That should do it."

"Vhonderful. So I'll let you out."

An intricately patterned sphere formed in the air in front of me. A breeze blew out of it. I reached for it, feeling a sort of ridge in space all around the sphere. I dug in my fingers and pulled. The little sphere was a sort of porthole. I slid through it and landed back on the pink outer hide of Babs, the bad sex sphere. Once again I could move my limbs kata and ana, once again I was free in hyperspace.

TEN

the film burns through

The floodlights through the windows covered the ceiling with a complex pattern of squares and triangles. Sybil stared up at the design, trying to ignore the pain in her arms and legs where the ropes dug in, trying to breathe shallowly under the crushing weight of Virgilio. Beatrice, the hard-faced American terrorist, had thought it would be funny to tie up her two hostages in this position: naked and bound ankle-to-ankle, wrist-to-wrist, and with a tight band ringing their two waists.

For the first half hour it had been exciting ... they'd even fucked again. Ironically, this had been one of Sybil's favorite fantasies as a teenager, the fantasy of having a man *tied onto her* with *no clothes on*. But now several hours must have passed and her joints were numb. She wanted nothing more than to get out from under.

"Come on, Virgilio," she hissed. "Let me on top."

"I can't move," he moaned. "My leg hurts too much."

The red-haired German boy, Peter Roth, had tied a rag around Virgilio's wound, a simple in-out bullet-hole in the right calf. There hadn't even been much bleeding, and at first Virgilio had seemed to be recovering. He'd certainly been as ready as Sybil for their little mondo-bondage sexhibition. But now he was weak and whimpering. *Basically, women are much stronger than men*, Sybil thought to herself. She jerked her left leg sharply.

"Don't," Virgilio begged. "Don't move!"

Sybil jerked her leg again. "Let me on top."

"*Malditti Americana putana!*" Hissing with histrionic pain, he rolled over, away from his bad leg. Sybil rolled with him. It felt much better on top, like lying on a bear-rug. She planted a kiss on Virgilio's tense mouth. Somewhere outside a bullhorn boomed. In the room next door, Beatrice shouted a hoarse response.

"What are they saying now, Virgilio?"

"They've brought in a professional negotiator. He's trying to win Green Death's confidence. He tells them they are very clever to have assembled an atomic bomb. But he is offering nothing but a fair trial."

Virgilio wriggled beneath Sybil, trying to get comfortable. "Move your foot up, *cara*."

Sybil drew her leg up, lessening the pressure on Virgilio's wound. "Is that better, you poor darling?" Now that she was on top she could afford to be sympathetic. Drawing up her leg had pressed their privates together. It still felt good. She kissed Virgilio, then pushed her tongue into his mouth. His strong shaft stiffened against her. She rocked her hips, feeling blindly for his tip. This was crazy. They were making their own pheromones now.

Virgilio moaned, though not in pain, and shrugged

himself down a bit. Sybil bore down, engulfing his strength in one smooth motion. Doing this made her wonder again what had happened to Alwin. He'd jumped in the giant ass, and it had shrunk to a little ball. The ball was in her purse. And where was the purse? The terrorists had taken it along with their clothes when they moved to a different room, a central room with only one window. In there they were yelling into the night, and in here Sybil and Virgilio were naked and all alone.

While all these thoughts passed through her head, Sybil kept gently jouncing, being careful not to jar Virgilio's wounded leg. She let her face slide down to rest in the hollow of his neck. This felt *so good*. She was bad to have started at all—she should have fought Virgilio off—but right now it was still fun. The guilt would come later. Sybil wondered what had come over her to let Virgilio fuck her next to "The Rape of Persephone." She'd always heard that the imminence of death makes you horny. Or maybe that sex sphere had something to do with it. Virgilio was coming now, she could feel the twitching of his penis and the distant gush of seed. She pressed against him and came as well. Sweet sex, sweet fuck, sweet cock and cunt.

The noises around them came filtering back in. Beatrice was screaming in Italian, her voice rough and cracked. Sybil raised her head, trying hard to understand.

"What's going on?"

"She asks," Virgilio paused, listening, "she asks that an armored car come for them to drive to the airport. She wants to fly to Libya with ten million dollars and the bomb." Beatrice's voice ranted on, rhythmic and musical. "She wants all the imprisoned *Brigate Rosse* terrorists released with her. Also Mehmet Agca."

"Who's he?"

"Don't you remember? The man who shot the Pope. She's crazy."

"But what if she sets off the bomb?"

"I think she wants to. It's a shame I have to deal with such people." Virgilio seemed relaxed and comfortable again. Sex as anaesthetic. "Madmen and terrorists. I just try to make a little money for my family."

"You're married?" Sybil felt an unreasonable stab of jealousy. Tied up naked here she felt she could say anything. "Do I fuck better than her?"

Virgilio shrugged beneath her. His limp penis slid out. "*E possibile*. But where is your husband? What happened to him?"

"That big sphere of skin," Sybil said. "It must have something to do with what the TV said about Lafcadio Caron. A spacewarp or something. Supermatter. Alwin jumped in. Maybe he saw the bomb dropping." Not knowing whether he was dead or only hiding, Sybil couldn't decide how to feel about Alwin's disappearance. He'd deserted her in the face of danger, hadn't he? And been unfaithful to her with garter-belt Giulia. Somehow the memories of Alwin seemed so unreal—like remembering a dream. Virgilio was no hallucination—that was for sure. Some boyfriend, a professional kidnapper. Sybil's train of thought was interrupted by more cries from Beatrice.

"She sets a deadline," Virgilio whispered. "One half hour. But the police are stalling. I don't think they will give in."

"Oh, Lord," Sybil moaned. "We've *got* to get out of here. I don't want to die. Come on, damn you. Stand up."

She rolled them over onto Virgilio's good side and drew that leg up. Then, hopping a bit and pressing their hands against the floor, they rose. Virgilio's clenched teeth were a white grid in the dark of his face.

"Good boy," Sybil murmured. "Now let's go downstairs and surrender to the police."

Their wrists and ankles were still bound together. A single tight strip of cloth encircled their waists. The two-backed beast. Now that they were standing, it was quite easy to move. They eased out of the wood-floored room, out into the marble hall.

The staircase was at the other end of the hall. They shuffled lightly along, then paused by the door of the room holding Peter, Giulia and Beatrice. Should they just dart past and hope for the best? With agonizing slowness, Sybil eased one eye past the door frame and peered in. The three were glued gangster-style to the far wall.

Beatrice held the bomb and stood on one side of the window. Giulia stood on the other side, holding an Uzi and half-facing the door. Peter slouched on the floor. Beatrice was berating him in English.

"Why didn't the cocksucking bomb go off? I fucking *wanted* it to when I shot that wop bastard Virgilio. Don't tell me I got plutonium poisoning just for a shitass dud!" She coughed hoarsely. "I can already feel it. My lungs are going."

"Alwin panicked us for his own purposes," mused Peter. "The Styrofoam is in fact so rigid that the force of a conventional explosive is needed to sufficiently compress the device."

"The pigs are ready to charge and I'm sittin' here with a fuckin' dud." Beatrice spat on the floor. "Look at that *blood*, Peter. Help me out, baby."

The bullhorn shouted, and Giulia shouted back. More silence, then a sudden crash as Beatrice threw the bomb across the room. Sybil snapped her head back and Virgilio took a jerky step away from the door.

But, again, there was no blast. Just the gongy *roing-roing-roing* of the steel mixing bowls rolling around.

"Look out," cried Peter. "You've split the seam."

"That's what I wanted," grated Beatrice. "I'm gonna play the cymbals, man. I'm ready to rock and roll. I'm gonna get out those pieces of plutonium and . . ."

"Giulia! Help me grab her!"

Sybil and Virgilio spidered past the door. Glancing sideways, Sybil thought she saw Beatrice wrestling Giulia's gun away from her. But then they were scuttling crab-style down the stairs, Virgilio giving a little grunt of pain with each step.

There was a burst of machine-gun fire and a scream. Giulia. Peter was yelling, loud and louder. Another burst of gunfire and he fell silent.

"Quick," Sybil hissed. "Let's go outside."

"No!" Virgilio's voice was sharp. "We go out, they grab us, the bomb goes off, we die. Or it doesn't . . . and I go to jail. No! Come this way."

He waltzed Sybil around to a door set under the staircase. "Down here!"

"Hide in the basement from an atomic bomb?" Sybil had trouble keeping her voice down. "Are you crazy?"

"*Lágrimas de Cristo!* There's a tunnel, you dog-bitch, a tunnel to the zoo. I *know* this."

Sibyl struggled for a second, then gave in. Virgilio was too strong to drag out the front door. She could hear Beatrice banging metal upstairs. As one wo/man, Sybil and Virgilio hurried down the basement steps.

Set into the stone of the basement wall was a steel door, just as Virgilio had promised. He raised his hands and did something to the latch. Then they were dragging the door open, rusty metal scraping stone. There was total dead blackness in there.

Spiders, thought Sybil, *broken glass, oubliettes.* "I don't want to go in there, Virgilio."

He didn't bother to answer. There was no alternative, and she knew it. They tangoed on in. As the meters of close darkness bumped past, there was nothing to occupy Sybil's mind but images of what Beatrice might be doing with the bomb.

There's blood all over the marble floor. In the dark, everything's black-and-white. Black puddles, white floor, gray flesh-tones.

Giulia: slouched just under the window, disabled by a shattered femur. Her long-fingered hands clutch to stanch the spurting blood. Her eyes are big and shiny, her mouth is straight. Her Uzi rests by the door, well out of reach.

Peter: twisted into a rag-shape no living body takes,

dead in the middle of the room. His mouth and chin are gone to black smash.

Beatrice is on all fours, crawling around the room. Her hair hangs over her eyes. You see only her mantis chin, her feral mouth. Dark blood on her lips, the lips moving, crooning disconnected lyrics to unheard neo-rock.

She has the steel mixing bowls, and is slamming one on the floor.

"In the time of the flood." *Fwuuunmmmp.*

"Dead mountain of God." *Whannng.*

"Sweep broken angels in a seedbed cloud." *Plumpp.*

She lifts up the loose hemisphere of plutonium, holds it high with cupped hands. Her chalice. Touches black lips to it, coughs, starts pounding the other mixing bowl.

"Suddenly inside a mirror." *Blannk.*

"The priestess merry with intrigue." *Fwuunnng.*

"The rooster shrieks my midnight." *Plampp.*

Both chunks of plutonium are free now, and she holds one in each hand, weighing them like Blind Justice. In the background, Giulia watches, empty, black-and-white. There are clothes next to her, Sybil's purse on top. The purse eases open like a stealthy clam. Inside we glimpse a gleam of happy Babs.

The bullhorn outside is talking, sounding a little nervous now, after the gunfire and the silence. "*Bay-ah-tree-chay!*" beseeches the bloated voice. "*Arriva l' autoblinda!*" They've brought that armored car too late.

Beatrice is kneeling now, kneeling over her dead lover, with half an A-bomb in each hand. Her eyes meet Giulia's for an instant. Yes. A tiny nod. Yes.

Beatrice's hands rise slowly up, accelerate into a sweeping cymbal crash. Her graven face. White light: the film burns through.

Sybil *felt* the blast rather than heard it, felt it with her whole body. It seemed to go on for a very long time. Part of the noise was the tunnel behind them collapsing. The air they breathed grew thick and dusty. Sybil coughed and laughed and cried. She could barely remember that man Alwin's name.

"*Avanti*," urged Virgilio. "I tell you this tunnel comes out at the zoo. It's not much further."

Loose rocks had slid down from the tunnel walls in several places. Blindly they stumbled along, gritting their teeth to filter out dust. And then finally there was a door. Their mated hands . . . her left, his right . . . dragged it open. Up a flight of stairs, unlatch another door, step out.

Sirens and police-horns were sounding everywhere. Looking over the zoo buildings, Sybil could make out a small mushroom cloud. It glowed light X-ray purple. Its underside was red-orange, lit by the fires the blast had set.

Something nudged Sybil in the thigh. A penguin. They'd stepped out into the penguin pit. The calm short birds crowded up to them, turning their heads this way and that. There was a strand of barbed wire along one wall of the pit. Sybil and Virgilio used it to saw through the wrist ropes, and then they untied the other bonds. Finally they stood there, free and naked beneath the stars.

"We'd better get out of here," Sybil said after a while, gently disengaging Virgilio's arm from her waist. "There'll be fallout."

"The Rape of Persephone," Virgilio said, shaking his head. "Blasted to radioactive dust."

"And all those poor police."

"*E vero.*"

One of the feathered little gents chanced a peck at Sybil's hand. "Shoo," she said. Somehow the bird reminded her of Tom in a baseball cap. Same height.

"Good-bye, Virgilio."

"Good-bye. But we see each other again, *eh?*"

"I don't know yet. I'll be at the Savoy, under Burton."

"Burton?"

"My last name."

They kissed almost tenderly, then helped each other out of the pit. One of the penguins aaaawrked *arrivederci*.

"This way," said Virgilio. "I know the man at the front gate. He can give you clothes."

"And you."

They walked through the park, the zoological garden, naked in the strangely warm night. Sybil had an unreal, larger-than-life feeling ... as if she were a person in a book.

In the magic of the moment, Virgilio divined her sentiments and said, "We are a painting come to life. The dust has settled."

Sybil could feel the truth of this. The soul of some placid Dark Ages Eden scene, A-bombed into energy, was passing through.

And then they were at the gates. Behind them frightened animals roared. Virgilio hammered at the guardhouse door. No answer. He kicked the door once, twice, thrice, then stopped to nurse his battered foot. The door swung open.

At first Sybil was relieved ... she'd begun to fear the guard was dead. But then the light hit the guard's face. Burned blind. Virgilio asked a rapid question, the man croaked something back.

"He was looking out the window," said Virgilio. "Trying to see what the police were doing."

The man's cracked skin was weeping lymph, his eye-whites were bright red.

"Let's hurry and get away from this awful place," begged Sybil.

Virgilio strode over to the guard-room closet and found a flimsy plastic raincoat. "Take this." He fumbled in the blind man's pocket and pulled out a ten-thousand lire note. "And this. Run now. The door to the right of the gate is open. I will help my friend to his car. Luigi."

Blind Luigi leaned against Virgilio, babbling and hugging his arm. Sybil slipped on the raincoat, smiled a last good-bye at Virgilio, and rushed into the radioactive night.

The main gate was flanked by two columns holding up snaky white elephants. To the right, just as Virgilio had said, she found a door that opened.

Sybil walked a few hundred meters along the zoo's outside wall. Then came a street with traffic. A taxi, a real one this time, stopped. The excited driver had to take a circuitous route, skirting the cordoned-off streets near ground zero. He wanted to talk about it. But he spoke no English. Sybil kept quiet, trying to put her thoughts in order.

The hardest thing to think about was ... Alwin? His face and voice were gone ... had she been married? But she had three children, didn't she? Or was it two? Sorrel, Tom and ... Ida?

Sybil entered the Savoy Hotel from the side, in case there were reporters in the lobby, and got the elevator up to their floor. Her parents had the TV on so loud that she could hear it down the hall.

"Let me in!" she shouted, pounding the door. "It's Sybil."

A child opened, a wet-faced little girl in a yellow dress. "Mama!" she cried. "Mama why were you gone so long? There was a bomb!"

"I know, Ida." Sybil leaned to kiss her younger daughter's tense face. "I was there. I barely got away."

"My name's not Ida, Mama. My name is Sorrel."

Sorrel? Sorrel was eleven, not six. Or ... ? "Well, look, where's Tom?"

"Granma put him in the crib with a bottle. Where's your clothes?"

"Sybil." Lotte Burton, Sybil's mother, came rushing out of the suite's living room.

She was a frail, pessimistic woman, originally Viennese. She'd met Cortland Burton, Sybil's father, on a youthful visit to America. He'd wooed and won her, and she'd settled there with him in Baltimore. And now Cortland had a big engineering-management job in Frankfurt.

"Sybil, where have you been? You could have been

killed! Have you heard? Have you heard what that Anarchist Archimedes did?"

A jog of memory. "My . . . Alwin? They're blaming him for the bomb?"

"You knew him? Oh, what will we do with you? And where did you get that dreadful raincoat?"

"I . . . a man gave it to me."

"And took your clothes? Sybil, even if you're single, you still have a child!" Lotte gestured at the diapered little girl crawling on the floor.

Feeling dizzy, Sybil raised a hand to her face. Hadn't . . . ? She looked down at the tiny child. Sorrel? The shrinking baby slid onto its stomach and let out a newborn's mewling cry. Then disappeared. The children were all gone. They'd never existed.

the machinery of the world

I was crawling *kata* towards our space when the bomb went off. I couldn't tell if Sybil got away. But at that point I had problems of my own . . . big problems.

In effect, the A-bomb burned a fleeting hole in the film of space that held Babs captive. She yanked her knotted tail free and bounded off like a bubble in deep water. I slipped and went tumbling *ana*.

At first the tumbling had me totally disoriented. With each degree that I turned, the images around me would deform and change. Three given blobs might split or merge to two or five, while some other shape's angular facets would sprout interlocking crystals. It was a little like trying to make out a human body by watching a slideshow of three hundred sixty microtomed cross sections.

But after a while some higher brain-center cut in, and I began mentally fitting the wildly changing scenery into a coherent four-dimensional whole. The process was really no more devious than the process by which one integrates the two hundred lines of a TV-screen picture into a single two-dimensional image . . . which is in turn interpreted as a three-dimensional scene. It's just a matter of processing information. Impossible? *I saw.*

I saw Rome stretched out below me like a bright glass model, all open to the fourth dimension. Scanning further away, I could see Italy, Asia and the Arctic wastes . . . and the Earth's interior as well.

Still further out coursed moon and sun, and planets bright and wee. The stars spread out the tangled skeins that knot to galaxies. The sprinkled whorls of starshine filled up man's mundane space; and looking down from up above, the celestial curve I traced.

Oh yes.

The space of our universe is the hypersurface of a vast expanding hypersphere. Babs had set me flying somewhere outside of it, all of me . . . and all my past.

"What is man but a poor forked radish?" asks the Bard. Bad Babs the sex sphere had yanked me out of history like a carrot. Looking at my right hand I could see it through time as: a baby's chubby fist, a toddler's grubby paw, a schoolboy's ink-stained hand, an old man's trembling claw. There were the stitches I had in ninth grade, the ring I'd worn in college, the fashionable fingernail polish I might wear when I'm old. All at once.

Earlier, I'd had glimpses of this, crawling *ana* Babs's breastline. My complete spacetime body was here, all of the Alwin Bitters sewn together in a long, four-dimensional stack. My awareness was primarily at the thirty-two-year mark. But all up and down my life I could feel myself as faintly real.

I was aware of the past selves by means of a series of eidetic memory flashes . . . memories so bright and detailed as to be momentarily indistinguishable from the original events.

My awareness of my future selves was a bit different. The future isn't fixed. A person's unlived lifeworm is, most often, a lashing blur, a constant skittering among the zillion options. When I tried to see into my future it was like watching all the world's TV channels at once: a multiplex information tangle adding up to white noise.

I was floating high *ana* . . . or later than . . . normal space. Space was in motion, expanding like some huge bubble. I noticed that as space grew up past any given cross section, that level of the worms would stop lashing and freeze into known history. *Ana* where I was, all the worms were still active, still flickering among many possible states.

Free in hypertime, I writhed and hissed among the forms, transcendently aware. These variable futures were all in sync, dancing the music of mad cosmic glee, dancing the world's joy at its *is*ness.

My awareness sped up and I peered at one of the nearby forms, trying to make her out. It was Sybil, a few days hence, indeterminate, hypernow happy, hypernow sad. Looking at her form more closely, I could make out the fine grain, the individual atoms.

A person's lifeworm is a tangle of atomic worldlines. A braid. The dotty little atoms trace out smooth lines in spacetime: you are the pattern that these lines make up. There is no one single atom that is exclusively yours. I breathe an atom out, you breathe it in. Your garbage helps my tomatoes grow. And so the little spacetime threads weave us all together. The human race is a single vast tapestry, linked by shared food and air.

There are larger links as well: sperm, egg and umbilicus. Each family tree is an organic whole. Your spacetime body tapers back to the threads of mother's egg and father's seed. And children, if you have them, are forever rooted in your flesh.

I'd dragged a lot of threads after me. Far down, at my spacetime body's thinnest end, my parents were deranged. And halfway up me dangled the three children: root hairs on my long stem of past. There was a certain slack, but now I'd drifted far enough to pull them out of normal space like me. I could feel the tugging in my groin.

The four of us might have tumbled ever *ana*, ever farther from the moving present, pulling after us all traces of our pasts. But Sybil held. Unbreakable cords stretched from her to the children, and from them to me. For an instant the kids and I strained at Sybil's stable womb. And then my momentum was exhausted. The four of us went coiling back towards space's bright advancing curve.

The children landed well, plugging right back into the holes they'd left, but I . . . I landed badly. It took a minute's wriggling to worm my way back into the compost of history.

The sudden thump brought Sybil bolt upright in bed. The children! Feeling her way in the dark, she hurried into the bedroom next door. There they were, the three little ones. Her treasure. Sorrel and Tom slept in the big double bed, and Ida nestled in the snowy whiteness of a roll-a-bed's crisp sheets. Everything was . . .

"Ssshibyl?"

The husky whisper seemed to come from the floor. Something long and thick was writhing there. Snake!

"Ssshybil, it'sh me, Alwin."

Alwin? A coil of flesh the size of a man's arm lay at her feet. A long pair of lips ran all along one side of it, strangely uniform lips which parted to reveal a single, unnaturally broad tooth.

"I'm sshidewaysh," slobbered the long mouth. Rising up near one end of it was a sort of eye-stalk, a slit-irised eye some two meters long. A broad foot the size of a dining table leaned against Ida's bed, and a hugely distended beer-gut danced in midair.

"What's the matter with you? The children . . ." She counted heads once more. "Were they gone with you?"

"Yesh. Now hang on. I've got to get untangled."

The mouth and eye withdrew. Two stacks of hands appeared next to the great jiggling belly. The foot over by Ida's bed skipped sideways . . . and then all the globs were gone. Sybil sat there silent. Once again her memories of Alwin took on solidity, and then he was in the room, the same as ever.

A: Hello.

S: Hi. You're back.

A: How did you get away from the A-bomb?

S: You wouldn't know, would you? Virgilio saved me. He took me out through a tunnel. It led to the zoo.

A: No kidding. Virgilio. I hope you're not in love with
him just because he fucked you.

S: I'm not allowed to love anyone, not even you.

A: Why do you say a thing like that? Look, you know
where I was?

S: Inside a giant ass. You jumped right in. It must have
reminded you of Giulia.

A: Is she dead?

S: They're all dead, all three. And lots of police, too.

A: What about me?

S: What *about* you?

A: Do they blame me?

S: I'm not sure. They probably will now. For the last
few hours everyone sort of forgot you ever existed.
We survived.

A: The children pulled me back.

S: Yes, it was horrible. They got younger and younger
and disappeared. I certainly hope you don't do that
again.

A: Aren't you curious about where I was?

S: So tell me.

A: I was in the future. The universe is a cross section moving up through hyperspace. Through
four-dimensional spacetime. Babs pulled me
up there and the worldlines of my sperm cells
dragged the kids after. I'm surprised you didn't
pull loose, too.

S: Who's Babs?

A: Babs the bad hypersphere. But why . . .

S: Is that what the giant ass calls itself? It talks?

A: I can't understand where she went. I didn't see her anywhere after the bomb went off.

S: Let's go back to Heidelberg tomorrow. My father will buy us plane tickets.

A: There must be a *fifth* dimension, a direction you can move in without worrying about time and your past self. Yes! That's it. At first, when I first peeked out of Babs, it was much more complicated than timeworms. That's what you are, you know.

S: A timeworm?

A: And we're all made of tiny hairs that are braided together. All men are brothers, all women are sisters ... it's really true. We're patterns in a huge tapestry that weaves itself. But there must be other tapestries. A whole stack of them like in a rug store. The lashing *ana* ends might lead ...

S: Call the airport, Alwin.

A: Do you think they're on duty this late? What time is it?

S: Eleven-thirty. Oh shit.

A: What?

S: I just realized that it's going to be impossible to get tickets.

A: The bomb?

S: That's right. A lot of people are panicking about the fallout, even though they said on TV it won't amount to much.

A: Of course they said that on TV. That doesn't make it true. Any idiot can figure *that* out.

S: Don't start calling me names, Alwin, or I'll leave you flat.

A: And do what? Go home with your parents?

S: I don't want to hear your nasty comments about my poor parents. It's thanks to them we have this nice room.

A: What happened to the other nice room? The one I paid for?

S: That dump? We moved out when you got yourself kidnapped. *If*.

A: If?

S: Maybe the paper was right. You're the one who called himself the Anarchist Archimedes aren't you? Nobody really made you build that bomb. You wanted to. I bet you volunteered.

A: You're nuts.

S: All I know is that the police could show up here any time.

A: God, this sucks. Babs was right.

S: That is just so typical of you, Alwin, to be in love with a giant ass. I can tell, I can tell.

A: I don't know why I'm on the defensive here. That stupid greaser Virgilio was really pumping it to you, last I saw. You loved it. You probably think he's something great just because he has an accent.

S: He saved my life, Alwin. *You* got me into trouble and ran away. Virgilio stayed and helped me.

A: He only helped because he had to. Green Death had him *tied* to you, for God's sake.

S: How could you see what we were doing?

A: I was out in hyperspace. At first I must have been in the fifth dimension. But when Babs took off I slid down to four-dimensional spacetime, and then just this. There's a great line in *Flatland*, you know, when A Square has been out in real space and he's falling back onto his two-dimensional world and sees how awful it is.

S: It must be a real burden, Alwin, to have to be back with your family.

A: The line goes like this: "One glimpse, one last and never-to-be-forgotten glimpse I had of that dull level wilderness—which was now to become my Universe again." *That dull level wilderness*. Can you dig it?

S: No.

A: God. No wonder you wouldn't come loose when the children and I were tugging at you. You've got about as much sense of intellectual adventure as . . .

S: Oh, shut up, Alwin. Let's get in bed.

A: Where are my pyjamas?

S: Your suitcase is over there.

A: Thanks. Thanks for bringing it.

S: You know, we still haven't done the Forum.

A: The Forum.

S: Do you think it'll be safe outside tomorrow? Or do you really think the fallout . . . ?

A: I didn't see how big the blast was. Did it leave a crater?

S: I don't think so. They showed it on TV. Most of that little museum is gone, of course, but you can still

see a bit of the foundation and the front steps. And
you know it's raining now. That's good, isn't it?

A: Should be. Should wash it all into the river. Whatever you do, don't drink any more water here. It
could have plutonium in it. Or eat any fresh sea-
food. Didn't they mention me on TV?

S: Just at first, as the Anarchist Archimedes. As long
as you were with *Babs*, you didn't seem quite real.
It was like remembering a dream or a movie. I still
can't get over that. It was like I'd never met you or
anything. I felt so . . .

A: What? Happy, free and liberated? Today's modern
woman?

S: Never mind.

A: Look, if you hadn't yanked me back, I'd still be
in hyperspace. I should have followed Babs. She
moved sideways, like. Into the fifth dimension.
The bomb set her free.

S: How was that?

A: This guy, a physicist called Lafcadio Caron . . .

S: The man you killed in the Colosseum. Had you
heard of him before?

A: I didn't kill him, the snoids did. He was crazy.
Heard of him? Yeah, I'd seen his name a few times,
and I'd read one of his papers. What happened was
that he did a proton-decay experiment and they
trapped a hyperparticle, a piece of Babs. They sta-
bilized it with a higher-dimensional force field. In
physics, you see, we have infinitely many dimensions on the microlevel, but now . . .

S: Can I turn out the light? It's after midnight.

A: Sure. Yeah, look at that rain.

S: Can we do the Forum tomorrow? After we go see the Pope?

A: What about the police? Do you really think they're after me?

S: They probably think the bomb blew you up with the others.

A: Great. Wonderful. I can do anything.

S: What do you mean?

A: Well, if everyone thinks I'm dead, then I can take on a new identity and a new life.

S: And if I killed you right now and got rid of the body, it would be the perfect crime.

A: You don't want to kill me, do you?

S: No. Actually, I'm glad you're back. You feel nice in bed. Happy Easter.

A: You too. Do you want to fuck?

S: Maybe. But I wish you'd take a shower first.

A: Because of Giulia?

S: And the giant ass.

A: Did *you* take a shower? What if you're pregnant? Virgilio didn't use a rubber, did he? I'm probably the only man in the world who has to wear rubbers to fuck his wife. And then you let that goddamn greasy thug bastard . . .

S: No, Alwin, he didn't use a rubber. But you don't have to get all red and worked up. My period's supposed to start tomorrow.

A: It better. I'm not gonna raise Virgilio's kid. If you're pregnant it's abortion. Abortion or divorce.

S: If you're going to get like that, how do I know you don't have VD? She looked like the type.

A: She's dead. Keep your mouth off her.

S: You sure didn't.

A: Oh, shit. Let's just go to sleep.

S: About tomorrow, Alwin. We'll give the children their Easter candy and then go see the Pope in St. Peter's Square. And do the Forum. Okay?

A: But then let's get the night-train back to Heidelberg.

S: If we can get seats.

A: Tomorrow would be good. With the holiday and the crowd they won't check the passports. In case I'm wanted by the pig.

S: What about in Germany? You know how organized they are.

A: I don't know. The main thing is to get out of Italy.

S: Did you know that seeing the Pope on Easter makes up for one mortal sin?

A: That's handy. What'd you get the children?

S: Three big chocolate eggs with toys inside. And my mother got stuff.

A: Give me a kiss.

S: I wish you'd take that shower, Alwin. You smell funny.

A: All right, I'll take the shower. But don't go to sleep on me. Is there any beer?

S: Sure. See the fridge under the TV? My father got a lot of Heinekens for when we got you back. He's been so nice. Why don't you wake him up and tell him you're safe?

A: In the morning, in the morning. Do you want one?

S: Okay. And bring me my cigarettes.

A: I really wish you wouldn't smoke in the bedroom. That's like super-unhealthy.

S: Look who's talking. The Anarchist Archimedes.

A: Virgilio was standing over me with a *gun* when I wrote that, my callipygous Xanthippe. I'll have a cigarette, too. Move the ashtray. God, this beer's good. And there's a whole case of it.

S: So you won't have to go roaming the streets.

A: Yeah, that's how it started. I went out for a beer. Remember? We'd been drinking wine and doing sixty-nine and then you fell asleep. I hope you don't expect me to kiss you down there tonight.

S: You'll have to take a shower first.

A: I mean it.

S: So do I. You know where we came out? In the penguins.

A: I wonder if she'll be back? The sex sphere.

TWELVE
ball, ball, ball, ball

Joe Bone threw the empty soda bottle high over the black dirt, and Udo fired a rock at it. Miss. Joe's turn.

He looked for a good rock while Udo retrieved the bottle from the mounded rows of the asparagus field. In Heidelberg the farmers keep their asparagus white by making it grow up through half a meter of sunless mulch.

"Okay, Joe," Udo called. "*Raketen los!*" The big liter bottle arced up, twirling end-over-end and whistling. Completely in sync for that one second, Joe flung his clot of asphalt. He nicked the bottle, but it didn't break. Solid German construction.

Just then Udo's mother started yelling from the house. Joe couldn't understand her dialect, but he liked her voice. She had strong legs and big breasts and red hair. Too bad he didn't have a mother like that. Too bad he didn't have a mother.

"I must eat dinner," Udo explained in the clean High German they taught at school. "You can have the bottle since you hit it first."

"Thanks. Why don't you come over to the base tonight? They're showing *Grease*." It was Joe's favorite non-science-fiction movie. Dark and wiry, he himself looked like one of Travolta's friends.

"*Schmiere?* In English?"

"Naturally. In *Amerikanisch*, man. It's at the Patrick Henry Village theater. I'll get you in." Patrick Henry Village was the name of the American Army base in Heidelberg.

After Udo left, Joe walked into the asparagus field to get the bottle. It would be good for a twenty-pfennig refund, enough for a sweet-bun at the market he passed on the way to the US Army base where he lived with his father.

The mounds of mulch over the asparagus were patted smooth. Here and there you could see a little bump where a ripe stalk was about to break through. The watery, insistent April sunlight brought a rich earth-smell up from the field. An occasional car whizzed past, emphasizing the silence.

As Joe picked up the bottle, he noticed something shiny lying on the next mound over. A bright little sphere, like a big ball-bearing or a silvered glass Christmas-tree ball. An odd thing to find in an asparagus field. Yet somehow not surprising. An avid reader of SF, Joe had always imagined that he might someday find an alien artifact. Could this be it?

He hopped over the intervening mound and leaned over the little mirror-ball. The sky was in there, and his face and the horizon and the field. Neat. But wait. It wasn't the *same* in there. The field in the little reflected image was pink and crowded with towering . . . machinery, beautiful high-tech alien machinery, tapering in toward the image's center. It looked sort of like the fairground where Joe and Udo had just spent the day . . . no school on Easter Monday.

But if the ball was showing a fairground, it was an alien fairground with what looked like time machines and matter-transmitters and . . . God! Here came a woman, pressing her face up the ball's surface. She pursed her lips as if to blow him a kiss.

Joe scrutinized her features. She had dark hair, a straight full-lipped mouth, high cheekbones and an elegant Roman nose. She was the woman of his dreams. It was as if someone had looked into his mind to design her.

Smiling enigmatically, she beckoned to some moving shapes behind her, calling them. More faces crowded up. Two, three, five . . . small and distorted in the mirror's curve. Women. Naked women with pubic hair and big tits.

Joe leaned closer, then gave the ball a test-poke with his bottle. It rolled off the mound. Nothing in the image changed. The central figure held up her hand and made signs. Her large breasts shifted. Nipples the size of silver dollars. Above her head, Joe could make out a tiny rocket plane moving across the curved sky, moving away and away, dwindling towards the infinitely distant central point. He could see a whole universe in there! This was a window between the dimensions, just like in a science-fiction book! The woman beckoned him closer.

"Wait," Joe muttered. "I'll take you home. I can't stay here."

But he wasn't ready to touch the sphere. Maybe if you touched it they could pull you through. He took out his wool scarf and laid it on the ground next to the shiny ball. He planned to use the bottle to nudge the ball onto the scarf. But he didn't have to. As if sensing his plan, the little SF sphere rolled right over.

Joe picked up the scarf by its corners. The ball seemed very light. That figured, if it was really just a curved space bridge between two parallel worlds. Joe tried to remember the *Analog* article he'd read on Einstein-Rosen bridges. Back at the road, he stowed the sphere and the bottle in the knapsack he used for a school satchel.

The bike-ride from Udo's to the Army apartment blocks usually spun past in a happy blur of physical power. Joe was good on his bike, a ten-speed his Dad had given him for his fifteenth birthday.

But today the bike felt like an Exercycle. Like a pedal-powered generator feeding hidden movie projectors that were back-imaging filmed Heidelberg scenes onto a spherical plastic screen, a three-meter fake universe centered on Joe's head . . .

KLA-BRANG-BRANNG-BRANNNNG! Ow. Almost hit by a streetcar. Easy there, Joe, you're freaking out. Wasn't he ever going to get home? It was like he just kept going half the remaining distance.

Feeling too shaky to ride anymore, Joe dismounted and wheeled his bike down the crowded 4:00 pm sidewalk. Alien faces streamed past. All he could think of was the infinite universe in his knapsack. The fairground and the naked women.

"Joey! Hey, Joey!"

Vernice came skipping up to him, smiling and breathing hard. She was a preteen pest, a real Army-brat. She
lived in the same building as Joe, right next door. Her
father, Ronnie Blevins, Senior, worked as an MP with
Joe's father, old Bing Bone.

"What are you doing off base?" asked Joe.

Vernice's eyes glowed. "Mama sent me to baah some
waaahne. Ah'm allowed to in Germany! How was *German
school* today, Joey?"

Joe was one of the few Army kids who didn't go to Army
school. He had hopes of growing up cosmopolitan. With
a full-blooded gypsy for a father, he had a leg up on it.
Vernice already thought he was an international playboy.

"The Germans don't have school on Easter Monday. I
spent the day at a fair. It was highly stimulating. Will you
watch my bike while I go in the market?" He could have
locked it, of course, but if Vernice was watching it, then
she couldn't follow him into the store.

"Sure, Joey. Ah was already in theyure. Look!" She held
up her shopping bag. "Real waahne, and *ah* bought it!"
She stuck out her bud-breasts and pursed her pinkened
lips.

Joe walked past the bright vegetables and into the shop.
Little did Vernice realize that he, Joe Bone, was perhaps
the most important man in the universe. He selected a
twenty-pfennig sweet-roll and opened his knapsack to get
out the empty soda bottle.

A face filled with womanly pleading stared up at him.
The scarf had come undone. The other universe had its

own light . . . Joe could make out the bright pinpoint of a distant sun. Some antigravity hover-cars were driving around on the field behind the woman. *Out*, she gestured, holding her hands together and rapidly parting them. Her jutting breasts pointed at him. *Take us out of the bag!*

Joe vibrated his hands in front of his face in the *calm-down* gesture. He tapped his watch and held up a *just-a-minute* finger. Smiling and waving *good-bye for now*, he took out the bottle and rebuckled the knapsack.

"Do you have a little animal in there?" asked Frau Weiss as he traded the bottle for the sweet-bun. She was a pleasant skinny lady, who liked Joe for knowing German. Most other Germans didn't trust him because his skin was so dark. But ever since Frau Weiss had wormed out of Joe that his mother was a suicide, she'd treated him like a grandson.

"*Ja*," Joe nodded, thinking fast. "*Ein Meerschweinchen.*" A guinea pig.

"How nice," Frau Weiss beamed. "Take yourself another sweet-roll."

"Thanks."

On the sidewalk, Vernice was acting her age for once . . . staring blankly at the traffic and picking her nose. Feeling like a big brother, Joe gave her the extra bun. He wondered what it would be like to have a sibling, someone close enough to share his secret with. Maybe he could show it to Udo tonight . . . if Udo's parents let him come. But they probably wouldn't. They didn't like the Army.

He said good-bye to Vernice and rode the rest of the way home without any trouble. He was learning to control his excitement over the sphere. This was a terrible responsibility he'd been given, and he'd have to handle it like a man.

The apartment was a pigsty, an empty pigsty. Joe's Dad usually went straight to the noncoms' bar when he got off duty. He was a guard at the Army jail these days. Joe checked the fridge . . . nothing but milk and his father's beer . . . then went to his room.

Joe's room was the one nice spot in the apartment. He had a good stereo from the PX, travel posters on the wall, a couple of plants, and his model rockets. The furniture was GI, but at least it was neat.

His heart pounding, Joe rolled the science-fictional sphere onto his bed. The woman waved her hands in greeting, then began staring this way and that, taking it all in. She could only see half the room from the side she was on, and Joe was about to turn the ball so she could see the rest. But then she . . . turned it herself.

It was strange to watch this happen. One of the woman's hands came closer and closer to the ball's surface, and the image of her fingers covered almost everything. The fingers seemed to hold and turn the ball, universe and all. The fingers let go, the hand drew back and the woman was on the other side of the ball. Joe could see the back of her head.

He leaned over the ball and looked down at her from above. Her black hair flowed halfway down her back. She had a lovely behind. Fully humanoid. Amazing. How had she turned the ball? Joe could almost grasp it. She wasn't inside the ball any more than Joe was. The ball was just the region where their two spaces touched. They could see each other through it as through a lens. If he could move the lens, then so could the woman. This was really incredible; this was the greatest scientific discovery of all time.

The woman could see Joe's bookcase from where she was now, and it seemed to be of particular interest to her. She raised an arm and pointed. The arm-image curved halfway around the ball.

Still leery of actually touching the SF sphere, Joe went and got a book and brought it over ... a tattered copy of Heinlein's *Starman Jones*. The woman held up what seemed to be a camera, and he riffled through the pages for her. Her machines would be able to learn English and translate for her.

Excited by this idea, Joe showed her all his science-fiction books and then ... of course! ... the dictionary. At the end of an hour he was feeling hungry and weak from excitement. The boobs on those chicks!

Right now they were busy setting up something that looked like a TV set. Probably the translator. Joe took the opportunity to go into the kitchen for some milk.

When he came back the women had the TV screen working. Funny how they were all naked. Funny how there were no men in that other world either. It was almost too good to be true. Suddenly some English words appeared on the little TV screen ... English, but with some peculiar misprints.

HELLO. MY NAME IS BABS. VHAT IS YOUR NAME?

Hands shaking, Joe fumbled out a pen and one of his little blue school notebooks.

HELLO, BABS, he printed. MY NAME IS JOE. WHERE ARE YOU FROM?

I AM IN A ZPACETIME CONTINUUM PARAL-LEL TO YOURS. VHE ARE COMMUNICATING ZROUGH A HIGHER-DIMENSIONAL TUNNEL. I AM ZO GLAD YOU ARE ZERE. ONLY A MAN LIKE YOU CAN HELP US.

WHAT DO YOU NEED?

ALL OF ZA MEN IN OUR VHORLD HAVE BEEN KILLED BY ZA RULL. VHE NEED YOUR ZEED, CHOE. VHOULD YOU EVER CONZIDER MAT-ING VIZ ME?

Babs reached out and pressed two fingers against the ball's surface. Then she . . . picked up the surface and moved it around. The images in the ball swept and curved. Now he saw the top of her head, now the cheeks of her ass and now . . . oh now . . . now she set the ball down and stood right over it. Joe could see clear up to her crotch, plain as day. In his innocence, he'd never realized that women have their pussies quite so far down between their legs.

Just then the apartment door slammed. His father!

"Joe?" the drink-blurred voice called. "Are you here?"

"Yeah, Dad." Joe put his handkerchief over the ball.

"What a day," continued his father. "What a bitch of a day. The Heidelberg police arrested that guy Bitter who set off the A-bomb day before yesterday. And *we* have to put him up in our jail."

The voice trailed into a mumble. The fridge door opened and a beer-can popped. Light footsteps approached. "What are you doing in here?"

Bing Bone was a slight man, a bantamweight gypsy with a metallic voice. He was an alcoholic, a lifer retread sergeant, a lonely man who had never forgiven his wife for escaping into suicide. His eyes looked flat behind his flesh-colored GI glasses. Flat but observant.

"What's all the books for? And what's that under the hankie? You're not smoking pot, are you?"

Joe snorted contemptuously. "Sure, Dad, that's all kids these days do. I'm loaded on smack. And meanwhile I'm writing up a report on science-fiction for my literature class."

"So what's with the snot-rag, already?"

Before Joe could stop him, his father had flipped off the hankie. There was Babs—her face, thank goodness—and another woman, a tired-looking woman with reddish hair.

Bing grunted like a man punched in the heart. "That's her," he croaked. "That's your no-good traitor mother who left me all alone."

The tired-looking woman pushed Babs aside and stared intently out at Joe's father. A mocking smile played over her lips.

"You're crazy," Joe said, shaking his father's shoulder. "This has nothing to do with you."

Bing grabbed his son and stared at him. "Was it your Aunt Rose taught you the black art? But where'd you get the crystal ball?"

"This is *science*," Joe protested. "This isn't gypsy mumbo-jumbo. That's a parallel universe in there."

"It's *not*," shouted Bing. "That's your mother, safe in heaven and sneering at me."

The tired-looking woman made as if to spit at Bing.

"I'LL GET YOU ARLENE!" shouted Bing, suddenly maddened with rage. He snatched up the ball and threw it against the wall. The wall seemed momentarily to bulge out at them, and then the little sphere was gone.

"I busted it," said Bing with satisfaction. "I busted your crystal ball. Smashed it to bits."

Joe wasn't so sure. To him it had looked as if the concrete-block wall had ... made way for the ball and let it through. What was on the other side? He groaned inwardly. Vernice's room.

"Where'd you get that thing?" demanded Bing.

"I bought it from a Turk," Joe lied. "At the fair. It's too bad you're so drunk and crazy you thought you saw Mom in it."

"Look here ..." began Joe's father. But then he let his anger go. "Ah, forget it. I wanna see the news. Come watch with me; I might be on."

A major American terrorist was apprehended by German authorities today, said the Army news announcer. *Professor Alwin Bitter, a theoretical physicist visiting the University of Heidelberg, was arrested at his apartment early this morning. Bitter did not resist. He has been implicated in connection with the nuclear bombing of a museum in Rome this Saturday. He was known to his fellow terrorists as the Anarchist Archimedes. This afternoon, the German security police handed him over to US custody. Bitter is now awaiting questioning in the Patrick Henry ...*

"Look, Joe," cried Bing. "That's me in the background there!" But Joe was gone. Joe was in the apartment next door.

"Come on, Vernice, hand it over."

"Ah don't know whut you're after, Joey. Pushin' into a girl's room this-a-way." She strutted over to her dresser and gave her colorless hair a few licks with a hairbrush. "Supposin' ah diyud have your little picture-ball . . . what would you give me for it?"

"I'll break your neck, you stupid twerp!"

Vernice studied him briefly, and then began to shout. "Mah-meee! Joey's in here pickin, on me!"

"Don't you be fightin' with Vernice, Joe. Ron Junior's not here," called Cora Blevins from the kitchen. Ron Senior, her husband, was the MP who shared brig duty with Bing Bone. This week Ron Senior had night-shift and Bing had day.

"I won't hurt her, ma'am," shouted Joe. Vernice sat down on her desk, ready for protracted negotiations.

"You shouldn't ought to be lookin' at dirty pictures, Joey," she remarked primly. "Where'd you git that thing anyway? Downtown to the Sex Shop?"

Joe felt like tearing out his hair. Make that Vernice's hair. Here he'd found some kind of window into another universe, and this brat thought it was a machine for showing dirty pictures. Just because the women were naked. The women. Naked. *He'd seen everything when Babs stood over the ball.*

"Give it to me, Vernice, and I'll take you to *Grease* tonight. Just you and me. I'll take you, and afterwards I'll buy you a hotdog at the stand where all your friends can see. You can tell them I'm your boyfriend."

"Really?" Vernice's voice rose to an excited squeak. "Willya kiss me goodnight?"

"Give me that ball and don't push your luck or I'll break . . ."

"Here!" She took it out from under her pillow. "Take your dumb dirty pictures. I found 'em on mah bed. Were you in here lookin' at them with Ron Junior?"

"Just keep quiet about it, Vernice. Please. I'll meet you at the movie theater at 7:30."

"No. Y'all meet me *here*. Ah want Becky James to see us walkin' over theyure together."

"All right. On the steps downstairs. 7:15. Don't tell your mother; she'll think I've lost my marbles."

"Baah-Baaaah, Joey-Joe."

Vernice watched Joe rush off with his little picture-ball of machines and naked women. Boy-stuff. She hadn't told him that she'd found a whole *bunch* of the little balls on her bed. One was just for her. The others had drifted off.

She eased her bedroom door closed and got her ball back out of her desk drawer. A rough-featured man stared out at her adoringly. He said his name was Kenny Babs. He looked a little like Joe, but he had a mysterious European accent.

"You're my vhoman, Wernice," said Kenny. "Let me zhow you our love."

The little scene inside the ball clouded, then cleared. Vernice could recognize herself, all grown up and wearing a bride's dress. It was so *pretty*. The two of them were at a romantic candle-lit restaurant. Kenny came around the table and kissed her.

She held the ball up to her mouth, trying to feel his image. Firm, good-smelling lips pressed against her. Her head swam. It was just like she'd always dreamed it would be.

Joe couldn't stop himself any longer. He locked himself in the bathroom and let down his pants.

"Yes," mouthed Babs, smiling and licking her lips. "Giff me your zeed, dollink." She cupped her hands under her breasts and pointed the stiff nipples out at Joe. Then slowly, slowly, she slid the ball down between her legs.

Oooooh. Joe rubbed the warm beauty of the little ball against the tip of his cock. He'd thought Babs looked too innocent for this, but it seemed like she knew the score. How could his sperm ever travel through the solidity of this hyperspace window, though?

Babs held the ball out in front of her body now, breasts swaying, tongue licking, hips churning. Her fingers were pressed to the ball's surface. Pressed to the surface and . . . through. The ball grew projections, became Babs's hand with the red fingernails, caressing Joe so skillfully, so knowingly, so nastily.

Even as the blood rose to his head, Joe wondered how this was possible. It was all too good to be true. Babs had to have been lying to him all along. This peep-show hand-job SF sphere was no window in the dimensions. This was an alien blob, a creature of some kind, possibly dangerous; he should . . .

Babs's long forefinger reached down to tickle Joe's balls. Connected thought became impossible. Oh Babs, oh Babs . . .

The glow of satisfaction at seeing himself on TV wholly eclipsed Bing's rage at his dead wife. When the news was over he went to the kitchen and popped open another Stroh's. Or tried to. The pull-ring tore off and he had to look for a church key. *Can do*, Bing thought expansively, *no problem for a TV personality such as myself.* Just then he noticed something stuck to his thumb.

A bright little speck of crystal, probably from that ball Joe'd had. Just then the kid came running back into the apartment.

"Hey Joe! You missed me on TV."

"Sorry, Dad. Tell me in a minute. I've got . . . I've got to go to the john."

Bing shrugged and focused back on his thumb. Was it a glass splinter stuck in there or what? Suddenly the bright bit expanded like a balloon. Bing found himself holding a copy of his dead wife Arlene's head.

He tried to drop it, but it was stuck to his thumb, stuck like some horrible giant wart. Bing hesitated between rage and horror. But then the head began to talk.

"I'm zo glad to be free of you, you crummy little gyp. And you can't do a zing about it."

"Shut up, Arlene." He gave the head a slap with his free left hand.

"You zink I feel zat? *You* can't hurt me."

Panting a little, Bing gave the head a harder blow, this time with his fist. Another. Another. How many times he'd dreamed of this, dreamed of a chance to get back at Arlene! Real or not, this was a gift from God! The head felt good and solid ... he could feel his knuckles crunching bone. His whole body began to tingle with excitement.

"You little vhorm," taunted the head. "You're no man at all."

Bing fumbled open the kitchen drawer and found a paring knife. "You're gonna get it, Arlene. Now you're really gonna get what's coming to you." Just then he heard the toilet flush. Hide!

"Joe, I'm gonna take a nap," Bing called. And then he took Arlene into his bedroom and locked the door.

Next door, Cora Blevins was standing over her stove, watching some potatoes boil. She took another sip of wine. The heavy steam and heat reminded her of summer in Killeville, Virginia. A dizzy spell hit Cora just then ... she was seven months pregnant ... and without really meaning to, she sat down on the floor. The burbling of the boiling potatoes was like a hot river around her. She closed her eyes and remembered Sawyer's Island.

Sawyer's Island in the muddy James, summer camp for the Christian Children's Morality Crusade. There was a big meeting-house and little cabins laid out on a grid. Loudspeakers. Cora had her first vision of God there ... a sinful vision not found in the Good Book. She'd been alone in her cabin, touching herself, and the buzzing growing roar of some approaching train had seemed like the Lord's own voice. Hot, hot. God, it was hot.

Her eyes snapped back open. Some ... presence was here. There, o there, floating in front of her, was a white eye. God's eye. God knew her secrets; God always watched.

Cora rolled down her Supp-Hose and opened her legs. The roaring in her ears grew louder.

thoughtland

The Germans are nuts on the subject of terrorism. They had our apartment staked out, and busted me as soon as we got home: around noon on Easter Monday. This was no big surprise to us; Cortland had warned us to expect it. He'd already hired a lawyer for me in Heidelberg, and the lawyer got the Germans to turn me over to the US Army. I had my own 23 cubic meter cell in the Army lockup. It was just big enough to lie down in.

And lie I did. I was bone-tired from the big Easter, and from the long train-ride back. We'd all agreed on the strategy Sunday morning: enjoy Easter, get out of Italy and only then let the pig catch up with me. For the moment, thanks to my trip into the higher dimensions, I was still off the public radar.

Cortland, Sybil's father, got the hotel to send up breakfast for all of us: prosciutto, melon, rolls, omelets, hot coffee and pitchers of foamy hot milk.

The kids each had a giant chocolate Easter egg with a toy inside. Tom got the highest-bouncing Superball I've ever seen, Ida got a fuzzy little round mouse that rolled around when you wound up his tail, and Sorrel got a nested set of spherical doll's heads . . . each one wearing a funnier expression than the last.

Then we went to see the Pope in St. Peter's Square. The radio said the fallout was all washed away, and there was the biggest crowd ever. It was weird, the way all the streets were full of people, all walking in the same direction. It made you feel like an iron filing . . . or a pilgrim. We saw the Pope, all right. You want to know what he looks like? Find a white drawing-pencil and hold it out at arm's length. See the tiny lead tip? That's the Pope on Easter.

There were vendors selling special, perfectly round balloons . . . real shiny. Mylar or something. When the Pope came out, everyone let his or her balloon go . . . everyone except Ida. I said a prayer for Giulia, and one for me and my family. It felt good there in St. Peter's Square. The sun was really hot.

When the Pope got through, the kids were sort of tired, so Cortland hired an open horse-drawn carriage for fifty dollars or something. Lotte and Cortland wanted to go back to the hotel, and we dropped them off near it. Sybil and I decided to stay away with the kids . . . in case there were cops or reporters nosing around. By now the chase might be on again.

We five bought some sandwiches at a stand, and had a sort of picnic in the Roman Forum. It's like a meadow with ruins and broken stone. A big place. Lots of Italians were doing the same thing as us. There were plenty of excited children, all dressed up and playing with the neat round toys from their chocolate Easter eggs.

We passed most of the day at the Forum, had a late supper in a cheap restaurant, and caught the nine-o'clock night-train north. Sybil had managed to reserve us five sleeping couches under her maiden name. Good old Cortland met us on the platform of the Rome train-station with our suitcases and one of his spare passports. The picture even looked vaguely like me, not that it mattered. The night-train crosses the Italian-Swiss border at 3:00 am.

When we got to Heidelberg the *Polizei* were waiting for me. *Bullen*, the Germans call their police. "Bulls."

So Monday night I was lying there in my Army cell, my mind running a mile a minute. I was tired, but I couldn't sleep. There was music outside. I wanted to see where it was coming from.

By standing on tiptoe on my cot I could see out of a high, mesh-covered window. Now I could tell what the music was. *Grease*. They were showing *Grease* as a special Easter Monday treat for the folks on the American Army base. It was the last big song, "We'll Always Be Together," with the title phrase repeated a zillion times amid a sea of shang-langs and doo-whop-a-whops.

My mouth twisted in contempt. The fifties are supposed to be some golden age when the pig had everything his way. That's what TV and the government wants us to believe: there was a time when no one made trouble. What about Kerouac, you assholes? What about Neal Cassady?

I was the only one in the clink, except for the night-shift guard. The day-guard had been a lifer alky called Bing. He'd sold me a pack of Old Golds. I got one out and lit it, then went back to staring out the window.

The crowd was drifting out of the theater, gliding groovily on the beat of the title song. *Grease is the word: it's got rules, it's got meaning.* I sort of wished I had another A-bomb handy. It's being in jail that makes you feel that way.

Just then I noticed something really odd. Almost every single person coming out of the theater was carrying a shiny ball. Free Christmas-tree ornaments? On Easter Monday?

Without even thinking it through, I knew that those balls had something to do with Babs. And—oh, oh—so did the balloons at St. Peter's. And all those spherical toys. Sybil and the kids were home with three of them! Holy shit.

Two kids stopped under my window. I strained my hardened criminal ear against the mesh, trying to overhear.

"You shouldn't have done it, Vernice," said the boy. A dark-skinned kid, maybe sixteen. He held his shiny ball clutched against his body. Made me think of Lafcadio, the loving way he held it.

"Oh yeah?" sassed back the girl. Thirteen and with short dishwater hair. She looked like a sharecropper's daughter. "Yew promised me a real date to the movies an' then you dint even watch. You were jest starin' at naked wimmen in yore little crystal ball. Well, ah got one at home, ah'll have you know. Mama does, too."

"*Every*one has one now," groaned the boy. "When you threw mine at the screen, about two hundred copies blew off. I could have been the only one to know about them if it weren't for you, you stupid noisy brat." He made as if to shove the girl with his free hand.

She danced out of his way and slapped his ball out of his other hand. "Yah, Joey, keep lookin' at dirty pictures and you'll go blaaahnd. And *ah* know *whaah!*"

The little ball fell slowly in the night air. As it fell, other shining balls appeared in its wake. It was a little like soap-bubbles coming off a waving bubble-wand. A sudden updraft caught one of the bubbles and whisked it against my window. The glass shivered briefly, and then the ball was right in my cell. I grabbed it eagerly and sat down on my bed. Outside the two quarreling voices receded.

At first all I saw in the ball was Travolta's bestial, moronic, sensitive-lizard smile. Then Olivia, the tacky Cybis china doll that costs more than a car. Music tinkled up at me. "Summer Lovin'." Good, solidly blocked chords, I had to admit. But . . .

"Come on, Babs, I know it's you."

"Tell me more, tell me more, was it love at first sight?" Girls' voices. Babs was obliquely talking to me.

"You know I love you."

"Tell me more, tell me more, did she give you a treat?" Boys' voices.

"Did Sybil? Don't ask me about Sybil, Babs. Why don't you give me a nice blow-job and then we can talk things over." Invitingly, I unzipped my fly. *Goin' trollin'*.

The little sphere grew larger and pinker. The dark nipples and pubic hair came fading in like photographed features in a safe-lit bath of chemicals. That musky dusky sex sphere odor floated up, and I was instantly hard. But she didn't go for the knob-job. Instead she planted her luscious quim on my sturdy staff and rode the cattle to St. Louie. My zipper teeth were chewing hell out of my cock-skin, but for the moment this didn't seem to matter much. We kissed and came.

"What's the story, Babs? Are all those other spheres you, too?"

"Sure zing, dollink." For the first time, her red waxy lips talked to me. I hadn't been sure they could do anything but suck. "I'm more zan four-dimensional, you know. Not just a simple hyperzphere. My real home is Hilbert Space."

"Infinite-dimensional space? Could you take me there?"

"Vhell, I vas about to, last time. After I got zat stupid knot loose, I rushed to Hilbert Space to check it vhas okay. First I laid you down in four-dee spacetime. I zought you'd vhait for me. But vhen I came back, vhas nozzing zere."

"How was I supposed to know you'd be back? I couldn't stay there anyway. My children pulled me back."

"*Tchildren?* Don't you love me more zan zem?"

"Will they keep me from going to Hilbert Space?"

"No, no, dollink. Vhe can go out zrough za fifth dimension, or za sixth. Zen is no problem vhiz za timevhorms. Are you ready?" She began to grow again, getting bigger and bigger like at the Borghese museum.

"First answer my question. Why are you splitting apart like this? Lots of copies of you in Rome, and lots of copies at the movie theater."

"Yeah, I'm everyvhere, svheetie. All zings to all men . . . and vimmens, too!"

"But what's your motive?"

"I vhant you all to come togezzer. I vhant to get your group-mind loose. Come on, svheetie, get naked."

Without thinking about it too much, I went ahead and stripped. The giant cunt-lips slid over me headfirst. I didn't resist.

Babs must have plugged me right into her nervous system this time. When she swallowed me up, things got bright and brighter. I was seeing hundreds, thousands, of images at once. I was seeing what Babs was seeing out of each of her earthly cross sections.

Dreamy girls, panting boys, excited women, grunting men; moistened lips, pumping hands, spreading legs, pushy cocks. Babs was having a good time.

But not many of Babs's partners were women. And not everyone was glad to see her. There were some twisted faces out there, some people screaming in fear and anger. Fists and knives flailed in, but Babs never budged.

The aggression on those faces gave me pause for thought. What *was* Babs up to? A full-scale invasion of Earth? I didn't feel right, wedged deep down inside her vagina like this. I thought of the wasps who lay eggs in paralyzed prey. Was I to be Earth's first casualty in the Attack of the Giant Ass From Hilbert Space?

"Hey Babs!" I tried to shout. "Let me out!" But my face was smothered in the slick folds of her wet flesh. Good God! Why had I stood still for this? Yet, all the while, I had a soggy, stubborn hard-on.

The multiplexed image of Babs's lovers and haters faded out, and it was dark. There was a sensation of motion. I

struggled and struggled, trying to find my way back out
to light.

And then, all at once, I was free.

Well ... how do you want it? Music and a light show?
Strobing image-montage? Men in funny hats? Did you
see Ken Russell's *Altered States?* My favorite part was after
the guy takes the mushroom potion in the FZAAAAT
cave ZUZZZUZZZUZZ and THUBBZZZT reels out.
Lizard out there. Or his wife. Lizard. Sphinx. Tits. The
sand is blowing hard. They're both gray with sand, she
sphinxing on her elbows, he fetal on his side. The wind
blows and blows and blows. The sandblast eats away at
the two figures, which go from real to rudimentary to
elemental. Then there is only the wind and the rippled
desert.

Start with the noise of that wind. It's a sound you may
have heard before, some night when your brain kept running though your body was asleep. What is a dream really
like? How can we forget them so easily?

What is it like in Hilbert Space? You should know. You
live there.

At the most elemental level, reality evanesces into
something called Schrödinger's Wave Function: a mathematical abstraction which is best represented as a pattern
in an infinite-dimensional space, Hilbert Space. Each
point of the Hilbert Space represents a possible state of
affairs. The wave function for some one physical or mental system takes the form of, let us say, a *coloring in* of
Hilbert Space. The brightly colored parts represent likely

states for the system, the dim parts represent less probable states of affairs.

The arrangement of the color shades is a subtler affair. A system's tendency, for instance, to move from State A to State B, but not from State B to State A . . . a tendency like this is not any specific event which you can point to in space and time. These nonspecific properties correspond to overall *gestalts* in the Hilbert Space coloring. Alternating bands of red and green might, for example, represent a particle which is moving from left to right but which has no specific location. A good mood could be a golden haze not tied to any particular cause.

We can think of Hilbert Space as a vast cataloging of all possible events. The events are arranged along infinitely many perpendicular axes: right/left, happy/sad, near/far, sober/drunk, past/future, hot/cold, true/false, male/female, wet/dry, sun/moon, bitter/sweet, matter/antimatter, etc.

Each part of the universe makes its own contribution. You are reading, I am writing. Two spots of brightness. Going out from you are various bands of color, indicating your moods and predilections. Bands emanate from me as well . . . and where our color-bands cross each other there is interference. You change me and I change you. Each part of the universe makes its own contribution.

Taken as a whole, these individual contributions add up to the world as it is: a certain coloring in of Hilbert Space: the Universal Wave Function. Keep in mind that time itself is coded into the pattern. The pattern is not something that evolves: the pattern *is*.

Theologically, this idea is expressed by saying that God

creates the whole universe *now*. God makes yesterday, today and tomorrow at the same time. Has to, since everything depends on everything else. The image is of a heavyset white-haired figure throwing a bucket of mingled paints at a wall. SPLAT, *fiat lux*, the job is done.

For whatever reason, we find it easier to "read" Hilbert Space patterns in terms of time, even though the patterns exist outside of time. Thinking timelessly is not some unusual skill: when you remember last night's supper you sense a whole meal, rather than a chew-by-chew replay. To know a novel's action is not to memorize the word-for-word order; it is simply to grasp the four-dimensional spacetime whole described.

When Babs released me in Hilbert Space I was outside of time, outside of hypertime, outside of all that tick-tick-tock. I have always been there, and I am still there as I write this. You are there as well; there's no place else to be. What does it look like?

It looks like the stuff that's inside your head. Your mind is a direct window into Hilbert Space. Infinite-dimensional? Sure. Look past the words, at the continual dark flowing of thought-forms. It's especially vivid when you come.

Japanese landscape, rotten corpseface, bedpan, bible-lips, flying carpet, Old Glory, potter's wheel, ten years, Ixtlan, 5.297890718, dog with human legs, what Maisie knew, fireworks, smell of Scotch Tape, the Supremes, flume-ride, the turrets and blue waters.

The flash of orgasm lights up this tangle, like lightning over Venice, like a Very flare over the Amazon. It's always too much to take in; it's always the same.

Matter, mind, spirit: all are patternings of Hilbert Space. I saw this and let my awareness move out and out from Alwin Bitter. The whole is/was there in flashes, but each time I touched it, "I" jittered back as a limited seeker. Babs was near me and I knew her mind at last.

Babs herself was once a whole race of beings. She began as a sort of group-mind or racial memory. The beings she derives from no longer bother to exist ... they have passed fully into her. This is as it should be. A form in Hilbert Space is, after all, any race's ultimate evolutionary stage. Penultimate, really, for at the end lies the joyous dissolution into White Light.

But what about physical existence? Isn't that a lot to give up? Physical existence is, in Hilbert Space, a purely relative notion. Relative to you, the letter images of these words have physical existence. Relative to *me*, Alwin Bitter, Babs has physical existence. The Donald Duck archetype is a reality for Daisy. Romeo, meet Juliet; Juliet, Romeo.

The race of beings Babs derives from were never in fact "real" for you. They were not even organisms ... they were a certain class of mathematical theorems, I suspect, or something to do with spacetime fault-lines in one of the alternate universes.

When Lafcadio trapped that cross section of Babs she was well-embedded in Hilbert Space, on the verge of a final union with the One. Part of her mind-stuff was doing duty as this or that exotic particle. Lafcadio caught hold of a piece and knotted it. Looking *kata*, Babs saw our world and resolved to fight free. So, at her direction, the bomb took shape and blew her loose. But then, but then ... she chose to return.

In her contact with the human race, Babs was like God's
tongue finding a shred of food in some fissured tooth. We
rotted here all blind and lonely until our new Redeemer
found us. Babs came to bring us all together. *Swing low,
sweet chariot, comin' for to carry me home!*

At some point I was back. Finally I understood the meaning of Babs, and I comprehended the great task before me.

I sat up on my cot. The shiny sphere was gone ... I
had no need of it now. I wished to be free of these prison
walls. I closed my eyes and saw in Hilbert Space. A bright
spot, my body. Probably in jail, less probably not. Rejoic-
ing in God's love, I let my *is*ness flow from here to there,
quantum-tunneling across the profane barrier.

I opened my eyes and stood there for a moment in the
parking lot next to the Army jail. It was dark. I could see
glowing sections of Babs drifting around here and there in
the cool night. Noble Babs wanted all to share my vision.

I started walking. I was barefoot. The asphalt felt nice.
I walked past some Army housing-units. I wondered how
many in there were communing with Babs. Soon all would.

My mind was boiling with plans to bring Babs to
everyone. I saw myself as John the Baptist or even—why
not?—Jesus.

Messiah. I said the word to myself, relishing the sound.
Messiah. Somewhere behind me a harsh alarm-bell
sounded. The guard must have noticed my escape. Fool.

Where to go? Not home, not yet.

Huba. I'd visit my friend Huba Moller. How to get
there? Why not fly!

what do women want?

Why is Daddy in TV again?" demanded Ida. "I want him right here."

"He has to go to jail," said Sorrel. "Was Daddy bad, Ma? Pass the ketchup, please."

"BOOM!" shouted Tom. "Remember, Ida? BOOM!"

"Will you be quiet?" snapped Sybil. "I'm trying to hear the news."

The well-fed, blond German newscaster-woman continued talking on their rented TV. She wasn't plump exactly . . . just very solid. Buxom. Sybil wondered, once again, how the Germans could eat so well, yet look so trim.

"Do you children want more spaghetti? Ida, you haven't touched your food. There'll be no dessert until you empty that plate."

"Mean!" shouted Ida, bursting into tears.

"S.A.D.," taunted Sorrel. "*Shrink And Die*. Mommy, Ida's going to shrink and die."

"Hush, Sorrel."

"Well that's what Daddy always says when we don't eat."

"BOOOOM!" bellowed Tom. The picture of the smashed museum was on the screen again. Sybil thought briefly of Virgilio.

"I'm sure that Daddy will be back tomorrow," she told the children comfortingly. "The bomb wasn't really his fault. He just has to explain to the police how it happened."

"What's for dessert?" inquired Ida.

"Canned pineapple. At least eat your meatballs."

"Okay." The sound came out a fat quack. "But *no* buscadey."

"Mommy?" asked Tom, looking up. "Mommy, if you dreamed that you died would you never wake up?"

"You always wake up."

"But what if you have a heart attack?" put in Sorrel. "From being scared to death!"

"Do you children have bad dreams?"

"Night before last I did," said Sorrel.

"In Rome?" asked Tom, glancing at her.

"Yeah, everything was all mixed up like scrambled eggs."

"I had bad dweams, too," added Ida. "It was *awful*."

"You poor children. That dream was from something Daddy did. You helped to bring him back."

"He's not here now."

"I'm sure he'll be home tomorrow. Now let's put the dishes in the sink, and you'll get pineapple."

The girls helped, but Tom crawled under the table to look for his new Superball. When Sybil brought out the pineapple the way the kids liked it, in bowls with toothpicks, Tom had found his ball and was bouncing it between floor and ceiling.

BAT-a-PAT-a-Bat-a-Pat-a-bat-a-pat-a-babab'b'b'b'
bbbbbbbrrrrrrrthok. It bumped to a stop against the table
leg. Tom retrieved it and flung it down on the floor again.
BAT-a-PAT-a- . . .

"Tom, would you sit down and have your dessert?"

. . . 'b'b'bbbbbbrrrrrrrt. The ball was stuck under the
couch this time. Tom wormed about on the floor, trying
to get his arm in far enough.

"That's a neat ball," said Sorrel. "Have you looked
inside it, Mommy? You can see things moving in there.
Like our dream."

"What do you mean?"

"It's magic. All three of our Easter toys are magic.
Right, Ida?"

"Rwight. My mousie whispers to me. She's alive, *rweally!*"

"And your special pillow talks, too, doesn't it, Ida?"
Sybil gave her little daughter a kiss.

"No, no, Ma," insisted Sorrel. "I heard the mouse
talking. And my doll-heads smile at me when no one's
looking."

"I think you children are still dreaming. It's time for
bath and bed. Come on, Tom, you can get that ball out
tomorrow."

The kids had a happy, noisy bath together. Afterwards
Sybil read them *Mr. and Mrs. Pig's Evening Out*, the cur-
rent favorite. Kisses, prayers, kisses, lights out, last kiss.
Tom was already asleep.

Sybil closed the bedroom door and sat down on the
couch where she and Alwin usually slept. It was hard
to believe they were living in a two-room apartment.

A bedroom and a dining/living room with a couch for sleeping. Just a year ago they'd had a four-bedroom house. But then Alwin had lost his teaching job and had gotten a grant to do research in Heidelberg. A two-room apartment in the foreign visitors' housing complex was all they could afford.

In a way it was liberating not to own anything. But why did the apartment floor have to be concrete with a thin covering of green felt? Inexplicably, the expected wood parquet floor was mounted on the ceiling. Wood ceilings and green felt floors. Worst of all, the couches had no arms.

Sybil went to the kitchen and opened a green liter-bottle of white wine. That was the one thing that was cheap in Germany. Cheap and good. She drank off a quick glass and took a refill. Thank God that sex sphere, that Babs thing, was gone now. All Alwin had to do was tell the police how he'd been kidnapped. After being threatened by Cortland Burton and his lawyers, Vice-Consul Membrane had agreed to support Alwin's story.

When Sybil went back into the living room, the lack of arms on the couch suddenly maddened her so much that she set down her glass and shoved the couch across the floor. Scooted it over to the bookcase so she could rest her arm on the lowest shelf. There. She lit a cigarette, tilting her head back to keep the smoke out of her eyes. The light was better here, too. Now, where was that new book?

Something bright glistened on the floor where the couch had been. Tom's ball. But it was *moving*, oh no, and *growing* just like at the museum!

"Babs?" Sybil had trouble getting out the name. "Are you the sex sphere?"

The glistening globe hovered in front of her. Images swam in it like fish in a bowl. It was as if Sybil kept seeing what she expected to see: color swirls, Giulia, ass-cheeks, bloody teeth, an A-bomb. How she wished Alwin or Virgilio were here.

The sphere shrank a bit and took on the form of Virgilio's face. "Hey, svheetie. You okay?"

"Oh, stop," protested Sybil. "Don't."

"Vhant to fuck?" purred the sphere. Virgilio's features furred over and his nose grew into a stiff mauve prick. Nodding suggestively, it glided closer.

"That's *not* what I want," cried Sybil, lashing out with her fist. "Don't!"

The sphere smoothed over and went blandly yellow. Two black dot-eyes and an upcurved black line-mouth. A living Smiley button ... with a Hungarian accent.

"Why are you back?" asked Sybil. "Alwin said his bomb set you free."

"I vhant to set humanity also free," intoned the yellow face. "Alwin understands."

"Can't you leave poor Alwin alone? He's done enough for you!"

"Alwin is za Savior of za human race, you vhill see. But vhy did you reject me just now?"

"You want to know why I didn't let you stick that gross penis-shape in me?"

The great yellow head nodded.

"Well, why should I? It was just an organ with no *person*

attached. That kind of thing may be all right for *men*. But women . . ."

"Vhat is it zat vimmen really vhant?"

The same question that had stumped Sigmund Freud. There was still hope for humanity if this alien invader had to ask that.

"If you don't know by now," said Sybil, lighting another cigarette, "Don't mess with us."

"I have no time to mess. Vimmen must join me, and if not vhillingly, zen unvhillingly. If necessary I vhill eat you all up!" The long mouth-slash opened, and the sphere drew closer.

Just then the phone rang. Sybil picked it up.

"Hello, Sybil? Guess where I am?"

"Alwin! Did you get out of jail? Should I pick you up? The sex sphere is back. She's threatening me."

"I know. Dear Babs. She showed me everything. I'm like a god. Guess where I am!"

"You're in a bar on Hauptstrasse."

"Guess again!"

The sex sphere squeezed up next to Sybil and the receiver, trying to eavesdrop. Sybil hit it as hard as she could.

"Alwin, I don't really *care* where you are. Come home and help me!"

"I'm in the sky, Sybil. I'm floating in the sky about three hundred meters above you. And get this: I'm not using a telephone!"

"You're still in jail, aren't you, Alwin. Are you *on* something?"

"I'm high all right, but not on false drugs. Step outside and look up if you don't believe me. Are the pigs there?"

"You mean the children?"

"The police, Sybil. Have the police showed up yet?"

"No . . ."

"They will. Tell them to get fucked. Tell them the Second Coming is here and I'm it. Tell the newspapers."

"I thought it was over, Alwin. I thought everything could go back to normal."

"Step outside, I tell you. Look up!"

The sex sphere darted over to the patio door and began tugging at its handle as if she were some pet dog eager for her walk. Sybil got the door open and stepped out onto their tiny concrete patio.

The foreign scholars' Gästehaus apartments were located on a promontory some hundred meters above the Neckar River. As Sybil opened the door she could hear a barge's diesel engine laboring upstream, the barge way down there on the water, its long dark bulk lit by the headlights of cars speeding along the highways on either side of the river. There on the near road was the flashing blue light of a police car coming this way.

Sybil tilted back her head, looking up past the brambles, up past the tall German pines. It was a clear, star-besprent night. High up there hovered something dark and ragged. Sybil shuddered with the deepest fear she'd ever felt.

The sex sphere bounded up to join the bewitched form, and in the sphere's pale light, Sybil could see for sure: Alwin. Alwin floating, flying up there with his arms outstretched—oh Alwin, are you gone for good?

Already there was heavy pounding on the apartment

door, then the grating of a passkey in their lock. A child cried out. Sybil ran in to face the intruders.

Herr Blöd was in the lead, his furious purple face aglow. He was the building superintendent, and hell on kids. They called him the "Killer Tomato." Close on Herr Blöd's heels were two aging American MPs with night-sticks, followed by three green-capped German *Polizei* packing automatic weapons.

"*Wo ist der Herr Professor?*" cried Herr Blöd. "*Er ist gesuchte Terrorist! Ihre Familie ist ab morgen ausgewiesen, Frau Professor!*"

Frau Professor. That was about the worst thing Sybil had ever been called. The title had no organic connection to anything relating to her existence as an individual person. "Wife-of-professor."

"Get fucked," Sybil said, unconsciously following Alwin's advice.

"What is it?" screamed Sorrel, standing terrified at the bedroom door. The *Polizei* noticed the open patio door and rushed on out. Alwin's voice came down from the sky, high and faint, shouting something garbled, something of a religious nature.

"*Da is' er!*" barked one of the *Polizei*.

"*Aber unmöglich! Fliegt er denn?*"

The MPs peered apologetically into the bedroom, while Herr Blöd examined the bathroom.

"Whut all are they sayin'?" one of the American MPs asked Sybil with a nod towards the patio.

"That my husband can fly. It's true, he really can."

The man's eyes bulged out, and his mouth worked for

words. In the silence Sybil had time to read the name on his uniform. RON BLEVINS, SR. With some vague intent of lodging a complaint, she read the other soldier's name as well. BING BONE. That one looked drunk. Dark, wiry and shifty . . . a little pirate of a man. The first one, Blevins, had a fat body and sticklike arms . . . arms that waved about like an excited potato bug's feelers. A pirate and a potato bug, our nation's finest.

"What's going on, Mommy?" Sorrel clung anxiously to her leg. In the next room Ida had started to cry.

"Go in there and take care of Ida, honey. The police won't hurt us. They just made a mistake."

"But, Mommy . . ."

"*Please*, Sorrel!"

"I'm scared."

"I'll tuck you back in." Glaring her hardest at Herr Blöd, Sybil ushered Sorrel into the bedroom. All three kids were upset and full of questions. She shushed them as best she could, and returned to the living-room.

"Did you say your husband can fly?" asked Bing Bone, the little pirate. He made a flying gesture with his left hand, and Sybil noticed some rust-red stains under his nails. Blood?

"Mah waafe had her a Baahble vision just this naaht," put in potato-bug Blevins. "She phoned me up. After the call is when ah noticed yore husband had made good his escape. You say he rilly flaaaahs?"

"I . . . I saw my dead wife," put in Bone.

"These are the last taahms!" bleated Blevins.

"*Was sagen die Soldaten?*" asked one of the *Polizei*.

Apparently Sybil was supposed to be translator for her husband's international hunting-party.

"*Quatsch*," she said simply. "Nonsense."

"*Wir suchen weiter.*" The three *Polizei* trotted out of the apartment, weapons held smartly across their bodies. Herr Blöd stayed, eyeing Sybil and the soldiers with blind suspicion. Actually she was glad he was still there. Crazed yokels like Blevins made her nervous. And that sinister little pirate with blood on his hand, talking about his dead wife. Ugh!

"I'm terribly sorry I can't be of any further help," Sybil said in her best upper-class accent. "Good-bye."

Blevins looked like he wanted to stay and discuss the Book of Revelations, but Bone had the decency to lead him out.

"Good-bye, Mrs. Bitter."

"Baa-aaah," chimed in Blevins. "And, ma'am, you should take yore Baahble in yore lap tonaaht. It's done mah waafe a world of good."

Purple-faced Herr Blöd got off the last shot. "*Ab Morgen sind Sie ausgewiesen.*" "Tomorrow you have to move out."

"*Nein!*" shouted Sybil, forgetting all her German but the word for no. "*Nein, nein, nein!*" She slammed the door behind Blöd and hooked the inner chain. Good thing they already had a lawyer.

The children were in an uproar, and it took a half hour to calm them down. Finally that was done, and Sybil could sit back down with her cigarette and glass of wine.

The phone rang again. Something in Sybil snapped. Gritting her teeth, she yanked the phone cord out of the wall. The phone kept right on ringing. With a sigh, she picked up the receiver.

"Hello, Alwin."

"How'd you know it was me?"

"Where are you?"

"Do you think the line's tapped?"

"No. I just pulled it out of the wall."

"What for? Are you in a bad mood? You sound cranky."

"Alwin, I'm leaving. I'm taking the children and flying back to America tomorrow. I can't take this . . . this sitting around and being Frau Professor while you're in dimension Z."

"Where will you get the money for the tickets?"

This gave Sybil pause. Their bank-account was low. Her father would never pay to have her go back to the US . . . he'd want Sybil to stay and keep her mother company in Frankfurt. The horror and helplessness of her situation welled up, and she began to cry.

"Hey," came Alwin's voice over the phone. "Hey, Sybil, don't cry. I'll get the money. I'll put it in our account at the Deutsche Bank."

"How."

"I can do anything. I can! I'll just reach into their computer and . . ." his voice broke off. Sybil sat there for a minute, holding the dead phone.

Holding a dead, unplugged phone. She must be hallucinating. Oh, this was bad. This was the worst it had ever been. She had to get back to America, back to some friends. She could go stay with the DeLongs or . . .

"Sybil? Sybil?" Alwin's voice was back on the phone. "I've done it. Switched twenty thousand deutsche marks over to our account. That's about ten thousand dollars. Get it tomorrow, get it in cash dollars before they straighten things out. Deutsche Bank has a branch at the Frankfurt airport. Go ahead and go to America. Go first class! I'll look for you there, once I get things rolling here. I'll miss you, baby."

"Where . . ." Sybil had trouble controlling her voice. "Where should I go? How will I take care of the kids alone, Alwin? You can't just send me off like this."

"I'll be there. I promise I'll be there . . . next week or sooner. Why don't you go up to Maine. I'll meet you there." Alwin's family had a summer cottage near Boothbay Harbor.

"I'll be all alone."

"Get my mother to come. Or one of your friends. Get Nancy from Boston."

"Where are you, Alwin?"

"I'm in a tree right now. Outside Huba's. I might spend the night at his place. He can help me get things rolling."

"Get *what* rolling?"

"The end of the world. The apocalypse. Babs is going to help the whole human race move to a higher plane. It's gonna be great. Don't you want to learn to fly?"

"I'd rather have a husband. And a father for my children."

"Sybil, I don't want to get into all that. This is much bigger."

"For you."

"Good-bye, honey. See you in Maine, if not in heaven first."

"Oh, good-bye."

The phone went dead again. Sybil put the receiver in

its cradle. It was almost midnight, but there was no hope of sleeping.

Something came rolling out of the bedroom. Ida's mousie. Babs again.

"Get out of here!" cried Sybil in sudden fear. She snatched up the mouse, went in the bedroom and found the set of doll-heads, took them all out on the patio and threw them up into the sky.

I don't want the next world, she thought. I want this one.

FIFTEEN

fishing with huba

I didn't want to startle Huba too much, so I entered his apartment the normal way: by ringing his bell and walking up the stairs. His wife Ute opened the door.

Ute was German. Short and swarthy, yet quite attractive. Huba was a Hungarian refugee who'd come out through Yugoslavia a few years back. By marrying Ute he'd been able to get German citizenship. He worked in a place that made dentures, and she worked in the local grocery. They lived quite comfortably, and they loved to party, especially Huba.

"*Professor Bitter*," cried Huba from the living room when he heard my voice. "*Phantastisch! Wein, Ute! Musik! Rolling Stones!*" Although neither of us spoke perfect German, it was the one language we had in common.

"So what brings you here so late?" asked Ute in the front hall. "Where's Sybil?"

"Didn't you see the news?"

"What for news?"

"They arrested me as a terrorist. I've just escaped."

At this Huba stuck his head out from the living room. He was a big, tall man with curly hair and a bushy beard.

He had made a denture with four false teeth for himself. Sometimes, when we were drunk together, he'd take the bridge out and put it in upside down.

"*Waaas?*" he said, eyes dancing. "*Terrorist?* I knew it all along."

"Does Sybil know you've escaped?" asked Ute, leading me into the living room.

"Yes, I just talked to her on the . . . phone. The bulls were already there looking for me. Can I spend the night here?"

"But, naturally," said Huba. "You take Ute and I'll take the couch." He didn't mean this, of course . . . This was just typically exaggerated Hungarian hospitality.

"*Schwein*," scolded Ute with a laugh. Then, to me, "It's really no problem for me to fix the couch. It's meant as an extra bed. But why are the *Polizei* after you?"

I hesitated. It was such a long story. Why bother telling it word-by-word in my inelegant German? Instead, I let my consciousness flow out and mingle with Ute and Huba's. An instant later they knew the whole chain of events. There was a moment's silence while it sank in.

"What . . . ?" said Huba slowly. "I didn't catch at the end what you want to do now?"

"He's a devil," cried Ute, looking frightened and backing away. "Make him leave, Huba!" Later I would realize that she'd seen Babs's plans better than any of us.

"But no," protested Huba, jumping to his feet. "Alwin is my best friend. How about some of that good French wine, Alwin? Drink, listen to music . . . I got a new disk, you know. Pink Floyd. Ute, bring the wine, bring *two* bottles. Here, Alwin, have a cigar." I could tell Huba was thinking over what I'd just "told" him, but for the moment he was playing his usual host persona.

Ute sighed heavily, then went to get the wine.

"This sex sphere," asked Huba as soon as his wife was gone. "Can I see her?"

"I think she's outside. She was out there with me a few minutes ago. I told her to wait till I told you."

"Well, let's go out on the balcony."

Huba's apartment building was sandwiched between the Neckar highway in front and a railroad track in back. The balcony jutted out over the track. The steep hill to the Gästehaus apartments rose up right beyond the track. Looking up, I could see Babs hovering there like a full moon. I beckoned her with my mind.

In a flash she was at our sides, round and lovely: the sex sphere.

"*Was für ein Asch!*" exclaimed Huba, running an exploratory hand over her peachcleft. "What an ass! First class. But really, Alwin, that's not the only . . ."

Ute's step sounded in the living room. I hurriedly got Babs to shrink down to pocket size. Huba and I went back in, and Ute joined us in a round of wine. Her initial shock had worn off.

"So, Alwin, you see yourself as the Savior of mankind. But what about women?"

"Women, too," I insisted. "I want everyone to start living in Hilbert Space. We can totally dissolve present-day reality."

"Just for an ass?" Huba questioned. "There's more to life than that, Alwin. I like the physical as much as the next man, but it's conversation that counts. The life of the mind."

"You don't understand," I said shortly. "Neither one of you does. But I love this wine." It was an excellent sweetish and a bit tart. Like condensed sunshine. Huba and Ute had bought it at a vineyard near Strasbourg.

"Listen to this," urged Huba, passing me the earphones. "Pink Floyd."

I put on the phones. A single sharp drumbeat whhACKKed, and then a whole cream-pie of guitar lines splatted me. I closed my eyes. For a minute I forgot I was the Messiah and just dug the sounds.

When the song ended I took the phones off. There was an abrupt silence. They'd been talking about me. It occurred to me that I had no way of knowing if they'd properly decoded the information I had beamed them earlier. If you say something out loud, then there's a definite skein of words to go back to. But if you telepathically put information into someone's head, there's no objectivity, no way of going back and extirpating errors. There was no telling what garbled notions Ute and Huba might have about my mission.

"More wine?" asked Huba too hastily.

"Sure." Suddenly I felt very tired. I hadn't slept on a real bed for days. Thursday night on some rags in the Colosseum, Friday night on a couch in the Green Death hideout, Saturday . . . well, yeah, Saturday I'd slept at the Savoy with Sybil. Fucked and slept. But Sunday had been on some horrible fart-scented pallet in the train, and today I'd had to put up with being arrested. I sucked down the wine Huba poured me and held out my glass for more.

"Can you get off work tomorrow?" I asked him. "I'd like to have a chance to discuss this stuff with you. I'm not sure the direct thought-transmission worked right."

"Did you really set off an atomic bomb? I think I heard something about that. That was you?"

"It was on the news, Huba. What have you been doing all weekend?"

"We were in Mannheim. I have a friend there . . . what a party. You wouldn't believe it. Whole kegs of beer and cases of wine, a roast pig, a cheese this big . . ."

"Are you hungry, Alwin?" asked Ute politely.

"I'm tired. God, I'm tired."

"I'll fix the couch. Just stand up." Ute went out to get some sheets and pillows. A good, organized German housewife.

"Look," said Huba, "I'll call in sick tomorrow. We'll go fishing . . . right down there by the Neckar. It's the last place the bulls would think to look for you. And . . ." He glanced over his shoulder, checking that Ute was out of earshot. "Give me that sphere. I want to try it after the wife's asleep."

"Okay." I took the soft little bean out of my pocket and handed it over. "Just make a kissing noise with your lips when you want her."

Huba woke me at 6:00 the next morning.

"Come on, *Herr Professor*. The fish are biting."

Ute had already left for work at the grocery. She and her boss went to the farmers' vegetable market at 5:00 every day. Huba gave me some coffee for breakfast, and a stale bun. In Europe they don't really understand about breakfast.

Sipping my coffee, I stared out the kitchen window. The Neckar was covered with mist. Cars streamed into Heidelberg, bumper-to-bumper, everyone's lights on and the whole procession looking like a pearl necklace.

"She's Hungarian," said Huba suddenly.

"Who is."

"Your *Sex Kugel*. Babs."

"You fucked her?"

He looked a bit embarrassed. He wasn't Westernized enough to be comfortable talking dirty. "Well . . . if you so flatly ask, I have to say yes. But she talks too; she talks Hungarian."

"That's because . . ." I was about to explain how Babs had eaten Zsuzsi, then thought better of it. What if Babs decided to chew up all the women who wouldn't go along with her? No point upsetting Huba. I myself felt oddly neutral about this prospect. "Oh, never mind. Do you have a fishing-rod for me?"

"But naturally. How about a little *slivovitz*?" He reached down a medallion-shaped bottle of plum brandy from the cupboard. My stomach heaved.

"Maybe later."

"I'll bring it along. We're going only right down there." He pointed out the window to the grassy band on the other side of the road. "Did I show you my movie of the rats?"

"No."

"This you have to see. In the apartment across the hall live two old women. Cows. Always complaining about noise. Sisters. They put bread down there, down on the railing by the river. They think they are feeding the swans.

They are like *this*, these women." Huba widened his eyes and let his mouth go slack, then moved his open palm slowly back and forth in front of his face, miming the unresponsiveness of extreme idiocy. "Rats eat their bread, lots of big rats. From here, from this window I made a movie of them. Wait!" Huba rushed into his dining room and set up his film projector. "Look, Alwin, look at the rats!"

He really did have a film of river rats as big as cats creeping through the grass, then climbing onto the railing to get the bread. More and more rats came, a fight started, the film ran out, the projector squeaked.

"And they won't listen to me," muttered Huba.

"You should show them this movie."

"Stupid cows. Before I woke you today, they were already fighting. I'm surprised you didn't hear the screams. You'd think they were being eaten alive. *Ach*, let's go fish, away from women."

"Okay. But could you lend me a sweater? It looks chilly out there."

"Sure, of course, take mine."

When we got down to the river, the sun was starting to show. The river was still foggy, foggy in an interesting way. Instead of just coming up all over like steam, the fog seemed to come off the river along certain lines. It was as if there were invisible atmospheric vortex rings over the river, and the fog could appear only at the boundaries between cells. There was a picnic table to sit on. I took a bit of *slivovitz*. The rats were lying low.

"Bacon rind," Huba was saying. "That makes the best bait. You see? I use a long piece that's shaped like a little fish."

He baited a hook for each of us and we cast. His cast went a good ten meters, but I did it wrong and landed my hook in the shallows. Some tiny fish, minnows smaller than the hook, nibbled at my bacon rind. A long barge chuffed past and the backwash pulled the little minnows upstream, then down. I tried another cast.

"Let it sit on the bottom," urged Huba. "There's eels down there. Delicious, but very hard to kill."

The sun was out in earnest now, burning away the fog and dew. I laid down on the grass and closed my eyes. The sunlight through my eyelids was a pleasant yellow-or-ange. It was nice not to have any women around. I drifted toward Hilbert Space.

"Don't you want her back?" asked Huba just then.

"Who?" I shaded my eyes against the sun.

"The sex sphere."

"There's lots of copies, all connected in some higher dimension. Like fingers. Babs plans to saturate the Earth, and to make everyone fall in love with her. I'm supposed to make speeches that she's good for you." But today I barely had the energy to sit up, let alone go out and start a new religion.

"I don't see how you and Babs can enlist the women," said Huba. "They don't think like us, you know."

"Babs doesn't have to be just a big ass," I protested. "She can be a crystal ball showing nice things, or a man's head. Don't you think women would like a man's head that always listens to them and agrees?"

Huba shrugged. "Women have no fantasy. They want the world just like it is. With all the little touches and details."

"Yeah . . . maybe you're right. Women care about specifics. Men care about generalities, about abstract principles. I'm ready to wipe out all the details of the world as it is, just for the sake of the beautiful general principle of Hilbert Space. Sort of like selling the family silver to buy drugs. The women won't like it. But . . ." My voice trailed off. It was as if Babs had hypnotized me.

"What can the sex spheres do to the women?"

In the distance I heard a siren. And faint screams? How many copies of Babs were loose in Heidelberg? One for each woman? Oh God, what if she was killing them? I let my mind spread out into Hilbert space, trying to set things right. A strange, twinkling interval of time passed.

"You've caught something, Alwin," exclaimed Huba. He'd set the two rods into special holders, so all we had to do was watch the tips. Mine was twitching.

Rather than sitting up, I reached out with my magic energy field. Whirl, whirl, whirl, the reel wound in. Something slithered ashore . . . something odd.

"*Mein Gott!*" shouted Huba. "What is going on?"

Lying there on the grassy riverbank was a sort of little . . . man. Instead of arms and legs he had only a single wheel at the bottom, a small spoked wheel like from a tricycle. Running up from the wheel was a long tubular leg . . . or was it a neck? . . . and at the other end from the wheel was the creature's head. His skin was yellow and hairless, his bald head was long and thin. He had a projecting cucumber-nose and a smiling, lipless mouth-slash.

"Hi, Rubber," said the little man, spitting out my hook and sitting up. "I'm Wheelie Willie. Remember me?" He had a high, lively voice. By way of jogging my memory, Wheelie Willie straightened out his body and putt-putted around me in a small circle, riding his wheel like a unicyclist. "Hooray for Rubber v. B. Tire!" he piped.

Remember? Of course I remembered. Wheelie Willie was a character I invented back in graduate school at Rutgers. I used to draw his adventures for the college paper, the Rutgers *Daily Targum*. You could look it up. Most of the strips were about drugs and radical politics, so I used a pseudonym: Rubber v. B. Tire.

"What were you doing in the river?" I asked him.

"Looking for women." His smile broadened. "It's hard because there aren't any. There's hardly any women left in Heidelberg."

"*Was ist den los?*" asked Huba for the second time. "What's going on?" Wheelie Willie and I were speaking English, of course, which left Huba in the cold.

"This is Wheelie Willie," I explained. "He's from a cartoon strip I used to draw."

"Then, why is he real?"

"This is *Doktor Bitter*'s doing," said W.W. in German. "He is like a hole in the fabric of reality. All around him it starts now to unravel."

"Ah, German he speaks," exclaimed Huba. "But why doesn't he have arms?"

"I can't draw arms," I apologized. "I can never get the shoulders right. And his nose stands for a dick."

"I'm a muffdiver!" shrilled W.W. "A man about town."

"Do you know Babs?" Huba asked him. "She'd be perfect for you." Huba fumbled in his pocket and pulled out the soft bean. Before I could stop him, he'd *smeep*ed Babs up to standard size.

"Cowabunga!" cried Wheelie Willie.

"Alwin, I've been very bad," whispered the hovering sphere. A bedroom eye peeped out at me from beneath a puddled jumbo breast. In an instant, Wheelie Willie was beneath her, pumping at her slit.

"Hot dog!" yelped the yellow little clown presently. "I'm cookin'!" He buzz-sawed back a few feet and sneezed. A gusher of sperm shot from his nose—how disgusting. Babs looked like the old Sherwin Williams Paint Company's "Cover the Earth" logo, a sphere half-covered with dripping paint.

"Blurp," she blubbed, and bounded into the broad brown brook.

Just then Huba's rod-tip started twitching.

"You reel it in, Alwin," said Huba. "I'm scared."

"No thanks. If we keep fishing, this is going to look like a Bruegel engraving. Let's split before Babs comes back."

"Could you wipe my nose?" requested Wheelie Willie.

While I found a hankie, Huba took out a knife and cut his fishing line. We took apart the rods and hustled up the riverbank, Wheelie Willie in the rear.

"There's my car," shouted Huba. "Get in and I'll take you downtown. Me, I'm going to work. This craziness is more than I can outlast."

I got in front next to Huba, and Wheelie Willie installed himself on the floor between my legs. He was only about one meter tall. He wanted to know if I had any marijuana.

"It's *slivovitz* or nothing," I told him. "This is Germany. I haven't scored since I got here."

"Have you tried Turks?" piped the yellow little head. "Hash from Turks?"

"Shut th' fuck up."

I had to think, think about what was real. Start with Hilbert Space, the ultimate reality. Every possibility there, no one possibility chosen. Everything equals Nothing.

Yet there was something, call it U, something that I had in the past called the real world. The world as we knew it. The facts of the situation. U for universe.

There was something else, perhaps just as big: B. B for Babs. I was in some way coupled to Babs now. B wanted to absorb U. B wanted U to be a possibility instead of a reality.

There was a third thing, call it I. I was like a window from B to U, a hyperspace tunnel, a wave-function amplifier, a hole in the dimensions. Things were gushing into U through I, things like Wheelie Willie.

High on our left, the Heidelberg Castle slid by. There was still some mist in the trees beneath it, and the huge ruin seemed to float on the hillside, weightless and unreal. Then we were in the city itself.

"How about here?" suggested Huba, pulling over by Heidelberg's quaint and scenic *Alte Brucke:* the Old Bridge. In point of fact the Old Bridge is about thirty years old. Some nameless asshole blew up the original on the last day of World War II. But, hey, the replica is beautiful anyway. If you look down at it from the castle, the Old Bridge looks sort of like a dragon crossing the water:

regular arches for centipede legs, two towers like horns at the Heidelberg end, and a yawning portcullis mouth. It's a pleasant spot, sunny and mellow. But today something was wrong.

There were no women in sight. Just men and children. Men and children and sex spheres. I should have been upset, but—God forgive me—I wasn't. I was happy. Babs had really and truly gotten to me.

The spheres floated among the men, arousing no more comment than if they'd been real women. They wore clothes . . . skirts or tight jeans on the bottom, and T-shirts or blouses on top. You could see their mouths set down in the necks of the shirts, and below the breasts, the blouses had lacy holes for the eyes to peep out.

"Look what you've done!" cried Huba. "The sex spheres have eaten all the women! Ute! I have to go see about my Ute!"

I should really have ridden right back with him to check on Sybil. But, hell, I could fly back to her any second. Right now I just had to check out this action. Big guns boomed in the distance. That would be the Army, reacting.

Wheelie Willie and I jumped out of the car, and Huba sped away.

"I saw some super-funky Turks back there," coaxed Wheelie Willie. "For sure we could score off them."

I looked down at him, the personification of my 1972 psyche. Thin and yellow, he looked like a tightly rolled wheatstraw-paper joint. With a wheel at one end, and a cock for his nose. "It's great to see you in real life, Wheelie Willie. Would you settle for a beer?"

"You think they'll serve me?"

Two brightly dressed sex spheres brushed past. Shop-girls on an outing. Nice tits. Across the street a gangly young man was necking with his sex-sphere girlfriend. She wore a cute lavender dress. Right down the sidewalk were two mother sex spheres. One bounced along next to her two young children, keeping up a steady stream of chatter. The other hovered over a baby carriage, big fat tit hanging out of her sweater. Happy baby sucked his milk.

I led Wheelie Willie around the corner and into a place called the *Schnookeloch*. They have a good Munich beer on tap there: Hacker-Pschorr. A sex sphere in a white apron and a tight black top floated over. I ordered two big *Exports*.

"What does *Export* mean?" asked W.W.

"They have two types of beer," I explained. "*Export* and *Pils*. *Pils* takes longer to draw from the tap. It's bitterer and foamier. Don't worry though, *Export* is still German. You'll know you're in Heidelberg."

Three sex spheres were drinking together at a table near us. Looked like students from the University. Jeans, skimpy T-shirts and big knockers. They drank by tilting forward and sticking their rolled-up tongues into the beer. *Ssssuuuuuck*. Big mouths and strong tongues. One of them peeked over at me from under her breast. I waved.

"Like to get my nose in there," commented W.W. "Look how tight those pants are on her. Mother-far-fuck-ing-out!"

The waitress brought us our beers balanced between her breasts. Wheelie Willie sniffed hungrily at her bottom as

I took the beers. "*Zum Wohl des Herren*," she said, floating off with a slight waggle. "To the health of the gentlemen."

I took a long pull of the thick, heady brew, and then fed Wheelie Willie's glass to him. Some boys came in, students, and sat down with the sex spheres we'd been eyeing. One of the girls, the one who'd looked at me, excused herself and went downstairs.

The beer went down well on my empty stomach. I decided to order another round. But first I had to piss.

"Hey, Willie. Order a new round if the waitress comes by. I'll be back in a minute."

"And after that we score dope, hey, Alwin?"

Downstairs was a unisex john, not terribly unusual for Germany. I pushed in, half-hoping to surprise a sphere in action. My luck held. The cute young orb from upstairs was perched nude on the toilet.

I unzipped my fly and leaned over the sphere's upturned mouth. She wriggled with mock embarrassment . . . and got to work.

Man! This was really living!

SIXTEEN

the garden of earthly delights

Sybil made it out of Heidelberg before the sex spheres attacked. She'd spent the night packing, and when the sun rose she and the kids were on the autobahn to Frankfurt. Smooth move.

Nearing the Frankfurt International Airport, Sybil began to wonder at the amount of traffic. She flicked on the car radio, which was set to the US Army station.

". . . no panic at this time, with day-to-day life proceeding normally. Some authorities have challenged the story as a hoax, but telescopic observations have now confirmed it. A substantial proportion of the Heidelberg population has been transformed into what may be an alien life form. Evacuation of the surrounding areas is proceeding. All units are on Red Alert. Repeat, all units are on Red Alert. Report immediately to your superior officer."

The bulletin ended and was replaced by aimless easy-listening.

Sybil dialed another station and heard a more detailed report in German. Something had turned most of the women in Heidelberg into alien creatures, spherical in form. Yet the Heidelberg men were doing nothing. Emergency troops had been sent in, but instead of fighting they'd started a street-party.

It figured. That's all men really wanted anyway: sex spheres. Eyes slitted with fury, Sybil skidded onto the exit ramp for the airport. Thank God she and the kids had gotten out in time.

She abandoned the car in the airport's three-minute loading zone and led the children into the excited crowd. First to get money. Looking at a directory, she located a branch of the Deutsche Bank. Upstairs. Each of the children had a heavy suitcase to lug, and people kept jostling them. Briefly, Sybil took time to imagine cutting Alwin's throat. No ... that would be too fast, too easy on him. Better to break his legs and let him be eaten by hungry rats. Or stick knitting-needles in him, carefully avoiding vital spots as long as possible ... long, sharp, red-hot needles.

"There's the bank, Mommy. It's closed."

Of course. The men had it closed so no women could escape. Keeping their shit-cunt-money safe in their toilet-marriage-bank. Sybil slammed her suitcase into the thick glass doors. The doors didn't budge, but the suitcase burst open. If only she had a gun!

The PA system was making an announcement. First in German, then French, then English: "All outgoing flights are fully booked. If you have no ticket, please leave the airport. Repeat, all outgoing flights are fully booked for the next seventy-two hours."

The crowd around them surged this way and that.

There were many more women than men here; tough, pushy German women. What to do?

"If we can't get a plane today, then let's go visit Granma," suggested Sorrel. "Daddy can meet us there."

"Your *Daddy* is perfectly happy in Heidelberg. And if I ever see him again, I'll . . ." A sudden inspiration struck Sybil. There was a way. There was still a way. She gathered up her possessions and reclosed her suitcase. Her father would have weapons.

"I think you're right, Sorrel. We'll go stay with Grandma and Grandpa."

It took hours to get downtown, but finally they made it. Lotte and Cortland Burton lived on a walled estate, fully equipped with the latest antiterrorism devices. In America, Cortland had just been a good engineer; in Germany he was a military industrialist. His company produced a sort of particle-beam ray-gun which was supposed to provide Germany with a defense against missiles.

Cortland and Lotte were ecstatic to see their daughter and grandchildren safe. The maid fixed them a big dinner of Wienerschnitzel, the children's favorite food. Cortland and Lotte sat at either end of the long table, with Sybil and Sorrel at Cortland's end, Ida and Tom at Lotte's. Lotte was cutting up Ida's meat.

"But how do you *know* Alwin is safe?" she asked, fixing Sybil with a worried look. "Won't he starve in that jail?"

"Alwin is safe because he is a *man*," answered Cortland. "This whole invasion is in some sense a female problem. Perhaps it's related to sexual hysteria."

"Aliens are turning women into grotesque spheres, and

that's *our* fault?" snapped Sybil. "Really, Father, you go too far. Alwin is safe because this invasion is *his doing*. It's the final acting-out of heartless male chauvinism. *You* should go to Heidelberg. You'd love it there with the sex spheres."

Cortland refrained from answering, but Lotte sprang to his defense. "How can you speak to your father that way, Sybil? And in front of the children."

"What if the sex spheres come here?" asked Tom. "Will they eat Mommy?"

"Don't worry," said Cortland. "They're just in Heidelberg. And the army has them surrounded."

"Ha!" spat Sybil. "What good is an army against the sex spheres? Men lay down their arms and women get eaten. What weapons could stop the spheres anyway?" This wasn't a rhetorical question. She had a feeling Cortland would know the answer, if anyone did.

Cortland raised his eyebrows. "Sorrel, my sweetest grandchild, would you please close the kitchen door?"

Sorrel obliged, and Cortland continued, his voice lowered. "As you know, Sybil, my engineering firm develops new weapons. Today I was telephoned by Colonel Noschwet in Mannheim. Apparently the antimissile particle-beam laser which we have developed is capable of causing these . . . sex spheres to dematerialize. Several field tests have been successfully conducted. So I would not be unduly concerned. Whatever its cause, the invasion can indeed be contained."

"You only say *contained*. Why can't they take the lasers into Heidelberg and exterminate the sex spheres?"

"This will be attempted," Cortland sighed. "But, as you yourself have pointed out, the men who go to Heidelberg are won over and the women are eaten. In no case is a soldier likely to return, no matter how well-armed he or she may be. And we have only one portable PB laser."

"Ice crweam, please!" shouted Ida gaily. Ellie, the maid, came bustling back in.

"Wait," said Lotte. "Ida, you haven't eaten the nice spaghetti that Ellie made for you."

"I hate buscadey!"

Tom, not liking to see his little sister act spoiled and get attention, slid down in his chair and kicked her under the table. Ida's face did squeezed grapefruit. Sorrel punished Tom with a sharp poke under the ribs. Doubling up from pain and excitement, Tom knocked his water glass over. It hit and broke Sorrel's Meissen china plate, then rolled onto the floor and smashed. Ida, thinking a food fight had broken out, grabbed a leftover schnitzel and threw it at Sorrel for being bossy. It missed her and hit Cortland on the shoulder of his Lanvin suit. "Pig!" screamed Sorrel as loud as she could. Seeing the expensive plate broken, Tom crawled under the table and began roaring in terror.

Cortland looked accusingly at Lotte. Lotte passed the look to Sybil. "Really, Sybil, Do all American children behave this way?"

"It's Alwin's fault. He acts like a child himself."

Ellie was already clearing up the mess. Sybil pulled Tom out from under the table. "There'll be no dessert for you children. Go upstairs and put your pyjamas on."

"Can't we watch TV?" wailed Sorrel.

"Of course you can," put in Cortland. "And be sure to give me a good-night kiss me when you're all clean."

"Okay, Granpa."

The three little pigs surged upstairs. Sybil and her parents moved into the enormous living room, and Cortland served out a round of cognac.

"What do you know about these alien spheres?" asked Cortland. "And what exactly is their connection with Alwin?"

"I didn't tell you before, because it sounded so crazy. The original sphere was involved in the bombing in Rome. She calls herself *Babs*. I think all these spheres in Heidelberg are copies of Babs."

"What a vulgar name," put in Lotte. "Where does Babs come from? Underground? The planet Venus?"

"Not even from our space. From another dimension."

"Just like in your husband's book," said Cortland. "*Geometry and Reality*." He was referring to a little text on higher dimensions which Alwin had written. Thanks to this one publication, he'd been able to get his grant in Heidelberg.

"Yes," said Sybil. "But the main thing about Babs is her sexuality. She's all breasts and buttocks and lips and . . . you know."

"That sounds like Cortland's secretary," commented Lotte.

"This is no laughing matter," said Cortland sternly. "Apparently these sex spheres have destroyed and replaced all the women in Heidelberg. But why?"

Sybil shuddered, realizing how narrow her escape had been. "Alwin said something about destroying reality. The spheres connect to some higher realm that Alwin thinks is better. He wants the spheres to take us all up there. It's fine for the men. They just ... you know. But Babs has nothing to offer most women. I saw her myself—I threw her out of the apartment! She must have decided then that it was all or nothing. I think she's killing anyone who won't go along ... which is almost all the women."

There was a long, thoughtful silence. Finally Cortland spoke up.

"It must be then—if I can believe all this—that Alwin is in some way enabling the sex spheres to enter our space. For if he were not in some way instrumental, then the spheres could simply be appearing all over Earth at once. Yet we find them only in his vicinity, in Heidelberg."

"I have to kill him," said Sybil flatly. At first she thought she was only saying this for effect, but as the words hung there, she realized they were true. Killing Alwin was the only way to save her children—and the rest of the world. Oh, Alwin—how had it come to this?

"What are you saying?" burst out Lotte. "Leave the killing for the soldiers, darling. Leave it for the men!"

Cortland lit a cigar with slow, deliberate motions. Blue smoke obscured his features. Sybil's mind was racing. Kill Alwin, yes, that was the only answer, and put your damned emotions away. Nobody could approach Alwin better than her. But what if the sex spheres got to her first? Her father had mentioned a weapon ...

"I do have that one portable version of the particle-beam laser," said Cortland, fully in synch with his daughter's thoughts. "It's like a bazooka wired to a backpack.

An infiltrator would need this, and some conventional weapon as well. The Uzi machine gun is an excellent choice. Also I would recommend our night-glasses."

"So you'll help me?" said Sybil, feeling a sense of doom.

"Let me make some phone calls," said Cortland, rising to his feet. "You are prepared to go in thirty minutes, Sybil?"

This was all happening so rapidly! Was Cortland that eager to have his son-in-law killed? Sybil was, after all, his only child, his only daughter—maybe Cortland secretly hated Alwin for taking her away. But look how Alwin was behaving! Who *wouldn't* hate him!

"It's not about Alwin at all," said Cortland, once again divining Sybil's thoughts. "It's about saving the world. We have to think of it like that."

Sybil went upstairs to bathe and put on fighting clothes. Black jeans and a black turtleneck. Mountain boots. She tied her hair back in a bun. She took off her earrings and her bracelets. All from Alwin. Her wedding ring . . . she put her wedding ring in the dresser drawer. The kids didn't bother her, they were busy watching a Charlie Chaplin movie, *Modern Times*.

Downstairs in the kitchen, Sybil burnt a bit of cork and blackened her face. She drank two cups of coffee. High above the house a racketing noise drew closer. Cortland switched on the outside floodlights, and the helicopter landed.

The noise broke the children's concentration. Squealing with excitement, they tumbled down the stairs.

"Why's Mommy all black?"

"Where's Granpa's helicopter taking her?"

"Is Granpa going too?"

"Who's going to take care of us?"

"Your mother and I are going to a costume party," Cortland told the children. "Grandma will take care of you."

"Cortland," said Lotte in a strained voice. "Are you sure this is for the best?"

His answer was lost in the syncopated beat of the chopper blades. Sybil kissed the children and followed her father through the deaf wash of damp air. The helicopter rose up over Frankfurt, then followed the autobahn south.

"We'll go past Heidelberg," said Cortland, "then cut over to the Neckar and set you down there. You can come unobtrusively into town on this raft." He gestured at a bundle of black rubber. "But be sure to stop before the locks!"

"I'll get off by the castle," said Sybil. "Now show me how to use the particle-beam and the machine gun."

Half an hour later they were passing Heidelberg. There is a mountain—Konigstuhl—between Heidelberg and the autobahn, so there was no way to really see what was up. A pass directly over the city would have been too risky. The helicopter went on past Konigstuhl, then turned left to land by the Neckar near the village of Neckargemund, which lies ten kilometers upstream from Heidelberg.

Cortland's pilot, a taciturn German named Wolf, helped them inflate the raft. Sybil fired test-shots from the PB and the Uzi. *Zweeeeef! Brdrdrdrdrt!* The particle-beam was a pale-purple ray; the Uzi had tracer-bullets that shot like a Fourth of July fountain.

"Sybil," said her father, just as she pushed off shore. "Are you sure you want to do this?"

"There's no one else, Daddy. I have to."

"I know."

The helicopter got back aloft as fast as possible. The river was misty and very dark. But Sybil had a pair of Cortland's heavy night-glasses, his company's latest invention. The glasses were a pair of tiny infrared TV cameras coupled to two little screens, one in front of each eye. Looking through them, Sybil could see the riverbanks as pink shoulders sloping down to the yellow-green river. Her hands were hot red, the sky dark blue. The raft was streamlined and equipped with a silent water-jet engine, so she made good time.

Before long, Sybil was sliding under the Schlierbach-Ziegelhausen bridge, just one big bend away from Heidelberg. She hugged the left bank and stared anxiously at the sky. She held her PB at the ready. High on the left, the *Gästehaus* slid by.

Sudden sweet memories sandbagged Sybil: Alwin and the children catching a hedgehog, Alwin reading E. M. Forster to her on the long winter evenings, the two of them dancing to reggae tapes on Friday nights, the wine, the talk, the good sex . . .

Just then a sphere rushed past, right in front of the raft. Sybil leveled her PB and pressed the button. *Zweeeef!* Nothing left. Had this piece of Babs had time to tell the others? And where had it been going?

Sybil strained to push all her awareness out into the night. Just downstream glittered the lights of Heidelberg. She took off the night-glasses. Almost time to land.

She could see the castle up on the left, hovering like a thought. It was bathed in floodlights and lit by flares, as if for a holiday. A rocket shot up from the castle's octagonal belfry, then another and another. The hoarse roar of many men's voices drifted down. Something was going on up there, something big.

Sybil glided up to the locks and found a ladder. She slung the Uzi under her left arm and the PB tube under her right. Praying that Babs wouldn't pick this moment to pounce, she climbed to the concrete riverbank. So far, so good.

There were stairs to the street, deserted. Trying to look every which way at once, Sybil skittered across a bright intersection and darted into the shadows of some modern apartment buildings.

Another roar rose from the castle. The whole sky up there was red. A block away, two drunks hurried past. American soldiers. A bottle smashed on the cobblestones. Sybil stayed in the shadows.

Not far from here was a little-used trail up to the castle's L-shaped grounds. If she used this trail she would come out at the opposite end of the L from the castle, far from the crowd, and with a good view of what they were up to.

The drunks' clumsy footsteps and hoarse voices faded away. Senses strained to the limit, Sybil moved forward. *I'm ready to kill*, she repeated to herself. *I'm going to kill*

Babs and . . . and Alwin. She held a weapon ready in each hand.

In some of the buildings children were crying. But the streets were totally deserted. Everyone was up at the castle: all the men and all the sex spheres. Sybil found the path and hurried up.

As she climbed higher she could see more and more of the bizarre celebration. A lurid red glow illuminated the castle park; most of the trees were on fire. In the background were the jagged castle ruins, hollow and dead.

Set in the midst of the crowded park was a single huge sex sphere . . . a giant ass with gaping hell-mouth cunt. A few late-arriving sex spheres shot past and merged into the mass of the one great Babs. The air tingled with pheromones. The crackling trees bathed the scene in jump-jump eldritch light.

Men with horrible twisted faces pressed up to the giant sex sphere like sperms seething around an egg. One by one, they were worming their way into the gaping vaginal rent: damned souls entering the gate of hell, children following the Pied Piper under the mountain. Naked and distant, they looked rudimentary, like forked parsnips. In their sexual frenzy, some coupled together. Others hunched twitchingly against the sex sphere's sagging breasts, or rubbed their faces against the sphere's broad, glistening anus.

The livid mob surrounded the sphere's crack like a puddle. Body by body, the pool grew smaller, as one man after another reached his heart's desire, the stink wet hot dark embrace.

An odd little figure darted around the edges of the manpool, herding them forward. The figure was short and yellow, and seemed to have a wheel instead of feet. Occasionally he would pause in his feverish activity to stare attentively towards the top of the sphere. A single man squatted there near the sex sphere's summit, just beneath her huge, pleased mouth. Sweating and grinning, he shouted down instructions. He was the procurer, the Devil, the Pied Piper: Sybil's husband, Alwin Bitter, me.

SEVENTEEN
a happy ending

I could feel the bullets coming, sense them with my field. The first burst would have hit me in the head if I hadn't jumped clear.

I landed on a fat man wedged in between Babs's labia. Sybil was still firing her Uzi. I could see the tracer-bullets *thipp*ing past.

"*Pass doch auf, Sie doofe Narr*," hollered Fatman: "Look yes out, sir goofy fool." Skull-faced Thinman, just ahead, pulled Fatman fully in.

Men seethed around me. Ugly men with warts and wens, limps and humps, scars and age-spots, blind white eyes. I was lost in the crowd, and crazy Sybil was firing at random. Sudden blood-flowers bloomed th-th-th-th-there on Babs's hide. Men screamed like women. I stayed low and worked my way around to the shelter of the sphere's other side.

Wheelie Willie, I called with my mind, *come help me!*

Tilted over at a high-speed angle, the little rascal came buzzing round the great curve of flesh. After my *Schnookeloch* knob-job we'd scored him some hash, and he was in high spirits.

"Everything's right on, Alwin! Babs'll haul this whole bunch off to Hilbert Space in a few minutes. Is it really trippy there? Are we going too?"

"Not yet. I still have much to do. When I return to Hilbert Space it will be in glory. The reason I called you is . . ."

Suddenly the smooth wall of the sphere above us split open. A tightly collimated beam of pale-purple light punched through. I recognized it as a particle-beam. Sybil was shooting a particle-beam laser at Babs!

The beam had eaten a hole right through the sphere, but no important centers had been cut. Babs rose hugely off the ground, looking this way and that for her attacker. All but a few dozen of the men were lodged in her womb, and she moved heavily. Thirty meters away stood Sybil, a tiny courageous figure with a weapon in each hand.

"That's my wife," I told Wheelie Willie. "We have to save her."

The sphere's great mouth opened to show cruel teeth. "Vhell, vhell," she boomed. "Little Sybil Burton Bitter." A plump, struggling figure slid out of Babs's stuffed cunt and dropped maggotlike to earth.

Black-painted and tense, Sybil stood her ground. Another beam of purple light flicked forth. Babs dodged it and zoomed fifty meters straight up. Her bulk seemed to cover half the sky. For a moment, the angry firelit monster hovered, and then she dove.

With our minds tuned together, Wheelie Willie and I had formed a plan: a desperate suicidal rescue. As Babs dropped, he and I surged forward. I flew like Superman, my arms stretched out. He followed right behind, his wheel a screaming blur. Directly above us, the sex sphere's mouth was swooping down.

I snatched Sybil and sped away. Babs's piggy eyes were too far around her curve to see. Noble W. W. poised himself right on ground zero. He made there by his one oblation of himself once offered a full, perfect and sufficient sacrifice and satisfaction for my sins. He gave himself as substitute, fooling Babs's gross mouth.

In a flash I'd landed Sybil in the shelter of the *Gesprengter Turm*, the Sprung Tower. Babs thought she'd eaten Sybil, but she was looking for me with her eyes and her hypersenses. I used my mental powers to disguise our vibes: Sybil and I would scan as a rabbit and a slug. Babs searched vainly for another minute, then settled down to load the remaining men. Perhaps she thought I'd gone off to grieve.

"Let me *go*," said Sybil, waving her Uzi.

"Put that down."

The Sprung Tower was "sprung," or blown in two, by the troops of Louis XIV, some three hundred years ago. Half of it still stands, and half of it lies on the ground in one huge piece. Originally it was used as a fortress, with several floors and lots of gun-slits. What remains of the top floor is good and solid. Sybil and I were up there, peeking down at Babs through one of the tower's loopholes.

"I'm supposed to kill you, Alwin."

"Be reasonable, Sybil. I haven't done anything to you."

"You killed all the women in Heidelberg."

"Babs did that."

"You brought her here."

"I know this *looks* bad. But Babs is trying to bring freedom and immortality to everyone. You should see how things look from Hilbert Space, Sybil."

"Help me get rid of that sphere for good. Or else."

Sybil poked me with her Uzi. The same gun she'd been shooting at me before. With a twitch of my will, I melted the barrel. Sybil dropped the hot weapon with an exclamation of pain.

"There's only one way I know to stop Babs," I said. "And it's not any Uzi or particle-beam laser. You have to realize that she's infinite-dimensional. Nothing we can do to her in this space can amount to more than a pinprick. But there is maybe a way."

"Save us, Alwin. It's your duty."

"Why should I do listen to you if you're talking about killing me?"

"Think of the babies, Alwin. The poor children. Having the world disappear is fine for you . . . you're bored with it. But the little ones are just beginning. Shouldn't they have their chance, too?"

"Well . . ."

"All the children in Heidelberg are alone. Locked up and crying. Is that fair?"

"You don't realize what a sacrifice you're asking me to make," I complained. "Wheelie Willie already died for us, isn't that enough?"

"What are you talking about?"

"Wheelie Willie, the little man I used to draw at Rutgers. He was alive. I found him in the Neckar. And just now he let Babs eat him so she'd think you were taken care of."

"That's . . . impossible, Alwin. You must be going crazy."

I paused to recall exactly when Wheelie Willie had appeared. I'd been chatting with Huba. Just before that I'd been about to doze off; no, I'd been thinking about Hilbert Space. *Moving* in it. What must have happened was that I'd shifted the nature of reality. Probably the shift that made Wheelie Willie real had been the same as the shift that had turned all the Heidelberg women into sex spheres.

Enjoyable. It had been an enjoyable afternoon with Wheelie Willie, partying in the old town. Huba had turned back up, not really too pissed-off about his wife, and we'd gone barhopping. The funniest moment had come when we'd passed some really loud and plastic-looking American tourists. "*Deine Landsmänner*," Huba had said, nudging me. "Your fellow-countrymen." Around sunset, all the spheres had flown up to the castle, as if roosting there for the night. We men had followed them up and found that they'd merged into one humongous ass . . . Crazy? Sure. But I hadn't questioned it till Sybil came blazing her way in.

Duty. Should. Fair. Wife words. But maybe she was right. There was no rush, really, to destroy reality. In the Zen sense, there's nothing to destroy anyway.

A gleam of light from a gun-slit lit up Sybil's face. Wide mouth, deep eyes. A strong face, a good face. She smiled. I kissed her.

"All right. I'll save the world."

There are many possible realities, infinitely many. Yet most of them are not . . . alive. Most of them are like possible books that no one ever actually wrote. A group-mind, like humanity's, lights up one given world. What makes this world different from some ghostly alternate universe is that *we actually live here.*

In my trip to Hilbert Space I'd learned how to take hold of human reality and move it. The first thing I'd done was to fix it so that I had superpowers. And then I'd begun shaking things, trying to get our group-mind free, free like Babs. But now I was going to have to undo everything I'd done. More than that, I was going to have to move our group-mind across the dimensions to some other universe where Babs might not find us. Dodging her wasn't going to be easy.

"How will you do it?" Sybil leaned against me, familiar, intense.

"In a minute Babs will disappear. She'll take all those sex-fiends up to Hilbert Space. While she's gone we'll run away."

"To Frankfurt?"

I laughed shortly. "To a different layer of reality. I'll move the human race's group-mind to a different place and hope that Babs can't find us."

We peeped out of our stone loophole. The last man was in Babs now. Her sides swelled out like a hamster's cheeks. Then she shrank . . . smoothly sliding off into hyperspace.

"This is it," I told Sybil. "Say your prayers."

I let my consciousness flow out. First to Sybil. Her complex self: part bad-girl, part school marm. Past her, to the children down in Heidelberg. Then up and down the Neckar. Fleeting images, snatches of German. I flowed across Europe—holding it all—Asia, Africa, Australia, the Americas. The mystical body of Christ, of Brahma, Buddha, Allah, you, me too.

Suddenly I'm thinking of a children's book, *Make Way for Ducklings*, Father Duck looking for a place to land. God, the sunset's bright. Hurry up, the sphere is coming. Down there is a safe spot, a mote in golden light. Hurry. Circle down . . .

We live in Virginia now. I'm sitting at a typewriter. There's a magnolia outside my window. The kids are in school and Sybil's in another room, working on a painting. I think I'll go ask her if she remembers how we got here. One thing: if you see the sex sphere, I don't want to hear about it.

afterword

I wrote *The Sex Sphere* in Lynchburg, Virginia, in 1981-1982. This book is what I call a transreal novel, that is, it's a fantastical elaboration upon my actual real-life experiences.

In this case, the autobiographical core is that my family and I lived in Heidelberg, Germany, during the years 1978-1980, where I had a grant to do mathematical research on the nature of infinity. And we did indeed make a trip to Rome with our two younger children one Easter, staying at an inexpensive hotel off the Via Veneto. But, of course, in real life, I didn't get kidnapped, and I didn't meet the sex sphere.

Where did I get the idea for the sex sphere? I might blandly say that, as I'm interested in the fourth dimension, I wanted to echo the Flatland theme of a sphere that lifts a lower-dimensional being into higher space. But that doesn't address the real question, that is: Why did I write a book about a giant ass from the fourth dimension?

Visually, I think the sex sphere may have been inspired by the paleolithic Venus of Willendorf sculpture—perhaps I saw a photo of the little statuette in the Scientific American. Less highbrow inputs were drawings in the underground comix I read at the time—I'm thinking particularly of the work of Robert Williams.

Another reason why I wrote about the sex sphere was that, quite simply, I wanted to be outrageous and to flout conventional notions of propriety. I was chafing at the fact that I was living in the preppy home town of a then well-known right-wing television evangelist, while teaching mathematics at a namby-pamby college for women. I was well aware that I was likely to be relieved of my teaching job very soon, and I was singing lead in a short-lived punk band called The Dead Pigs.

In terms of iconography, the sex sphere interested me as she's an objective correlative for a certain way that men may think of women. And combining her appearance with higher dimensions makes her a male scientist's image of a love goddess. But it's important that, in the end, our hero Alwin would rather be with his real, human wife.

My editor for the 983 Ace Books edition of *The Sex Sphere* was Susan Allison. From time to time, I've worried that some might view *The Sex Sphere* as offensive. But Susan Allison was very accepting. I have a wonderful letter from her in my files, with a sentence that still warms my heart: "You've created a marriage here that for all its looniness is rounded and wonderful, and you may not even be aware how rare it is for a writer to be able to do that at all—to say nothing of doing it with one hand while playing the most unlikely arpeggios with the other." Thanks, Susan!

The Sex Sphere didn't sell well, and it wasn't in print for long. The reaction in the SF community was muted—although, *Fantasy and Science Fiction* did say, "You cannot know where modern science fiction has gotten to unless you are familiar with Rucker."

In 2008, the novel reappeared in paperback and ebook from the small publisher E-Reads. In my excitement, I did a cartoony over-the-top painting of the sex sphere herself for the book cover. My graphic-designer daughter Georgia Rucker incorporated the art into a nice design. I think she thought it was funny.

By 2016, I was regularly publishing titles as print and ebook editions under my Transreal Books imprint, and I decided to take over the publishing of *The Sex Sphere*. For this new edition I went with a less lurid cover painting, in hopes that the novel might someday find a wider audience. In my heart of hearts I've always hoped for my novels to become respected works of modern literature.

Hope you enjoy this one.

Rudy Rucker
Los Gatos, California,
September 19, 2016

turing & burroughs
a novel by
RUDY RUCKER

mathematicians in love
a novel by
RUDY RUCKER

saucer wisdom
a novel by
RUDY RUCKER

white light
a novel by
RUDY RUCKER

million mile road trip
a novel by
RUDY RUCKER

the big aha
a novel by
RUDY RUCKER

spacetime donuts
a novel by
RUDY RUCKER

jim and the flims
a novel by
RUDY RUCKER

the secret of life
a novel by
RUDY RUCKER

also from rudy rucker
and night shade books

Night Shade Books' ten-volume Rudy Rucker series reissues nine brilliantly off-beat novels from the mathematician-turned-author, as well as the brand-new *Million Mile Road Trip*. Conceived as a uniformly-designed collection, each release features new artwork from award-winning illustrator Bill Carman and an introduction from some of Rudy's most renowned science fiction contemporaries. We're proud to make trade editions available again (or for the first time!) of so much work from this influential writer, and to share Rucker's fascinating and unique ideas with a new generation of readers.

Rudy Rucker is a writer and a mathematician who worked for twenty years as a Silicon Valley computer science professor. He is regarded as a contemporary master of science fiction, and received the Philip K. Dick award twice. His forty published books include both novels and non-fiction books on the fourth dimension, infinity, and the meaning of computation. A founder of the cyberpunk school of science-fiction, Rucker also writes SF in a realistic style known as transrealism, often including himself as a character. He lives in the San Francisco Bay Area.